The

Ingredients

of

Love

The
Ingredients
of
Love

....

Nicolas Barreau

TRANSLATED BY BILL McCANN

St. Martin's Griffin
New York

This is a work of fiction. All of the characters, organizations, and events portrayed in this novel are either products of the author's imagination or are used fictitiously.

www.stmartins.com

ISBN 978-1-250-00670-7 (trade paperback)
ISBN 978-1-250-02088-8 (e-book)

First published as *Das Lächeln der Frauen* in Germany by Thiele Verlag

First U.S. Edition: January 2013

10 9 8 7 6 5 4 3 2

Happiness is a red coat
with a torn lining.

—Julian Barnes

The
Ingredients
of
Love

One

....

Last year in November a book saved my life. I know that sounds very unlikely now. Many of you may feel I'm exaggerating—or even being melodramatic—when I say so. But that's exactly how it was.

It wasn't that someone had aimed at my heart and the bullet had miraculously been stopped by the pages of a thick, leather-bound edition of Baudelaire's poetry, as so often happens in the movies. I don't lead that exciting a life.

No, my foolish heart had already been wounded. On a day that seemed like any other.

I can remember it exactly. The last guests in the restaurant—a group of rather noisy Americans, a discreet Japanese couple, and two argumentative Frenchmen—were as always sitting around quite late, and the Americans were licking their lips with lots of "Oohs" and "Aahs" over the *gâteau au chocolat*.

After serving the dessert, Suzette had, as always, asked if I still needed her and then rushed happily off. And Jacquie was in his usual bad mood. This time he was worked up about the tourists' eating habits and was rolling his eyes as he clattered the empty plates into the dishwasher.

"*Ah, les Américains!* They know *nothing* about French cuisine, *rien du tout*! They always eat the decoration as well—why do I have to cook for barbarians? I have a good mind to give it all up, it really depresses me!"

He'd taken off his apron and growled his *bonne nuit* at me before getting on his old bike and vanishing into the night. Jacquie is a great cook, and I like him a lot, even if he carries his cantankerousness around with him like a pot of bouillabaisse. He was already the chef in Le Temps des Cerises when the little restaurant with the red-and-white-checked tablecloths just off the lively Boulevard Saint-Germain in the Rue Princesse still belonged to my father. My father loved the chanson about the "Cherry Season," so lovely and over so soon—a life-affirming and at the same time somewhat melancholy song about lovers who find and then lose each other. And although the left wing in France had later adopted this old song as their unofficial anthem, I believe that the real reason Papa gave his restaurant that name had less to do with the memory of the Paris Commune than with some completely personal memories.

This is the place where I grew up, and when I sat in the kitchen after school doing my homework surrounded by the clatter of the pots and pans and a thousand tempting smells, I could be sure that Jacquie would always have a little tidbit for me.

Jacquie, whose name is actually Jacques Auguste Berton, comes from Normandy, where you can look out as far as the horizon, where the air tastes of salt and nothing obstructs one's gaze but the endless wind-tossed sea and the clouds. More than once every day he assures me that he loves looking far out into the distance—far out! Sometimes Paris gets too confined and too noisy for him, and then he longs to get back to the coast.

"How can anyone who's ever had the smell of the Côte Fleurie in his nostrils ever feel good in the exhaust fumes of Paris, just tell me that!"

He waves his chef's knife and looks reproachfully at me with his big brown eyes before brushing his dark hair from his forehead, hair that is more and more—I notice with a little sadness—flecked with threads of silver.

It was only a few years ago that this burly man with his big hands showed a fourteen-year-old girl with long, dark blond plaits how to make a perfect *crème brûlée*. It was the first dish I ever impressed my friends with.

Jacquie is of course not just *any* chef. As a young man he worked in the famous Ferme Saint-Siméon in Honfleur, the little town on the Atlantic coast with the very special light—a refuge for painters and artists. "It had a lot more style then, my dear Aurélie."

Yet no matter how much Jacquie grumbles, I smile inwardly, because I know he would never leave me in the lurch. And that's how it was that evening last November, when the sky over Paris was as white as milk and people hurried through the streets wrapped up in thick woolen scarves. A November that was so much colder than all the others I had experienced in Paris. Or did it just seem like that to me?

A few weeks earlier my father had died. Just like that, without any warning, his heart had one day decided to stop beating. Jacquie found him when he opened the restaurant in the afternoon.

Papa was lying peacefully on the floor—surrounded by fresh vegetables, legs of lamb, scallops, and herbs that he had bought at the market that morning.

He left me his restaurant, the recipe for his famous *menu d'amour* with which he claimed to have won the love of my mother many years before (she died when I was still very small and so I'll never know if he was pulling my leg), and a few wise bits of advice about life. He was sixty-eight years old, and I found that far too early. But people you love always die too early, don't they, no matter what age they live to?

"Years don't mean anything. Only what happens in them," my father once said as he laid roses on my mother's grave.

And when—a little nervous but still resolute—I followed in his footsteps as a restaurateur that autumn, the realization that I was now quite alone in the world hit me very hard.

Thank God I had Claude. He worked in the theater as a set designer, and the massive desk that stood under the window in his little attic apartment in the Bastille quarter was always over-flowing with drawings and little cardboard models. When he was working on a major job, he would sometimes go to ground for a few days. "I'm not available next week," he would say, and I had to get used to the fact that he actually refused to answer the phone or open the door even when I was ringing his bell like mad. A short time later he was back as if nothing had happened. He appeared in the sky like a rainbow—beautiful and unattainable—kissed me boldly on the lips, and called me *ma petite* while the sun played hide-and-seek in his golden blond curls.

Then he took me by the hand and led me off to present his designs to me with gleaming eyes.

I wasn't allowed to say anything.

When I'd only known Claude for a few months I'd once

made the mistake of expressing my opinion openly and, my head to one side, thinking aloud about what might be improved. Claude had stared at me, aghast. His watery blue eyes seemed almost to overflow, and with a single violent movement of his hand he swept his desk clean. Paints, pencils, sheets of paper, glasses, brushes, and little pieces of cardboard flew through the air like confetti and the delicate model of his set for Shakespeare's *Midsummer Night's Dream,* which he'd spent so much effort producing, was broken into a thousand pieces.

After that I kept my critical remarks to myself.

Claude was very impulsive, very changeable in his moods, very tender, and very special. Everything about him was "very," there seemed to be no well-balanced middle ground.

We'd been together about two years by then, and it would never have entered my mind to question my relationship with this complicated and very idiosyncratic man. If you consider it closely, we all have our complications, sensitive spots, and quirks. There are things we do or things we would never do—or only in very special circumstances. Things that make other people laugh and shake their heads and wonder.

Peculiar things that are ours and ours alone.

For example, I collect thoughts. In my bedroom there's a wall covered with brightly colored notes full of thoughts that I've preserved so that, fleeting as they are, they won't be lost to me. Thoughts about conversations overheard in cafés, about rituals and why they are so important, thoughts about kisses in the park at night, about the heart and hotel rooms, about hands, garden benches, photos, secrets—and when to reveal them— about the light in the trees and about time when it stands still.

My little notes stick to the bright wallpaper like tropical butterflies, captured moments that serve no purpose but to be near me, and when I open the balcony door and a light draft blows through the room they flutter a little, as if they want to fly away.

"What on earth is *that*?" Claude had raised his eyebrows in disbelief when he first saw my butterfly collection. He came to a halt by the wall and read some of the notes with interest. "Are you going to write a book?"

I blushed and shook my head.

"Good gracious, no! I do it . . ." I had to think for a moment myself, but couldn't find a really convincing explanation. ". . . you know, I just do it. No reason. Like other people take photos."

"Could it be that you are a little weird, *ma petite*?" Claude had asked, and then he had thrust his hand up my skirt. "But that doesn't matter, not in the slightest, because I'm a little bit crazy too . . ." He brushed his lips over my neck and I suddenly felt quite hot. ". . . crazy for you."

A few minutes later we were lying on the bed, my hair wonderfully disheveled, the sun shining through the curtains and painting little quivering circles on the wooden floor, and I could subsequently have stuck another note on the wall about *love in the afternoon*. But I didn't.

Claude was hungry, and I made us omelettes, and he said that a girl who made omelettes like that could be allowed any quirks she liked. So here's something else:

Whenever I'm unhappy or uneasy, I go out and buy some flowers. Of course, I also like flowers when I'm happy, but on days when everything goes wrong flowers are for me like the start of a new regime, something that is always perfect no matter what happens.

I put a couple of campanulas in a vase, and I feel better. I plant flowers on my old stone balcony that looks out over the courtyard and immediately have the satisfying feeling of doing something quite meaningful. I lose myself in unwrapping the plants from the old newspaper, carefully taking them out of their plastic containers and putting them in the pots. When I stick my fingers into the damp earth and root around in it, everything becomes absolutely simple and I lose all my cares in cascades of roses, hydrangeas, and wisteria.

I don't like change in my life. I always take the same route when I walk to work; I have a very particular bench in the Tuileries, which I secretly think of as my bench.

And I would never turn around on a staircase in the dark because of the creepy feeling that there might be something lurking behind me that would attack me if I turned round.

By the way, I've never told anyone the bit about the stairs— not even Claude. I don't think he was telling me everything at that time either.

During the day we both went our own ways. I was never quite sure what Claude did in the evenings when I was working in the restaurant. Perhaps I just didn't want to know. But at night, when loneliness descended over Paris, when the last bars had closed and only a few night owls walked shivering on the streets, I lay in his arms and felt safe.

That evening, as I switched off the lights in the restaurant and set off home with a bag of raspberry macaroons, I still had no idea that my apartment would be as empty as my restaurant. It was, as I said, a day just like any other.

Except that Claude, in just three sentences, had departed from my life.

• • •

When I woke up the next morning after what felt like a sleepless night, I knew that something was wrong. Unfortunately I am not one of those people who immediately spring into wakefulness, and so it was at first more a strange feeling of uncertainty and uneasiness that gradually penetrated my consciousness than a clear thought. I was lying on the soft, lavender-scented pillows; from outside the muffled noises of the courtyard entered the room. A crying child, the reassuring voice of a mother, heavy footsteps moving away, the courtyard gate creaking shut. I blinked and turned to my side. Still half asleep, I stretched out my hand and felt for something that was no longer there.

"Claude?" I murmured.

And then the realization came. Claude had left me!

What had still seemed strangely unreal the night before, and after several glasses of red wine had become so unreal that I could well have dreamed it, became irrevocable in the gray light of this November dawn. I lay there motionless and listened, but the apartment remained silent. No sound from the kitchen. No one rattling around with the big dark blue cups and cursing because the milk had boiled over. No smell of coffee to dispel tiredness. No quiet humming of his electric razor. Not a word.

I turned my head and looked over toward the balcony door: The thin white curtains were open, and a cold morning was pressing against the window. I pulled the covers more closely around me and recalled how I'd unsuspectingly entered the dark, empty apartment with my bag of macaroons the night before.

Only the kitchen light was on, and for a moment I stared blankly at the lonely still life that presented itself to my view in the light of the dark metal lamp.

A handwritten letter lying open on the old kitchen table, the jar of apricot jam that Claude had spread on his croissant that morning. A bowl of fruit. A half-burned candle. Two cloth napkins rolled up carelessly and stuck in silver rings.

Claude never wrote to me, not even a note. He had a manic relationship with his mobile phone, and if his plans changed, he would ring me or leave a message on my voice mail.

"Claude?" I called, and still somehow hoped for an answer, although the cold hand of fear was already grabbing at me. I lowered my arms and the macaroons fell out of the bag in slow motion. I felt a little faint. I sat on one of the four wooden chairs and pulled the letter unbelievably slowly toward me, as if that could have changed anything.

I had read the few words that Claude had penned on the paper in his big, sloping handwriting over and over, and eventually seemed to hear his rough voice, close to my ear, like a whisper in the night:

Aurélie,

I've met the woman of my dreams. I'm sorry that it had to happen just now, but it would have had to happen sometime anyway.

Take care,

Claude

At first I had sat motionless, just my heart beating like mad. So that was how it felt when the ground was pulled out from under your feet. That morning Claude had said good-bye to me with a kiss that seemed particularly tender. I didn't know then that it was a kiss of betrayal. A lie! How contemptible, just to slink away like that!

In a surge of impotent rage I crumpled the paper and threw

it into the corner. Seconds later I was sitting over it, sobbing loudly and smoothing the page out again. I drank a glass of red wine, and then another. I took my phone out of my purse and rang Claude again and again. I left messages—some desperately pleading, some wildly abusive. I walked up and down in the apartment, took another gulp to give myself courage, and shouted down the phone that he should call me back at once. I think I must have done that about twenty-five times before I realized, with the dull clarity that alcohol sometimes brings, that all my efforts would be in vain. Claude was already light-years away and my words could no longer reach him.

My head ached. I got up and padded through the apartment like a sleepwalker in my short nightshirt, which was actually the big—far too big, in fact—blue-and-white-striped jacket of Claude's pajamas that I had somehow pulled on during the night.

The bathroom door was open. I looked around to make certain. The razor had gone, as well as the toothbrush and the Aramis aftershave.

In the living room the burgundy cashmere throw that I'd given Claude for his birthday was missing, and his dark pull-over was not hanging carelessly over the chair as it usually did. The raincoat had gone from the hook to the left of the front door. I pulled open the wardrobe in the hallway. A couple of empty coat hangers knocked against each other, rattling gently. I breathed in deeply. Everything had been taken away. Claude had even remembered the socks in the bottom drawer. He must have planned his departure very carefully, and I asked myself how I had managed to notice nothing, nothing at all. Not that he was intending to go. Not that he'd fallen in love. Not that he was already kissing another woman at the same time that he was kissing me.

In the tall gold-framed mirror over the bureau in the hall the reflection of my pale, tear-stained face looked like a pale moon surrounded by quivering dark blond waves. My long hair with the center parting was as tousled as if after a wild night of love, except that there hadn't been any passionate embraces and whispered promises. "You've got hair like a fairy princess," Claude had said. "You're my Titania."

I laughed bitterly, went right up to the mirror, and examined myself with the ruthless gaze of the desperate. The state I was in with the dark shadows under my eyes made me look more like the madwoman of Chaillot, I thought. Above me to the right the photo of Claude and me that I liked so much was stuck in the frame. It had been taken on a balmy summer evening as we strolled over the Pont des Arts. A chubby African who'd spread his bags out for sale on the bridge had taken it for us. I still remember that he had unbelievably big hands—between his fingers my little camera looked like a doll's toy—and that it took ages until he finally pressed the button.

We were both laughing in the photo, our heads snuggling close together against the deep blue sky that tenderly embraced the silhouette of Paris.

Do photos lie or do they tell the truth? Pain makes you philosophical.

I took the photo down, put it on the dark wood, and leaned on the bureau with both hands. *"Que ça dure!"* the dark-skinned man from Africa had called after us in his deep voice with the rolling Rs. *"Que ça dure!"* Hope it lasts!

I noticed that my eyes were filling with tears again. They ran down my cheeks and splashed like heavy raindrops on Claude and me and the whole Paris-for-lovers crap, until everything became misty and indistinct.

I opened the drawer and shoved the photo in among the scarves and gloves. "So there," I said. And then once more, "So there!"

Then I pushed the drawer shut, and thought about how easy it was to disappear from someone else's life. Claude had only needed a couple of hours. And it looked as if the men's striped pajama top, which had been left—probably unintentionally—under my pillow, was the only bit of him that remained.

Happiness and unhappiness are very often close to each other. To put it another way, you could also say that happiness sometimes follows very strange and devious routes.

If Claude hadn't left me then, I would probably have gone to meet Bernadette on that gloomy November morning. I would not have wandered the streets of Paris, the loneliest person in the world; I would not have stood at twilight on the Pont Louis-Philippe for such a long time staring self-pityingly into the water, nor would I have fled from that concerned young policeman into the little bookshop on the Île Saint-Louis, and I certainly would not have found the book that was to turn my life into such a wonderful adventure. But let's tell things in the right order.

It was at least quite considerate of Claude to leave me on a Sunday, because Le Temps des Cerises is always closed on Mondays. It's my free day, and I always use it to do something nice. I go to an exhibition. I spend hours in Bon Marché, my favorite big store. Or I see Bernadette.

Bernadette is my best friend. We got to know each other on a train journey when her little daughter Marie tottered up to me and cheerfully emptied a mug of cocoa over my cream knitted dress. The stains have never completely gone, but by the end of that entertaining journey from Avignon to Paris, including our not very successful attempts to clean the dress with water and paper towels in a swaying train toilet, we were already firm friends.

Bernadette is everything that I'm not. She is determined, unflappably good-tempered, very clever. She accepts things that happen with remarkable calm and tries to make the best of them. She's the one who sorts out in a couple of sentences things I sometimes think are frightfully complicated, making them quite simple.

"Good grief, Aurélie," she says on such occasions, and looks at me with amusement in her dark blue eyes. "What a *fuss* you make about things! It's all really quite *simple* . . ."

Bernadette lives on the Île Saint-Louis and is a teacher at the École Primaire, but she could just as well be an advisor for people with complicated thought processes.

When I look into her beautiful, open face, I often think that she is one of the few women who look really good wearing their hair in a simple chignon. And when she wears her shoulder-length blond hair down, men follow her with their eyes.

She has a loud infectious laugh. And she always says what she thinks.

That was also the reason why I didn't want to meet her that Monday morning. From the very beginning, Bernadette could not stand Claude.

"He's a freak," she said, after I had introduced Claude to her over a glass of wine. "I know people like that. Egocentric—and never looks you in the eye properly."

"He looks into *my* eyes," I answered, and laughed.

"You'll never be happy with a man like that," she persisted.

I found that a bit over-hasty at the time, but now, as I spooned the coffee into the *cafetière* and poured in the boiling water, I had to admit that Bernadette had been right.

I sent her a text and canceled our lunch together with a few cryptic phrases. Then I drank my coffee, put on my coat, scarf, and gloves, and went out into the cold Parisian morning.

Sometimes you go out in order to get somewhere. And sometimes you just go out to walk and walk and go farther and farther until the clouds clear, despair calms down, or you have thought a thought through to the very end.

I wasn't going anywhere that morning; my head was strangely empty and my heart was so heavy that I could feel its weight and I involuntarily pressed my hand to the rough fabric of my coat. There were still not many people around and the heels of my boots clattered forlornly on the old cobbles as I walked toward the stone gateway that links the Rue de L'Ancienne Comédie with the Boulevard Saint-Germain. I had been so happy when I found my apartment on that street four years ago. I love this lively little district whose winding streets and alleys with their vegetable, oyster, and flower booths, cafés, and shops reach down to the bank of the Seine. I live on the third floor in an old house with worn stone steps and no elevator, and when I look out of the window I can look across at the Procope, the famous restaurant that has been there for centuries and is said to have been the first coffee-house in Paris. Writers and philosophers used to meet there: Voltaire, Rousseau, Balzac, Hugo, and Anatole France. Great names, whose spiritual presence gives most of the guests who sit and eat there on red leather banquettes under massive chandeliers a pleasant frisson.

"Aren't you lucky!" Bernadette had said when I showed her my new home and we were eating a really delicious *coq au vin* in the Procope that evening to celebrate the occasion. "When you just think of all the people who've eaten here—and you live only a couple of steps away . . . great!"

She looked around enthusiastically, while I speared a piece of wine-marinated chicken on my fork, contemplated it blissfully, and wondered for a moment if I was a Philistine.

To be honest, I have to admit that the thought that you could have eaten the first ice cream made in Paris in the Procope delighted me far more than the idea of bearded men putting their brilliant thoughts down on paper—but my friend would probably not have understood that.

Bernadette's apartment is full of books. They sit around in tall bookshelves that stretch over the door frames, they lie around on dining tables, desks, coffee tables, and bedside tables, and even in the bathroom I discovered to my amazement a few books lying on a small table next to the toilet.

"I simply couldn't imagine a life without books," Bernadette had said once—and I had nodded a bit ashamedly.

In principle, I also read. But most of the time something gets in the way. And if I have the choice, I'd sooner take a long walk or bake an apricot tart: then it's the delicious smell of that combination of flour, butter, vanilla, eggs, fruit, and cream wafting through the air that gives my imagination wings and makes me dream.

This is probably because of the metal plaque, framed with a wooden spoon and two roses, that still hangs in the kitchen of Le Temps des Cerises.

When I was learning to read in primary school and letters began to fit together into a big, meaningful whole, I would stand under it in my dark blue school uniform and decipher the words that were written on it:

The purpose of a cookery book is one and unmistakable: to increase the happiness of mankind.

This maxim had been written by someone called Joseph Conrad, and I still remember that for a long time I thought that he must be a famous German cook, so that I was all the more surprised when I chanced upon his novel *Heart of Darkness*. Out of loyalty to the name I even bought it—but never got round to reading it.

Anyway, that title sounded as gloomy as my mood that day. Perhaps this would have been the right time to get the book out, I thought bitterly. But I don't read books when I'm unhappy: I plant flowers.

At least, that was what I thought at that moment, not knowing that I would spend that very night leafing with almost unseemly haste through the pages of a novel that had, as it were, thrown itself into my path. Chance? Even today I still don't believe that it was chance.

I greeted Philippe, one of the waiters from the Procope, who gave me a friendly wave through the café window, passed heedlessly by the glittering display in Harem, the little jewelry shop on the corner, and turned into the Boulevard Saint-Germain. It had begun to rain; cars sprayed past me and I pulled my shawl tighter around me as I marched determinedly along the boulevard.

Why do awful or depressing things always have to happen in November? November is the worst time I could conceive of for being unhappy. The choice of flowers you can plant is very limited.

I kicked an empty cola can, which clattered across the pavement and ended up lying in the gutter.

It was just like that unbelievably sad song by Anne Sylvestre, *"La Chanson de Toute Seule,"* the one about the pebbles that first roll and then an instant later sink in the Seine. Everyone had abandoned me. Papa was dead, Claude had vanished, and I was alone as I had never ever been before in my life. Then my mobile phone rang.

"Hello?" I said, and almost choked. I could feel the adrenaline coursing through my body at the thought that it might be Claude.

"What's up, my love?" Bernadette went straight to the point, as always.

A taxi driver screeched to a halt beside me, hooting like a madman because a cyclist hadn't given way. It sounded like the apocalypse.

"My goodness, what's that?" shouted Bernadette, before I could say anything. "Is everything okay? Where are you?"

"Somewhere on the Boulevard Saint-Germain," I replied miserably and stepped for a moment under the awning of a shop that sold bright umbrellas with ducks' heads as handles. The rain trickled out of my wet hair and I was drowning in a flood of self-pity.

"Somewhere on the Boulevard Saint-Germain? What in heaven's name are you doing 'somewhere on the Boulevard Saint-Germain'? Your message said that something had cropped up!"

"Claude's gone," I said, and sniffed into my phone.

"How do you mean, gone?" As always when Claude was in question, Bernadette's voice immediately became a touch impatient. "Has the idiot gone to ground again without letting you know where he is?"

I had foolishly told Bernadette about Claude's tendency toward escapism, and she hadn't found it at all funny.

"Gone forever," I said with a sob. "He's left me. I'm so unhappy."

"Oh, good grief," said Bernadette, and her voice was like an embrace. "Oh, goodness gracious! My poor, poor Aurélie. What's happened?"

"He's . . . got . . . someone . . . else . . ." I sobbed. "Yesterday, when I got home, all his stuff had gone and there was a note . . . a note—"

"He didn't even tell you *to your face*? What an asshole," Bernadette interrupted me and took an angry breath. "I've always said that Claude's an asshole. Over and over. A note! That's just too bad . . . no, that really takes the cake!"

"Please, Bernadette . . ."

"What? You're not still defending that idiot?"

I shook my head wordlessly.

"Now listen, my dear," said Bernadette, and I narrowed my eyes. When Bernadette begins a sentence with "Now listen" it's normally the signal that she's about to let loose with deeply grounded opinions, which are often right, but often hard to accept. "Forget that creep as quickly as you can! Of course it's bad at the moment . . ."

"Very bad," I sobbed.

"Okay, *very* bad. But that man was really unspeakable, and deep inside you know that too. Now try and calm down. Everything will be all right, and I promise you that you'll soon find a very nice man, a *really* nice man who knows how to appreciate a wonderful woman like you."

"Oh, Bernadette," I sighed. It was all very well for Bernadette to talk: She was married to a really nice man who put up with her fanatical attachment to the truth with unbelievable patience.

"Listen," she said once more. "You just get in a taxi and go straight home, and when I've sorted everything out here I'll come over. Don't get so upset, please! No reason for drama."

I swallowed. Of course it was good of Bernadette to want to come over and console me. But I had a sinking feeling that her idea of consolation was a bit different from mine. I wasn't sure if I really wanted to spend the evening having her explain that Claude was the most useless guy of all time. After all, I'd been with him until the day before, and I would have found a little bit more sympathy rather nice.

And then good old Bernadette went over the top.

"I'll tell you something, Aurélie," she said in her schoolmarm voice that allows no contradiction. "I'm glad, yes, I'm actually very glad that Claude has left you. A real stroke of luck, if you ask me! You would never have managed to get rid of him. I know you don't want to hear this now, but I'll say it anyway: I see the fact that that creep has finally disappeared from your life as something to celebrate."

"Bully for you," I answered more sharply than I really intended, and I could feel that the subliminal realization that my friend was not entirely wrong was all of a sudden making me absolutely furious.

"D'you know what, Bernadette? You go off and celebrate a bit, and if your great euphoria allows it, just let me be miserable for a couple of days, okay? Just leave me alone!"

I ended the call, breathed in deeply, and then switched my phone right off.

Great! Now I was quarreling with Bernadette as well. The rain poured off the awning onto the street and I pressed myself shivering into a corner and began to think that it might be just as well to go home after all. But the thought of going back to an empty apartment frightened me. I didn't even have a little cat that would be waiting for me and would rub itself purring against me as I ran my fingers through its fur. "Look, Claude, aren't they just adorable?" I had said when Madame Clément, our neighbor, had shown us the tortoiseshell kittens tumbling clumsily over each other in their little basket.

But Claude was allergic to cat hair and didn't like animals anyway.

"I don't like animals, just fish," he had said a few weeks after we got to know each other. In fact I should have realized then. The likelihood of being happy with a man who only liked fish was for me, Aurélie Bredin, relatively small.

Resolutely, I pushed open the door of the little umbrella shop and bought a sky blue umbrella with white polka dots and a caramel-colored duck's-head handle.

It turned out to be the longest walk of my life. After a while the fashion shops and restaurants that stood on either side of the boulevard disappeared, to be replaced by furniture stores and bathroom suppliers, and then even these gave up and I wandered my lonely way through the rain, past the sandstone façades of the big houses that offered little diversion to the gaze and met my disordered thoughts and emotions with stoic indifference.

At the end of the boulevard, where it reaches the Quai d'Orsay, I turned right and crossed the Seine toward the Place de la Concorde. The obelisk in the middle of the square towered like a dark index finger and it seemed to me that, in its Egyptian sublimity, it had little or nothing to do with the hordes of little tin cars that hurtled hectically around it.

When you're unhappy, you either see nothing at all and the world sinks into meaninglessness, or else you see things preternaturally sharply, and everything suddenly seems to have meaning. Even the most banal things, like a traffic light turning from red to green, can decide whether you turn left or right.

And so a few minutes later I was walking through the Tuileries, a sad little shape under a spotted umbrella that bobbed gently up and down along the empty, newly swept paths of the park, then left it in the direction of the Louvre, glided along the bank of the Seine as twilight descended, past the Île de la Cité, past Notre-Dame, past all the lights of the city as they gradually twinkled into life, until I finally stopped on the little Pont Louis-Philippe, which leads over to the Île Saint-Louis.

The deep blue color of the sky lay over Paris like a velvet cloth. It was just before six, the rain was gradually stopping, and I leaned, somewhat exhausted, over the stone parapet of the old bridge and stared pensively into the Seine. The reflections of the streetlights quivered and glittered on the dark water— magical and fragile, like everything beautiful.

After eight hours, thousands of steps, and even more thousands of thoughts, I had reached this quiet place. It had taken that much time to grasp that the depths of misery that were weighing on my heart like lead were not due just to the fact that Claude had left me. I was thirty-two years old, and it wasn't the first time that a love affair had broken up. I had left, I had been left, I had known far nicer men than Claude, the freak.

I think it was the feeling that everything was crumbling,

changing, that people who had held my hand had suddenly disappeared forever, that I was losing my grip and that there was nothing between me and the great big universe but a sky blue umbrella with white polka dots.

That didn't actually make things any better. I was standing alone on a bridge, a couple of cars drove past me, my hair was blowing in my face, and I was holding tightly on to my duck-handled umbrella as if that too might fly away.

"Help!" I whispered quietly, and stumbled slightly against the parapet.

"Mademoiselle? Oh, *mon Dieu,* mademoiselle, don't! Wait, *arrêtez!*" I heard hurried steps behind me, and gave a start.

The umbrella slipped from my hand, turned half over, bounced off the parapet, and fell down in a spiraling dance to land flat on the surface of the water with a barely audible splash.

I turned around in confusion and found myself looking straight into the dark eyes of a young policeman, who was looking at me with great concern. "Is everything all right?" he asked agitatedly. He obviously thought I was intending to commit suicide.

I nodded. "Yes, of course. Everything's fine." I forced myself to give him a little smile. He raised his eyebrows as if he didn't believe a word of it.

"I don't believe a word you say, mademoiselle," he said. "I've been watching you for quite some time now, and no woman who's perfectly fine looks like you did standing there."

I was taken aback, and said nothing—I just watched the white-spotted umbrella for a moment as it sailed slowly off down the Seine. The policeman followed my gaze.

"It's always the same," he added. "I know these bridges. Only recently we fished a young girl out of the icy water a little bit farther downstream. Just in time. If anyone hangs around on a bridge for a long time you can be sure that they're either madly in love or just about to jump in the water."

He shook his head. "I've never understood why lovers and suicides have such an affinity for bridges."

He ended his little lecture, and looked at me suspiciously.

"You look quite upset, mademoiselle. You weren't going to do anything silly, were you? A lovely woman like you. On the bridge."

"Of course not!" I assured him. "And anyway, completely normal people sometimes stand on bridges for a long time, just because it's nice to look at the river."

"But you have such sad eyes." He wouldn't give up. "And it looked just as if you were going to jump."

"What nonsense!" I replied. "I was just feeling a little faint," I hurriedly added, and instinctively put my hand to my stomach.

"*Oh, pardon! Excusez-moi, mademoiselle . . . madame!*" He spread his hands in a gesture of embarrassment. "I couldn't have known . . . *vous êtes . . . enceinte?* In that case, you ought to look after yourself a little better, if I might say so. Can I see you home?"

I shook my head and almost giggled. No, at least I wasn't pregnant.

He tilted his head to one side and smiled chivalrously. "Are you sure, madame? The protection of the French police is at your service. I wouldn't want you to faint on me again." He looked protectively at my flat tummy. "When is it due?"

"Listen, monsieur," I replied in a firm voice. "I'm not pregnant, and am relatively sure that I won't be in the foreseeable future. I was just feeling a bit faint, that's all."

And no wonder, I thought, because I hadn't had anything all day except a coffee.

"Oh! Madame . . . I mean *mademoiselle!*" Obviously embarrassed, he took a step backward. "I'm very sorry, I wasn't trying to be indiscreet."

"That's all right," I sighed, and waited for him to go.

But the man in the dark blue uniform stayed put. He was the archetype of the Paris policeman of the kind I had often seen on the Île de la Cité, where the police headquarters are: tall, slim, good-looking, always ready to flirt. This one had obviously decided that it was his duty to be my personal guardian angel.

"Well, then . . ." I leaned back against the parapet, and tried to get rid of him with a smile. An elderly man in a raincoat went past, giving us an interested look.

The policeman raised two fingers to the peak of his kepi. "Well then, if there's nothing more I can do for you . . ."

"No, definitely not."

"Then take care of yourself."

"I will." I pressed my lips together and nodded my head a couple of times. This was the second man in twenty-four hours who'd told me to take care of myself. I raised my hand briefly, turned round, and leaned with my elbows on the parapet. I gave my full attention to studying the Cathedral of Notre-Dame, which rose like a medieval spaceship from the darkness at the end of the Île de la Cité.

I heard someone clear his throat behind me. I tensed my back and then turned slowly to face the street once more.

"Yes?" I said.

"Which is it then?" he asked, and grinned like George Clooney in the Nespresso commercial. "Mademoiselle or madame?"

Oh. My. God. I just wanted to be miserable in peace, and a policeman was flirting with me.

"Mademoiselle, what else?" I responded, and decided to take flight. The bells of Notre-Dame rang out toward me, and I walked quickly over the bridge to the Île Saint-Louis.

Many people say that this little island in the Seine, directly behind the much larger Île de la Cité and reachable only by means of bridges, is the heart of Paris. But that heart beats very, very slowly. I very rarely went there, and every time I did I was surprised anew by the calm that reigns in that district.

As I turned into the Rue Saint-Louis, the main street lined with peaceful little shops and restaurants, I saw from the corner of my eye that a tall, slim figure was following me at a respectable distance. My guardian angel was not giving up. What was this man thinking anyway? That I was going to try again at the next bridge?

I speeded up until I was almost running and then tore open the door of the first shop that still had its lights on. It was a little bookshop, and as I stumbled in I would never have thought that this step would change my life forever.

At first I thought that there was no one in the shop, but in fact it was so packed with books, bookshelves, and tables that I did not see the owner, who was standing at the end of the room with his head bent forward behind an old-fashioned counter stacked precariously with piles of books. He was deep in contemplation of an illustrated volume, turning the pages with extreme care. He looked so peaceful standing there with his wavy, silver-gray hair and his half-moon reading glasses that I hardly dared to disturb him. I paused for a moment in this cocoon of warmth and yellowish light, and my heart began to beat more calmly.

I carefully risked a glance outside. Through the window, which was inscribed in faded gold letters LIBRAIRIE CAPRICORNE PASCAL FERMIER, I saw my guardian angel standing, earnestly examining the display.

I sighed involuntarily, and the old bookseller looked up from his book and stared at me in surprise, then pushed his spectacles up.

"Ah . . . *bonsoir, mademoiselle*—I didn't hear you coming in," he said in a friendly way, and his kind face with his intelligent eyes and delicate smile reminded me of a picture of Marc Chagall in his studio. Except that this man wasn't holding a brush in his hand.

"*Bonsoir, monsieur,*" I answered in some embarrassment. "Forgive me, I didn't mean to startle you."

"Not at all," he said, raising his hands. "It's just that I thought I'd locked the door." He looked over at the door, where a bunch of keys was hanging from the lock, and shook his head. "I'm starting to get a bit forgetful."

"Then you're actually already closed?" I asked, taking a step forward and hoping that the guardian angel outside the window would finally fly away.

"Take your time and look around, mademoiselle. There's no hurry." He smiled. "Are you looking for anything in particular?"

I'm looking for someone to really love me, I answered to myself. I'm running away from a policeman who thinks I want to jump off a bridge, and I'm pretending that I want to buy a book. I'm thirty-two years old and I've lost my umbrella. I wish something nice would happen to me for a change.

My stomach rumbled audibly. "No . . . no, nothing in particular," I said quickly. "Just something . . . nice." I went red. Now he probably thought I was an ignoramus whose powers of expression were exhausted by the meaningless little word "nice." I hoped that my words had at least drowned out my stomach's rumblings.

"Would you like a cookie?" asked Monsieur Chagall.

He held a silver dish of shortbread out under my nose, and after a short moment's hesitation, I took one gratefully. There was something consoling about the sweet cookie, and it calmed my stomach immediately.

"Do you know, I haven't eaten properly today," I explained as I chewed. Unfortunately I'm one of those uncool people who always feel obliged to explain everything.

"It happens," said Monsieur Chagall, without commenting on my embarrassment. "Over there"—he pointed at a table piled with novels—"you may well find what you're looking for."

And I really did! A quarter of an hour later I left the Librairie Capricorne with an orange paper bag with a unicorn printed on it.

"A good choice," Monsieur Chagall had said as he wrapped the book, which had been written by a young Englishman and was called, pleasantly enough, *The Smiles of Women*.

"You'll like this."

I'd nodded and, red-faced, fumbled for the money. I hardly managed to conceal my amazement, which Monsieur Chagall probably thought was an attack of excessive anticipation of the pleasures of reading as he locked the shop door behind me.

I breathed in deeply and looked down the empty street. My new policeman friend had given up his surveillance. The probability that someone who bought a book would subsequently throw themselves from a bridge over the Seine was obviously very small from a statistical point of view.

But that was not the reason for my surprise, which gradually developed into excitement, causing me to walk much faster and then, with thumping heart, to take a taxi.

On the very first page of the book, which I was pressing to my heart in its pretty orange wrapping like a precious treasure, there was a sentence that bewildered me, aroused my curiosity—electrified me:

> The story I would like to tell begins with a smile. It ends in a little restaurant with the auspicious name "Le Temps des Cerises," which is in Saint-Germain-des-Près, where the heart of Paris beats.

It was to be the second night that I went without sleep. But this time it wasn't a cheating lover who robbed me of my rest but—who would have thought it of a woman who was anything but a passionate reader?—a book! A book that enchanted me from the very first sentences. A book that was sometimes sad, and at other times so funny that I had to laugh out loud. A book that was both beautiful and mysterious, because even if you read a lot of novels you will rarely come across one in which your own little restaurant plays a major role and the heroine is described in such a way that you seem to be seeing yourself in a mirror—even on a day when you're very happy and everything is going well!

When I got home, I hung my wet things over the radiator and slipped into a fresh white nightdress. I brewed a big pot of tea, made myself a couple of sandwiches, and listened to my answering machine. Bernadette had tried to reach me three times, and apologized for trampling on my feelings "with all the sensitivity of an elephant."

I had to smile when I heard her message: "Listen, Aurélie, if you want to feel sad about that creep, then feel sad, but please don't be mad at me any longer—get in touch. I'm thinking about you such a lot."

My resentment had evaporated a long time ago. I put the tray with the tea, the sandwiches, and my favorite cup on the rattan table next to my saffron yellow sofa, thought for a moment, and then sent my friend a text:

Dear Bernadette, it's so awful when you are right. Do you want to come over Wednesday morning? Looking forward to seeing you. I'm off to sleep now. Bises, Aurélie!

The bit about sleeping was a fib, of course, but everything else was true. I got the paper bag from the Librairie Capricorne off the bureau in the hall, and put it down carefully beside the tray. I had a peculiar feeling, as even then I sensed that this was going to be my very own lucky bag.

I restrained my curiosity for a while longer. First of all, I drank my tea in tiny sips, then I ate the sandwiches, and finally I got up once more and fetched my woolen blanket from the bedroom.

It was as if I wished to delay the start of the actual business of the moment.

And then, finally, I unwrapped the book from the paper and opened it.

If I were now to claim that the hours that followed seemed to fly by, that would only be half the truth. In actual fact I was so immersed in the book that I could not even have said if it was one or three or six hours that had passed. That night I lost all sense of time—I entered into the novel like the main characters in *Orphée,* that old black-and-white Jean Cocteau film, which I had once seen with my father when I was a child. Except that I didn't go through a mirror after pressing it with the palm of my hand, but through the cover of a book.

Time stretched out, contracted, and then vanished completely.

I was beside the young Englishman who ends up in Paris because of his Francophile colleague's passion for skiing (compound fracture of the leg in Verbier). He works for the Austin Motor Company and is now tasked with establishing the Mini Cooper in France in the place of the marketing manager, who will be unable to work for some months. The problem: His knowledge of French is as rudimentary as his experience of the French, and he hopes—in total ignorance of the French national character—that everyone in Paris (at least the people in the firm's Paris branch) understands the language of the Empire and will cooperate with him.

He is outraged not only by the adventurous driving style of Parisian drivers—who try to force six lanes of traffic into a two-lane carriageway, have not the slightest interest in what is happening behind them, and abridge the driving school's golden rule of "mirror, signal, maneuver" to its final element—but also by the fact that the dyed-in-the-wool Frenchman doesn't get his dents and scratches repaired and is totally unaffected by advertising slogans such as "Mini—it's like falling in love," because he would rather make love to women than to cars.

He invites attractive Frenchwomen to dinner, and then almost has a fit as, with a cry of *"Ah, comme j'ai faim!"* they order the entire (expensive) menu but then pick at their *salade au chèvre* a few times, take four forkfuls of *boeuf bourguignon* and two teaspoons of the *crème brûlée*, before dropping their cutlery charmingly in the remains of all that cuisine.

No Frenchman has ever heard of standing in a queue, and

no one here talks about the weather. Why should they? There are far more interesting topics. And hardly any taboos. They want to know why, in his mid-thirties, he still has no children ("Really, none at all? Not even one? Zero?"); what he thinks of American policy in Afghanistan or child labor in India; whether the hemp and Styrofoam artworks by Vladimir Wroscht in the Galerie La Borg aren't *très hexagonale* (he knows neither the artist nor the gallery—nor even the meaning of the word "*hexagonale*"); if he's satisfied with his sex life and where he stands on the subject of women dying their pubic hair.

In other words: Our hero moves from one tight spot to another.

He is an English gentleman who doesn't really like talking. And all of a sudden he has to discuss everything. In all possible and impossible places. At work, in the café, in the elevator (four floors are enough for a discussion of car burnings in the *banlieue,* the Paris suburbs), in the gentlemen's toilet ("Is globalization a good or a bad thing?"), and, of course, in the taxi, since French taxi drivers, unlike their London counterparts, have an opinion on every subject (which they also make known), and their passenger is not permitted to sit quietly keeping his thoughts to himself.

He has to *say* something!

In the end the Englishman puts up with it all with British good humor. And when, after many twists and turns, he falls head over heels in love with Sophie, a delightful and somewhat capricious girl, British understatement comes up against French complexity, leading at first to all kinds of misunderstandings and complications.

Until everything finally ends up in a wonderful *entente cordiale.* If not in a Mini, at least in a little French restaurant called

Le Temps des Cerises. With red-and-white-checked tablecloths. In the Rue Princesse.

My restaurant! There was no doubt about it.

I closed the book. It was six in the morning, and I once more believed that love was possible. I had read 320 pages and was not the least bit tired. The novel had been like an extremely exhilarating trip to another world—and yet that world seemed strangely familiar to me.

If an Englishman could describe a restaurant that, unlike La Coupole or the Brasserie Lipp, for example, doesn't crop up in every travel guide, and portray it so exactly, then he must actually have been there.

And if the heroine of his novel looked just like you—even down to the slinky dark green silk dress that was hanging in your wardrobe and the pearl necklace with the big oval cameo that you'd been given for your eighteenth birthday, then that was either a massive coincidence—or that man must have seen that woman at some time.

But if *that woman,* on one of the most miserable days of her life, chose *this very book* out of hundreds of others in a bookshop, then that was no longer a coincidence. It was fate itself speaking to me. But what was it trying to say?

Pensive, I turned the book over and stared at the photo of a likeable-looking man with short blond hair and blue eyes, sitting on a bench in some English park or other, his arm slung carelessly over the back of the seat, and smiling at me.

I closed my eyes for a minute and thought about whether I had ever seen this face before, this boyish, disarming smile. But no matter how long I searched through the drawers of my memory—I couldn't find that face.

The author's name said nothing to me either: Robert Miller.

I didn't know any Robert Miller—I didn't actually know any Englishmen at all, apart from the English tourists who occasionally wandered into my restaurant, and that British exchange student from my school days who came from Wales and—with his red hair and masses of freckles—looked just like Flipper the dolphin's sidekick.

I studied the short biography of the author carefully.

Robert Miller had worked as an engineer for a big English car manufacturer until he wrote his first novel—*The Smiles of Women*. He loved old cars, Paris, and French food, and lived with his Yorkshire terrier, Rocky, in a cottage near London.

"Who are you, Robert Miller?" I asked under my breath, and my gaze returned to the man on the park bench. "Who are you? And how do you know me?"

And suddenly an idea began buzzing around my head, and I found it more and more attractive.

I wanted to get to know this author, who had not only restored my will to live in my darkest hour, but also seemed to be linked with me in some mysterious way. I'd write to him. I'd thank him. And then I'd invite him to a really magical evening in my restaurant and find out what this novel was all about.

I sat up and aimed my index finger at the chest of Robert Miller, who at this moment was probably walking his little dog somewhere in the Cotswolds.

"Mr. Miller—I'll be seeing you!"

Mr. Miller smiled at me, and strangely enough I didn't doubt for one moment that I would succeed in tracking down my new (and only) favorite writer.

Little did I know that this author shunned the glare of publicity like the plague.

Two

....

"What do you mean, this author shuns the glare of publicity like the plague?" Monsieur Monsignac had jumped up. His massive belly quivered with agitation and the members of the editors' meeting sank down lower in their seats as the thunder of his voice grew ever louder.

"We've sold almost fifty thousand copies of that bloody book. This guy Miller is just about to jump onto the bestseller lists. *Le Figaro* wants to do a big feature about him." Monsignac calmed down for a moment, looked dreamily upward, and drew a gigantic headline in the air with his right hand.

"Title: *An Englishman in Paris*. Éditions Opale's surprise best seller." Then he slapped the table with such a crash that Madame Petit, who was taking the minutes, dropped her pencil in fright. "And you sit there and try to tell me in all seriousness that this man isn't capable of shifting his English ass to Paris for just one day? Tell me it's not true, André, tell me it's not!"

I saw his red face, his bright eyes darting bolts of lightning. There was no doubt about it: Jean-Paul Monsignac, publisher and owner of Éditions Opale, was going to have a heart attack any second.

And it was my fault.

"Monsieur Monsignac, calm down, please." I wrung my hands. "Believe me, I'm doing everything I can. But Monsieur Miller is an Englishman, after all. You know—*my home is my castle*. He lives in seclusion in his cottage, just tinkering with his cars most of the time—he's not at all used to dealing with the press and doesn't like to be the focus of attention. I mean, that's . . . that's what makes him so likeable . . ."

I could see that I was talking to save my life. Why hadn't I just said that Robert Miller was traveling around the world for a year and didn't have his iPhone with him?

"Tsk, tsk! Stop blathering, André! Just make sure that the Englishman gets on a train, zooms under the Channel, and answers a few questions and signs a few books over here. That's the least we can expect. After all, this guy was"—he picked up the book, glanced at the back cover, and then dropped it back on the table in front of him—"a motor mechanic—no, even an *engineer*—before he wrote his novel. He must occasionally have come into contact with the human race then. Or is he autistic?"

Gabrielle Mercier, one of the two editors, giggled behind her hand: I could have strangled the silly cow.

"Of course he's not autistic," I quickly replied. "It's just that he's a bit, hmm, a bit averse to human company."

"So is *every* intelligent human being. The more I see of men, the better I like my dog. Who said that? Well? Does anyone know?" Monsieur Monsignac looked expectantly around the table. Even now, he couldn't resist showing off his education. He'd been at the École Normale Supérieure, the Parisian elite school, and he never let a day go by in our publishing company without quoting some important philosopher or writer.

Strangely enough, Monsieur Monsignac's memory functioned in a very selective way. While it retained the names of great literary figures, thinkers, and Goncourt Prize winners with ease, it had great difficulty where light literature was concerned. Either he forgot the author's name immediately, and then it was "that man" or "that Englishman" or "that *Da Vinci Code* writer," or he indulged in ridiculous contortions like Lars Stiegsson (Stieg Larsson), Nicolai Bark (Nicholas Sparks), or Steffen Lark (Stephen Clarke).

"I'm not all that frightfully keen on American authors, but why don't we actually have a Steffen Lark on our list?" he had bellowed at the meeting two years before. "An American in Paris—that still seems to go down well, even today!"

I was responsible for our English-language books, and I had warily made him aware of the fact that Steffen Lark was an *Englishman,* who was actually called *Stephen Clarke* and wrote very successful humorous books about France.

"Funny books about Paris. By an Englishman. Well, well," Monsieur Monsignac had said, shaking his big head. "Stop trying to lecture me, André, and bring me someone like this Clarke instead. What do I pay you for? Are you a truffle hound or not?"

A few months later, I produced the manuscript of a certain Robert Miller from my briefcase. In terms of wit and wealth of ideas it was right up there with its popular predecessor. It all worked out: The book sold extremely well, and I was now paying the price. What's that great saying? Pride comes before a fall. And in the case of Robert Miller I found myself in free fall, so to speak.

The only reason that Jean-Paul Monsignac had finally retained the name of his new bestselling author ("What's that

Englishman called—Meller?") was that he had a famous name-sake ("No, Monsieur Monsignac, not Meller—*Miller!*"), who had already received the stamp of literary approval ("Miller? Is he related to *Henry* Miller in some way?").

While those round the table were still wondering if the quotation was from Hobbes or not, I suddenly thought that Monsignac, with all his terrible quirks, was still the best and most human publisher I'd met in all my fifteen years in the publishing business. I found it difficult to lie to him, but the way things were looking I had no choice.

"And what if we just give Robert Miller the questions from *Le Figaro* in writing and then pass his answers on to the press? The way we did with that Korean publisher. That worked very well." It was a last pathetic attempt to ward off the impending disaster—and of course, it failed to convince him.

"No, no, no! I don't like that at all!" Monsignac raised his hands defensively.

"Out of the question—that way we'd lose all spontaneity," interjected Michelle Auteuil, with a disapproving look over her black Chanel glasses. Michelle had been bending my ear for weeks now to get something done about "this charming Englishman." So far I'd been deaf to her entreaties. But now she had one of the most important papers on her side, and—what was much worse—my boss.

Michelle does our press relations, wears nothing but black or white, and I hate her for her apodictic remarks.

She sits there in her immaculate white blouse and black suit and says things like "That won't do *at all*," whenever you go to her with an idea that you think is great because you still somehow believe in the good in people who—just like that—get enthusiastic about a book. "There's no literary editor in the world who

seriously reads historical novels anymore, André—just forget it!"
Or she says: "A book launch for an *unknown* female author—and
one who writes *short stories* to boot? Puh-lease, André! Who is
that going to bring in out of the rain? Has she at least been
nominated for the Prix? No?" Then she sighs, rolls her blue eyes,
and fiddles impatiently with the little silver ballpoint that she always seems to have in her hand. "You really have *no* idea what
press relations are like today, do you? We need names, names,
names. At least try and find a celebrity to write the foreword."

And before you can say anything else, her phone rings again
and she's gushing effusively over one of those TV or journalist
guys in leather jackets who "seriously" don't read historical novels anymore and think themselves even cooler because a long-
legged beauty with smooth black hair is joking with them.

That all went through my mind as Michelle Auteuil now sat
before me like freshly fallen snow and waited for a reaction.

I cleared my throat. "Spontaneity," I repeated, trying to win
time. "That's precisely our problem." I looked meaningfully
around the table.

Michelle remained expressionless. She was definitely not the
kind of woman whose reserve can be broken down by rhetori-
cal maneuvers.

"This guy Miller is by no means as humorous and quick-
witted in conversation as you might think," I continued. "And
he is—like most writers—not very spontaneous either. After
all, he's not one of those . . ." I couldn't resist the dig and darted
a glance toward Michelle. ". . . TV celebrities who chatter on
day and night but need a ghostwriter to help them with the
books they write."

Michelle's blue eyes narrowed.

"I'm not interested!" Jean-Paul Monsignac's patience was

finally exhausted. He waved Miller's book around in the air, and I thought it was quite possible that he would throw it at me any second. "Don't be childish, André. Get that Englishman over to Paris for me! I want a great interview in *Le Figaro* with lots of photos, period!"

My stomach churned painfully.

"And if he says no?"

Monsignac looked hard at me and remained silent for a few seconds. Then, with all the joviality of a hangman, he said:

"Then you'd better make sure that he says yes."

I nodded apprehensively.

"After all, you're the only one of us who knows this Miller, aren't you?"

I nodded again.

"But if you don't think you're up to getting him here, *I* could talk to the Englishman. Or perhaps . . . *Madame Auteuil?*"

This time I didn't nod.

"No, no, that wouldn't be a good idea, absolutely not," I replied quickly, and felt the trap closing around me. "Miller is really a bit awkward, you know—not unpleasant, he's more like Patrick Süskind, not easy to get hold of, but we . . . we'll cope. I'll get in touch with his agent today."

I put my hand to my beard and stroked my chin with finger and thumb, hoping that no one would notice how I was panicking.

"*Bon,*" declared Monsignac, and leaned back in his seat. "Patrick Süskind—I like that!" He smiled benevolently. "Admittedly, his writing is not as intelligent as Süskind's, but on the other hand, he's better-looking, isn't he, Madame Auteuil?"

Michelle smiled maliciously. "He is indeed! Much better-looking. At last we've got an author we can present to the press without any worries. I've been saying that for weeks. And if our esteemed colleague manages to get around to sharing his wonderful author with us, there's nothing more to stop us."

She snapped open her thick black Filofax. "What do you think of a lunch with the press in the brasserie at the Lutetia?"

Monsignac grimaced, but said nothing. I don't think anyone but me knew that he wasn't very keen on the Lutetia because of its inglorious past. "That old Nazi dump," he had once said to me when we'd been invited to a publisher's reception in the old grand hotel. "Did you know that Hitler had his headquarters there?"

"Then we'll take our author on a shopping trip around Paris and its Christmas decorations," Michelle continued. "That will make a nice rounded story, and we can also finally take a few reasonable photos." She waved her silver pen busily and leafed through her diary. "Shall we look at the beginning of December? That would give the book a bit more of a push—for the Christmas trade."

I went through the rest of that afternoon's meeting in an impenetrable mist. I only had three weeks left, and I didn't have a plan. From far away I heard Jean-Paul Monsignac's voice. He made in-your-face criticisms, laughed out loud, flirted a bit with Mademoiselle Mirabeau, the pretty new editorial assistant. He inspired his troops—not for nothing were these meetings in Éditions Opale very popular and entertaining.

Yet that afternoon I had only one thought: I must call Adam Goldberg! He was the only one who could help me.

I made an effort to look at whoever was speaking and prayed that the meeting would end quickly. They discussed the dates of various events and went through the sales figures for October. Book projects were presented, and met with rejection ("Who on earth would want to read that?"), incomprehension ("What do the others think?"), or acceptance ("Great! We'll make her the new Anna Gavalda!") from Monsignac. Then, as the afternoon gradually drew toward its end a violent argument flared up: Should we offer the so far unknown author—owner of a Venetian ice-cream parlor—of a thriller that his sharp-nosed American agent praised to the heights as "a masculine Donna Leon" an advance for which any normal human being could buy himself a small palazzo? Monsignac put an end to the discussion by getting Madame Mercier to give him the manuscript and stuffing it into his old brown leather briefcase. "That's enough argument, we'll carry on tomorrow. Just let me take a look at it."

This could have signaled the end of the meeting, if Mademoiselle Mirabeau hadn't raised her hand at that very moment. Shyly, and with a wealth of detail that had everyone else yawning, she told us about an unsolicited manuscript. It was clear from the third sentence that it would never see the light of day in the world of books. Monsignac raised his hand to silence the unrest that was suddenly making itself felt in the room. Mademoiselle Mirabeau was so worked up that she didn't even notice the warning glances he gave us. "You did that very well, my dear," he said as she finally put down her last page of notes.

Mademoiselle Mirabeau, who had only been working in our editorial department for a few weeks, blushed with relief. "There's probably no question of its being published," she whispered.

Monsignac nodded with a serious expression. "I'm afraid you're right, my dear," he said patiently. "But don't worry about it. So much that we have to read is garbage. You read the beginning: garbage. You take a look in the middle: garbage.

The end: garbage. If something like that ends up on your desk, you can save yourself the trouble and . . ." He raised his voice a little, "there's no need to waste your breath on it." He smiled.

Mademoiselle Mirabeau nodded her understanding, the others grinned noncommittally. The publisher of Éditions Opale was in his element, and rocked back and forth in his chair. "I'll tell you a secret, Mademoiselle Mirabeau," he said, and we all knew what was coming, because we'd all heard it before. "A good book is good on every page," he said, and with these lofty words the meeting was finally at an end.

I grabbed my manuscripts, ran to the end of the narrow corridor, and burst into my little office.

Completely out of breath, I fell into my desk chair and dialed the number in London with trembling hands.

It rang a few times, but nobody answered.

"Pick it up, Adam, damn it!" I cursed under my breath, and then the answering machine cut in.

"Adam Goldberg Literary Agency. Unfortunately you are calling outside office hours. Please leave a message after the tone, and we'll get back to you."

I took a deep breath. "Adam!" I said, and even to my ears it sounded like a cry for help. "This is André. Call me back immediately, please. We've got a problem!"

Three
....

When the telephone rang, I was in the garden of a charming English cottage, pensively plucking a few withered leaves off a climbing rose that was growing up against a brick wall.

Birds were chirping, the morning was filled with an almost unreal sense of calm, and the sun was shining warm and mild on my face. The perfect start to a perfect day, I thought, and decided to ignore the telephone. I buried my face in a particularly opulent pink rose, and the ringing stopped.

Then I heard a click, and a voice that I knew well but that somehow didn't belong here spoke behind me.

"Aurélie? . . . Aurélie, are you still asleep? Why aren't you picking up the phone? Hm . . . funny . . . Are you just taking a shower? . . . Listen, I just wanted to tell you I'll be with you in half an hour, and I'm bringing croissants and *pains au chocolat*— you know you like them. Aurélie? Heeellooo! Hellohellohello! Pick up the phone now, please!"

With a sigh, I wrenched my eyes open and tumbled into the hall in bare feet to pick up the phone from its stand.

"Hello, Bernadette!" I said sleepily, and the English rose garden faded away.

"Did I wake you? It's half past nine!" Bernadette is one of those people who like getting up early, and half past nine is almost the middle of the day for her.

"Hm . . . hm." I yawned, went back into the bedroom, wedged the phone between my ear and my shoulder, and fished under the bed for my slippers with one foot. One of the disadvantages of owning a small restaurant is that you almost never have an evening free. However, the undisputed advantage is that you can always start the day in a leisurely manner.

"I've just had such a lovely dream," I said, and opened the curtains.

I looked up at the sky—no sun!—and became lost in thoughts of the summery cottage.

"Are you feeling better? I'll be there any minute!"

I smiled. "Yes. Much better," I said, and noticed to my surprise that it was true.

Three days had passed since Claude had left me, and even yesterday when, admittedly somewhat bleary-eyed but by no means unhappy, I had done my shopping in the market halls and then in the restaurant in the evening greeted the customers and recommended the *loup de mer* that Jacquie prepares so well, I had hardly thought of him once. I had in fact thought a lot more about Robert Miller and his novel—and about my idea of writing to him.

Only once, when Jacquie put his arm around my shoulder in a fatherly way and said, "*Ma pauvre petite,* how could he do that to you, the sonofabitch? Ah, men are such pigs. Here, eat a dish of bouillabaisse," did I feel a little pang in my heart—but at least it wasn't making me cry anymore. And when I got home last night, I sat down at the table with a glass of red wine, leafed through the book once more, and then sat for quite a while, pen in hand, with a sheet of white paper in front of me. I couldn't remember the last time I had written a letter, and now here I was writing a letter to a man I didn't know at all. Life was strange.

"Know what, Bernadette?" I said, and went into the kitchen to lay the table. "Something strange has happened. I think I've got a bit of a surprise for you."

An hour later, Bernadette was sitting looking at me in total amazement.

"You've read a *book*?"

She'd arrived with a little bunch of flowers and a gigantic bag of croissants and *pains au chocolat,* fully intending to console me; and instead of a miserable woman with a broken heart weeping into one paper tissue after another, she'd found an Aurélie who, with gleaming eyes, excitedly told her an adventure story about a spotted umbrella that had floated away, a policeman on a bridge who had pursued her, an enchanted bookshop where Marc Chagall had been sitting and had offered her cookies, and about the wonderful book she had reached out for. How one thing had led to another, what a twist of fate! That she'd spent the whole night reading that fateful book, which had driven away all her lovesickness and aroused her curiosity. About her dream and the fact that she'd written the author a letter—and wasn't all this just so amazing?

Perhaps I'd been speaking too quickly or too confusedly— either way, Bernadette hadn't understood the most important thing.

"So, you bought one of those 'Advice for the Lovelorn' books, and that helped you to feel better," was how she summed up my own little personal miracle. "That's wonderful! I admit I wouldn't have thought you were the type for self-help books, but what's important is that it helped you."

I shook my head. "No, no, no, you haven't understood, Bernadette. It wasn't one of those psychobooks. It's a novel, and I'm in it!"

Bernadette nodded. "You mean the heroine thinks like you do, and that's what pleased you about it."

She grinned and spread her arms in a theatrical gesture. "Welcome to the world of books, my dear Aurélie. I must say that your enthusiasm gives me hope. Perhaps we'll make a passable reader out of you!"

I groaned. "Bernadette, just listen to me, will you. Yes, I don't read many books, and no, I'm not freaking out just because I've read some novel. I liked the book—liked it a lot, in fact. That's one thing. And the other thing is: There's a girl in it, a young woman, who looks like me. Her name is Sophie, that's true, but she has long, dark blond, wavy hair, she's middling tall and slim, she's wearing my dress. And at the end she's sitting in a restaurant called Le Temps des Cerises in the Rue Princesse."

Bernadette said nothing for a long moment, and then she said, "And is the woman in the novel also together with a completely screwed-up weirdo called Claude who's cheating on her with another woman the whole time?"

"No, she's not. She's not with anyone and then later on falls in love with an Englishman, who finds French customs and behavior rather peculiar." I threw a piece of croissant at Bernadette. "Anyway, Claude *wasn't* cheating on me the whole time!"

"Who knows? Anyway, let's not talk about Claude! I want to see this wonderful book at once!"

Bernadette was obviously getting all fired up. Perhaps it was just that she would have found anything wonderful if it led me away from Claude and gave me back my peace of mind. I stood up and got the book, which was lying on the sideboard.

"Here," I said.

Bernadette glanced at the title. *"The Smiles of Women,"* she read out loud. "A nice title." She leafed through the pages with interest.

"Look . . . here," I said excitedly. "And here . . . just read that!"

Bernadette's eyes moved from side to side, while I watched expectantly.

"Yeeees," she said finally. "That is certainly a bit strange. But, *mon Dieu,* remarkable coincidences do happen. Who knows, perhaps the author knows your restaurant or has heard something about it. A friend who ate there on a business trip to Paris may have enthused to him about it. Something like that. And—don't get me wrong here, you're a very special person, Aurélie—but you're not the only woman with long, dark blond hair . . ."

"And what about the dress? What about the dress?" I pressed her.

"Yes, the dress . . ." Bernadette thought for a moment. "What can I say, it's a dress you bought sometime, somewhere. I assume that it's not a model that Karl Lagerfeld personally designed for you, is it? In other words—other women could also have a similar dress. Or it was on a mannequin in a shop window. There are so many possible explanations . . ."

I made a dissatisfied sound.

"But I can understand that this must all seem very surprising to you. I'm sure it would be the same for me at first."

"I can't believe that it's all just coincidence," I insisted. "I just don't believe it."

"My dear Aurélie, *everything* is chance or fate—if that's what people want to believe. For my part, I think that there's probably a simple explanation for all these remarkable coincidences—but that's only my opinion. Anyway, you found that book at just the right moment, and I'm truly happy that it's taken your mind off things."

I nodded, feeling a bit disappointed. Somehow I'd imagined a rather more dramatic reaction. "But you must admit that things like this don't happen very often," I said. "Or has something like it ever happened to you?"

"I admit everything," she said with a laugh. "And no, nothing like that has ever happened to me."

"Even though you read so much more than me," I said.

"Yes, even though I read so much more," she repeated. "Pity, really."

She glanced critically at the book and then turned it over. "Robert Miller," she said. "Never heard of him. But at least he's damned good-looking, this Robert Miller."

I nodded. "And his book saved my life. So to speak," I added quickly.

Bernadette looked up. "Did you tell him *that* in your letter?"

"No, of course not," I said. "At least, not directly. But yes, I did thank him. And invite him to a meal in my restaurant, which—as you said—he either already knows or has heard of." I said nothing about the photo.

"Oh, là là," said Bernadette. "You really want to know, don't you?"

"Yes," I said. "And anyway, readers often write to authors when they've really liked their books. That's not so unusual."

"Will you read the letter to me?" asked Bernadette.

"Not on your life." I shook my head. "Postal confidentiality. And anyway, I've already sealed it."

"And posted it?"

"No." Only then did I realize that I had no idea about the address. "What do you actually do when you want to write to an author?"

"Well, you could write to the publisher, and they could then forward it to him." Bernadette picked up the book again. "Let's see," she said, and looked for the publication details. "Ah, here it is: Copyright Éditions Opale, Rue de l'Université, Paris." She put the book back down on the kitchen table. "That's not far from here," she said, and took another sip of her coffee. "You could almost go there personally and hand the letter over to them." She winked at me. "Then it'll get there much quicker."

"You're so silly, Bernadette," I said. "And d'you know what? That's exactly what I'll do!"

And that's how I ended up that evening taking a slight detour and walking along the Rue de l'Université to stick a long, thick envelope into the mail slot at Éditions Opale. The envelope was addressed to "The Author Robert Miller/Éditions Opale." At first I'd just written "Mr. Robert Miller, c/o Éditions Opale" but "The Author" seemed somehow more formal and solemn. And I must admit that I felt a little solemn as I heard the letter landing softly on the other side of the big front door.

When you send off a letter, you are always setting something in motion. You enter into a dialogue. You want to communicate your news, your experiences, or your feelings, or else you want to know something. A letter always consists of a sender and a recipient. As a rule, it requires an answer, unless you're writing a letter breaking up with someone—and even then what you write is aimed at a living person and produces—unlike a diary entry—a reaction.

I could not have expressed clearly in words what sort of reaction I was actually expecting to this letter. It was at least more than simply putting a period after my thanks for a book.

I expected an answer—to my letter and my questions—and the prospect of getting to know the author who had ended his story in Le Temps des Cerises was exciting. But by no means as exciting as what then actually happened.

Four

....

The earth seemed to have swallowed Adam Goldberg. He didn't answer, and I became more nervous with every hour that passed. Since the previous evening I had tried to reach him again and again. The fact that someone could theoretically be called on four different numbers and was still, when it came down to it, unreachable, filled me with hatred for the digital age.

In his office in London the answering machine—whose announcement I by now knew by heart—just kept picking up. No one answered his business cell phone either—I could leave a message and the subscriber would also be informed of my call by text: how comforting! The telephone at his home number rang for several minutes before the answering machine cut in—with the babbling voice of Tom, Adam's six-year-old son.

"Hi, the Goldbergs are not at home. But don't you worry—we'll be back soon and then we can taaaaalk . . ." Then came some giggles and crackles and then the additional information that the head of the Goldberg family could be reached on his private cell phone if the matter was really urgent.

"In urgent cases you can reach Adam Goldberg on his mobile . . ." More crackling, then a whisper. "What's your mobile number, Daddy?" And then the child's voice recited another telephone number at full volume—one I didn't know. If you dialed this number, another friendly robotic voice informed you, "This number is temporarily unavailable, please try again later," and this time there wasn't even the chance to leave a message—just the instruction to "try again later." I ground my teeth.

Back in the office, I wrote to the literary agency first thing in the morning in the hope that, wherever Adam was, he would at least pick up his e-mail.

> *Dear Adam, I'm trying everything to reach you. Where on earth are you?! All hell's been let loose here!!! Please ring me back UR-GENTLY, preferably on my cell phone. It's about our author, Robert Miller, who's got to come to Paris. Yours, André.*

A minute later the reply came, and I sighed with relief, until I opened the message:

> *Sorry, I'm out of the office. In an emergency you can reach me on my mobile number.*

What can I say? The number was the one that, when you called it, was temporarily unavailable. And so the circle was completed.

I tried to work. I looked through manuscripts, answered e-mail, wrote some jacket copy, drank what felt like my hundred-and-fiftieth espresso, and watched my phone. It rang many times that morning, but my friend and business colleague Adam Goldberg was never at the other end of the line.

The first to ring was Hélène Bonvin, a French author who was very nice—and very time-consuming. She was always either writing away like mad, in which case she'd tell me about every minuscule idea she'd put down on paper—and if it had been up to her, she'd probably have liked to read me the whole manuscript over the phone. Or she would be suffering from writer's block, and then I had to do my utmost to convince her that she really was a superb writer.

This time it was the writer's block.

"I'm totally empty. I have no ideas whatsoever," she lamented.

"Oh, Hélène, that's what you say every time, and you always end up producing a fine novel."

"Not this time," she said in a gloomy voice. "The whole thing's a mess from start to finish. Do you know what, André? Yesterday I spent the whole day in front of this stupid machine, and in the evening I deleted everything I'd written because it was simply atrocious. Platitudinous, no ideas, and full of clichés. No one will want to read something like that."

"But, Hélène, it's not like that at all. You write so wonderfully—just read the enthusiastic reviews by our readers on Amazon. And anyway it's perfectly normal to feel a bit off from time to time. Perhaps you should just take a day off and write nothing. Then your ideas will start to flow again. You'll see."

"No. I've got a really funny feeling. It's not going to work. We'd better just forget about this novel . . . and I . . ."

"What nonsense you're talking!" I interrupted her. "You

want to throw in the towel just as you've reached the home stretch? The book is already as good as finished."

"Maybe. But it's no *good*," she replied stubbornly. "I'd have to rewrite the whole thing. Basically, I might as well delete it all."

I sighed. It was always the same with Hélène Bonvin. While most authors that I worked with circled anxiously around the first pages of their work and took unbelievably long to wind themselves up to get started, this woman always had her panic attacks when three-quarters of the manuscript was already written. Then suddenly nothing pleased her anymore, everything was total garbage, the worst thing she'd ever written.

"Now, Hélène, just listen to me. You're not deleting anything! Send me what you've written so far, and I'll look at it right away. Then we'll talk about it, okay? I bet it'll be fantastic as always."

I talked to Hélène Bonvin for another ten minutes before hanging up, exhausted. Then I stood up and went into the secretary's office, where Madame Petit was just having a gossip with Mademoiselle Mirabeau.

"Has Adam Goldberg called?" I asked, and Madame Petit, who had this morning swathed her baroque form in a brightly colored dress with large flowers, smiled at me over her coffee cup.

"No, Monsieur Chabanais," was her friendly reply. "I would have told you at once. Just one of the translators, Monsieur Favre, who had a couple more questions, but he'll call back later. And . . . oh yes, your mother called and wants you to ring back urgently."

"For heaven's sake!" I raised my hands in self-defense. Whenever my mother asked me to ring back urgently, it cost me at least an hour. But it was never urgent.

Unlike me, the old dear had plenty of time, and she loved to call me at work because there was always someone there to pick up the phone. If I wasn't available, she would chat to Madame Petit, whom she found "totally charming." I had once given Maman my number at work—for emergencies. Unfortunately, her idea of what constituted an emergency differed sharply from mine, and she had the uncanny knack of calling precisely when I was on the hop, when I had to rush to a meeting or was under severe pressure reading a manuscript that should if possible go to the typesetter by the afternoon.

"Just imagine, old Orban has fallen from his ladder while he was picking cherries, and now he's lying in the hospital . . . a fractured hip! What do you say to that? I mean . . . does he have to climb around in trees at his age?"

"Maman, please! I haven't got time right now!"

"*Mon Dieu,* André, you're always in such a state," she would then say, and you couldn't mistake the reproachful tone in her voice. "I thought you'd be interested; after all, you spent so much time at the Orbans' as a child . . ."

As a rule these conversations ended unhappily. Either I was actually sitting at my desk and let the conversation flow over me and then said "Aha!" or "Oh dear!" so often at the wrong time that my mother would eventually cry out indignantly, "André, are you actually listening to me?" or I would interrupt her immediately, snapping "I can't talk to you now!" and then have to listen to her saying I was extremely uptight and probably wasn't eating properly.

Then to prevent Maman being upset with me for a century

or so I would have to promise to call her from home in the evening "at leisure."

And so it was better for all concerned if she didn't get through to me at work. "If my mother calls, just tell her I'm in a meeting and I'll get back to her in the evening," I had constantly impressed on Madame Petit—but our secretary always took Maman's side.

"But, Monsieur Chabanais—she is your *mother*, after all!" she would say when she had disregarded my orders yet again. And when she really wanted to annoy me, she would add: "I also find you're sometimes a bit highly strung."

"Listen, Madame Petit," I now said with a threatening look. "I'm under a bit of pressure and under no . . . under no circumstances are you to put my mother through. And no one else who's going to waste my time—unless it's Adam Goldberg or someone from his agency. I hope I have made myself clear!"

Pretty little Mademoiselle Mirabeau looked at me wide-eyed. When I'd taken her under my wing in her first week and patiently explained to her the way things worked in the editorial department, she had smiled at me admiringly and finally said that I was just like that nice English publisher in the film of John le Carré's thriller *The Russia House*—the one with the brown eyes and the beard—but younger, of course.

I'd found that rather flattering. Well, I mean, what man would not like to be Sean Connery as a British gentleman publisher (but younger, of course): not only well read, but also intelligent enough to pull the wool over the eyes of all the world's secret services. Now I saw her dismayed look and ran a hand roughly over my short-trimmed beard. She probably thought I was an ogre.

"As you wish, Monsieur Chabanais," replied Madame Petit sharply. And as I went out I heard her say to Mademoiselle Mirabeau: "Is he in a lousy mood today! And yet his mother is such a delightful old lady . . ."

I slammed my office door and fell into my seat. I stared morosely at my computer screen and studied the reflection of my face on the dark blue surface. No, I had nothing at all in common with good old Sean today. Except that I was still waiting to be called back by an agent, who admittedly didn't have any secret documents but did share a secret with me.

Adam Goldberg was Robert Miller's agent. For some years now this eloquent, clever Englishman had run his little literary agency in London with great success and we had got on with each other from the moment we first talked. Since then we had been through so many book fairs and at least as many enjoyable evenings in London clubs and Frankfurt bars that we had become good friends. It was also he who had offered me Robert Miller's manuscript and sold it to me for a relatively modest sum.

At least that was the official version.

"Well done, André!" Monsieur Monsignac had said when I told him that the contract was safely signed, and I had felt a little low.

"Now don't get your knickers in a twist," Adam had said with a grin. "Opale wanted a Stephen Clarke, and now you've got one. You'll definitely bring in enough to cover the advance, and you'll save on the translation. Couldn't be better."

And now everything had gone a bit too well, and the demands were increasing. Who would ever have imagined that Robert Miller's little Parisian novel would sell so well?

I flopped down in my chair and thought back to the time when I'd been at the Frankfurt Book Fair sitting in Jimmy's Bar with Adam and told him about the kind of book our publishing firm was looking for.

On the wings of several cold, alcoholic drinks I had sketched out the rough outlines of a possible plot and asked him to keep a lookout for a novel like that.

"Sorry, but I haven't got anything like that on offer at the moment," Adam had answered. And then he had offhandedly said, "But I like the plot. My compliments. Why don't you actually write the book yourself? Then I can sell it to Éditions Opale."

And that was how it all started.

At first I'd turned him down with a laugh. "What an idea! Never. I couldn't. I edit novels, I don't *write* them!"

"Bullshit," Adam had said. "You've already worked with so many authors that you know how it works. You have original ideas, a good feeling for building up suspense, no one writes e-mails as funny as yours—and as for Stephen Clarke, you could beat him with one hand tied behind your back."

Three hours and several mojitos later I was almost beginning to feel like I was Hemingway.

"But I can't write the book under my own name," I objected. "I *work* for the company."

"You don't have to, man! Who writes under their own name these days? That's really a bit old school. I actually represent some authors who have two or three names and write for different publishers under them. John le Carré is really called David Cornwell. We'll invent a nice pseudonym for you," Adam said. "How about Andrew Ballantine?"

"Andrew Ballantine?" I pulled a face. "There's already a publisher called Ballantine, and as for Andrew—I'm André, and I'm buying the thing, people might feel . . ."

"Okay, okay, wait, I've got it: Robert Miller! What do you say? It's so normal that it sounds really genuine."

"And if things go pear-shaped?"

"They won't. You write your little book, I offer it to your company—or rather to you. I'll deal with all the contracts. You'll make a tidy pile, things like that always sell. You'll get your royalties. Old man Monsignac will finally have his novel à la Stephen Clarke. And ultimately everyone will be happy. And Bob's your uncle."

Adam clinked his mojito glass against mine. "To Robert Miller! And his novel? Or are you chicken? No risk, no fun. Come on, it'll be a great lark!" He laughed like a little boy.

I looked at Adam sitting cheerfully before me. Suddenly everything seemed so simple. And when I thought of my unspectacular salary and my permanent overdraft, the idea of an extra source of income was very tempting. No matter how good this profession was, as an editor, even as an editor in chief, you didn't exactly earn a massive amount—far from it. Many editors I knew worked as translators in their free time, or produced all kinds of Christmas or other anthologies to bump up their meager pay. The book trade was not the automobile trade. But at least the people had more interesting faces.

That always struck me when I was standing on the travelator at a book fair and whole phalanxes of chatting, thoughtful, or laughing book people came toward me. There was an animated buzz and flutter about the whole fair and the hall vibrated with millions of thoughts and stories. It was like a mercurial, intelligent, funny, vain, nimble-witted, effusive, over-lively, loquacious, and extremely intellectually active family. And it was a privilege to belong to it.

Of course, as well as the great publishing characters and

personalities who were admired or hated, there were also the glib manager types who maintained that in principle it didn't matter if you were trading in cans of cola or books, in the end it simply came down to professional marketing and, yes, I suppose, even just a little bit to the content. But in the long run even those guys could not remain untouched by the product they were dealing with every day, and ultimately there was a difference between holding a finished book in your hand rather than a cola can.

Nowhere else did you meet so many impressive, clever, intriguing, witty, curious, and quick people in one place. Everyone knew everything, and with the words "Have you heard the latest?" all the secrets that the business had to offer were revealed under the seal of strictest secrecy.

Have you heard the latest? They say Marianne Dauphin's having an affair with the marketing manager of Garamond—and she's pregnant. Have you heard the latest? Borani Press is bankrupt and is going to be sold to a perfume company before the end of the year. Have you heard the latest? The editors at Éditions Opale are now writing their own books and Robert Miller is in reality a Frenchman, hahaha!

I noticed the room beginning to spin around me. In those days you were still allowed to smoke, and at three in the morning Jimmy's Bar was a uniquely anesthetic combination of smoke, drinks, and voices.

"But why does it have to be an English name? It's all getting too complicated for me," I said lamely.

"Oh, Andy, come on! That's the whole joke! A Parisian writing about Paris—nobody wants that. No, no, it must be a genuine English author who fits all the clichés. British humor, a crazy hobby, if possible a good-looking bachelor with a little dog. I can see him right here in front of me." He nodded. "Robert Miller is perfect, believe me!"

"That's really clever," I said, impressed, and took a handful of salted almonds.

Adam knocked the ash off his cigarillo and leaned back in his leather seat. "It's not clever—it's brilliant!" he said, just like his favorite cartoon character King Rollo used to do every ten minutes in the TV series of the same name.

The rest was history. I wrote the book—and it turned out to be easier than I'd thought. Adam prepared the contracts and even contributed a photo of the author—a picture of his brother, two years older than him, a good-natured dentist from Devon who'd read a maximum of five books in his whole life and was now more or less made aware—less rather than more, actually— that he was the author of a novel. "How very funny," was, according to Adam, all that he said about it.

I had serious doubts about whether this placid man would still find it funny to come to Paris, talk to journalists about his book, and give a reading. Did he even know the city he was supposed, according to his biography in the blurb, to have such a liking for? Or had he never left his sleepy county? Was he likely to be up to speaking and reading in public? Perhaps he had a speech defect, or would refuse on principle to act as a ringer. It was only now that I realized that I knew nothing at all about Adam's brother, except that he was Libra with Libra in the ascendant (and so, according to Adam, a miracle of equilibrium) and a thoroughbred dentist (whatever that might mean). I didn't even know his name. No, of course I did: Robert Miller.

"Holy shit!" I laughed desperately and cursed the evening this whole lunatic plan had been hatched. "It's not clever, it's brilliant!" I mimicked my friend. Yes, that was in fact the most brilliant drunken idea that clever Adam had ever had and now everything was threatening to go off the rails and I was going to be in deep trouble.

"What can I do, what can I do?" I murmured, staring as if hypnotized at the screen-saver, which had flicked on and was showing a continuous series of dreamy Caribbean beaches. What wouldn't I have given to be that far away now, lazing on one of those white beach loungers under the palms with a mojito in hand, just staring into the empty blue sky for hours on end?

There was a timid knock at the door.

"What is it this time?" I barked, and sat up straight.

Mademoiselle Mirabeau came carefully into the room. She was carrying a big pile of printed paper and looked at me as if I were a cannibal who wolfed down little blond girls for breakfast.

"I'm sorry, Monsieur Chabanais, I didn't mean to disturb you."

Heavens, I must pull myself together!

"No, no, you're not disturbing me!" I tried a smile. "What is it?"

She stepped closer and put the pile of papers down on my desk. "This is that Italian translation that you gave me to edit last week. I've finished working on it."

"Good, good, I'll look at it a bit later." I took the pile and laid it to one side.

"It was a good translation. Didn't need much work."

Mademoiselle Mirabeau put her hands behind her back and remained in the room as if rooted to the spot.

"Glad to hear it," I said. "Sometimes you just get lucky."

"I've tried to write the jacket copy as well. It's on top of the pile."

"Wonderful, Mademoiselle Mirabeau. Thanks. Thanks a lot."

A gentle blush spread over her fine, heart-shaped face. Then she said abruptly: "I'm so sorry that you're having such problems, Monsieur Chabanais."

My goodness, she was really sweet! I cleared my throat.

"It's not that bad," I replied, and hoped that it sounded as if I had everything under control.

"Looks as if that Miller guy's being a bit difficult. But I'm sure you'll talk him round." She gave me an encouraging smile and went over to the door.

"Sure thing," I said, and for one happy moment forgot that my problem wasn't Robert Miller, but the fact that he didn't exist.

It was just as I expected. The very moment I unwrapped my ham baguette and took a hearty bite, the phone rang. I grabbed the handset and tried to maneuver the unchewed bite into the corner of my cheek.

"Hm . . . yes?" I said.

"There's some woman on the line. Says it's about Robert Miller—should I put her through or not?" It was Madame Petit, unmistakably still on her high horse.

"Yes, yes, of course," I managed to choke out, trying to swallow the lump of baguette somehow. "It's Goldberg's assistant, put her through, put her through!" Sometimes Madame Petit really had trouble adding two and two together.

There was a crackle on the line, and then I heard a somewhat breathless female voice saying: "Is that Monsieur André Chabanais?"

"That's me," I replied, having got rid of the baguette. Adam's assistants always had such pleasant voices, I thought. "Great that you've been able to call back so quickly, I need to speak to Adam urgently. Where's he been?"

The long pause at the other end of the line irritated me. I suddenly went ice cold, and I thought of that awful story the previous fall when an American agent had collapsed at the bottom of his stairs with a brain hemorrhage on the way to the book fair.

"Adam's okay, isn't he?"

"Er . . . well . . . I wouldn't know anything about that." The voice sounded a bit baffled. "I'm actually calling about Robert Miller."

She'd obviously read my e-mail to Adam. Adam and I had agreed at the time that we wouldn't tell *anyone* else about our little secret, and I hoped he'd stuck to the plan.

"And that's precisely why I need to talk to Adam," I said cautiously. "It's because Robert Miller is supposed to come to Paris, as you probably know."

"Oh," said the voice with delight. "That's just *wonderful*. No, I didn't know that. Tell me . . . did you get my letter? I hope it was all right that I just dropped it in like that. And would you be so kind as to forward it to Robert Miller? It's extremely important to me, you know."

I was gradually beginning to feel like Alice in Wonderland when she met the White Rabbit.

"What letter? I haven't received a letter," I bleated in confusion. "Tell me, you *are* from the Goldberg Literary Agency, aren't you?"

"Oh, no. This is Aurélie Bredin. Not an agency. I think I've been given the wrong extension. I wanted to talk to the editor who deals with Robert Miller," the voice said with cheerful certainty.

"That's me." I was gradually getting the feeling that the conversation was beginning to go round in circles. I didn't know anyone called Aurélie Bredin. "Now, Madame Bredin. What can I do for you?"

"I dropped a letter for Robert Miller at your office yesterday evening, and just wanted to make sure that it had arrived safely and will be forwarded to him."

At last the penny dropped. Nothing ever went quickly enough for these press people.

"Ah, now I know . . . you're the lady from *Le Figaro,* is that it?"

"No, monsieur."

"Well, but . . . who are you then?"

The voice sighed. "Aurélie Bredin, I've already told you."

"And?"

"The letter," the voice repeated impatiently. "I'd like you to forward my letter to Monsieur Miller."

"What letter are you talking about? I haven't received any letter."

"That can't be right. I brought it personally yesterday. A white envelope. Addressed to the author Robert Miller. You *must* have got the letter." The voice was becoming persistent, and now it was I who was beginning to lose patience.

"Listen, madame, if I say that there's no letter here, then you can believe it. Perhaps it may still come, and then we'll gladly forward it. Can we leave it at that?"

My suggestion seemed not to meet with much enthusiasm.

"Would it be possible to get Robert Miller's address? Or does he perhaps have an e-mail address where he can be reached?"

"I'm sorry, I'm afraid we don't give out authors' addresses on principle. They do have a right to a private life, after all." My goodness, what was the woman thinking of?

"Couldn't you make an exception just this once? It's really important."

"What do you mean—*important*? What's your relationship to Robert Miller?" I asked suspiciously. It was actually very unusual for me to ask a question like that, but the answer that now came was even more unusual.

"Well, if I only knew . . . I've read his book, you see . . . it's a really great book . . . and there are a few things in it that . . . well . . . I'd really like to ask the author a couple of questions . . . and thank him . . . he sort of saved my life . . ."

I stared at the phone in disbelief. This woman obviously wasn't right in the head. Obviously one of those overexcited female readers who pester authors mercilessly and, in their excessive enthusiasm write things like "I'd really *love* to get to know you!" or "You think just like I do!" or "I want to have your babies!"

Fine, I admit that in the readers' letters that had arrived for Robert Miller—that is, for me—there hadn't so far been any statements like that. But there had been a few enthusiastic missives that I had "forwarded." In other words, I'd read them and, since out of a certain degree of vanity I could not bring myself just to throw them away, I had stuck them in the very back corner of my steel cabinet.

"Now," I said. "I'm very glad about that. But I still can't give you Miller's address. I'm afraid you'll just have to make do with me. It's the only way."

"But you said you hadn't received my letter. If so, how can you forward it?" the voice asked in a mixture of truculence and despondency.

I would have liked to shake the voice, but it's an unfortunate quality of voices on the telephone that you can't actually shake them.

"Madame—what did you say your name was?"

"Bredin. Aurélie Bredin."

"Madame Bredin," I said, trying to keep completely calm. "As soon as your letter reaches my in-tray, I'll forward it, all right? Perhaps not immediately today or tomorrow, but I'll take care of it. And now I'm afraid I have to bring this conversation to an end, because I do have other things to do—admittedly not as important as *your letter,* but they do have to be done. I wish you good day."

"Monsieur Chabanais!" the voice shouted quickly.

"I'm still here," I responded grouchily.

"But what will we do if the letter is lost?" The voice trembled a little.

Exasperated, I ran my hand through my hair. In my mind's eye I could see an elderly lady with disheveled hair and a lot of time who scratched line after line on her paper with arthritic fingers, giggling quietly as she did so.

"Then, my dear Madame Bredin, you'll just have to write a new letter. And with that in mind, *bonne journée.*"

As far as I'm concerned you can write a hundred letters, I thought grimly as I slammed the phone back on its cradle. None of them will ever reach their target.

I'd hardly hung up when my office door opened and Madame Petit stuck her head round. "Monsieur Chabanais!" she said reproachfully. "Monsieur Goldberg has already tried to reach you twice and your line is always busy. I've got him on the line now, shall I . . . ?"

"Yes!" I shouted. "For heaven's sake, yes!"

My friend Adam was as always in a state of almost Buddhist serenity.

"About time too!" I snarled at him as he coolly murmured his "Hi-Andy-how's-it-going?" down the phone.

"Where on earth have you been? Have you any idea what's up here? I'm up to my neck in it, and you don't answer any of your crazy phones. Why's there no one in your office? Everyone's stressing me out about bloody Miller. Feral old women are ringing up here asking for his address. Monsignac wants a reading. *Le Figaro* wants a story. And do you know what'll happen when the old man finds out there's no Miller? I can pack my bags here and leave!"

At this point I had to pause for breath, and Adam used the opportunity to say something himself.

"Calm down, my friend," he said. "Everything's going to be all right. And which of your questions should I answer first?"

I growled into the phone.

"So . . . I was in New York for a couple of days visiting publishers, Carol came with me and Gretchen stupidly had food poisoning at the same time, which is why there was no one at the agency. My family used the opportunity to go and visit Grandma in Brighton. Emma had her mobile with her, but had forgotten the charger. And there's something wrong with my mobile at the moment, and perhaps the reception was poor— anyway your message only arrived in fragments and was so confused that I didn't understand what was happening. A classic case of Murphy's Law."

"Murphy's Law?" I asked. "What kind of stupid excuse is that?"

"It's not an excuse. Anything that can go wrong, will," said Adam. "That's Murphy's Law. But no need to get your knickers in a twist, Andy! First of all, you *won't* have to pack your bags. And secondly, we'll sort it out."

"You mean you'll sort it out!" I replied. "You'll have to make it clear to your nice dentist brother that he's got to show up here in Paris to play Robert Miller. After all, the idea of the photo was yours. I didn't want any photos at all, remember? But you couldn't get enough of all your silly details. Photo, dog, cottage, sense of humor." I interrupted myself for a moment. "Lives in a cottage with his little dog, Rocky. *Rocky!*" I literally spat the word out. "Who could land on the idea of calling his dog Rocky? That's completely gaga!"

"Completely normal for an Englishman," Adam insisted.

"Aha. Well! *Bon.* What's he like, your brother? I mean . . . does he understand a joke? Can he express himself? Do you think he's actually up to making a convincing appearance?"

"Oh . . . well . . . I think so . . . ," Adam muttered, and I heard a note of hesitation in his voice.

"What is it?" I said. "Don't tell me that your brother has since emigrated to South America."

"Oh, no! My brother would never get on an airplane." Adam fell silent once more, but he didn't sound as relaxed as usual.

"And . . . so?" I pressed.

"Well," he said, "there's just one teensy-weensy problem . . ."

I groaned, and wondered if our English non-author had shuffled off this mortal coil.

"He doesn't know about the book," Adam said calmly.

"What?" I shouted, and in a novel the letters would have been in a font size of at least 150 points. "You didn't tell him about it at all? I mean—is that supposed to be a joke, or what?" I was beside myself.

"No, not a joke," said Adam succinctly.

"But you told me that he'd said, 'How very funny.' 'How very funny'—those were his exact words!"

"Well . . . to be honest, they were actually *my* words," Adam said. "There didn't seem to be any point telling him about it at the time. The book has never appeared in England. And even if it had . . . my brother never reads. At best technical manuals about the latest developments in implant technology."

"My God, Adam," I said. "You've got a bloody nerve! And what about the photo? I mean, it is a picture of him, after all."

"Oh, that! D'you know, Sam's grown a beard since then—no one would recognize him from that picture."

Adam had regained his self-control. I, on the other hand, hadn't. "Oh, great! How very funny!" I shouted. "And now? Can he shave off the beard again? That's *if* he's even prepared to play along. *After* you haven't told him a single bloody word? Oh, hell! Oh, hell! *C'est incroyable!* Phew. That's it then. *Fini!* I might as well start packing up here."

My gaze wandered across to the overflowing bookshelves and the piles of manuscripts waiting to be edited. To the big poster from the last Bonnard exhibit in the Grand Palais, show-ing a cheerful southern French landscape. To the little bronze statuette on my desk that I'd once brought back from the Villa Borghese in Rome. It was of Daphne, at the very moment when, fleeing from Apollo, she is transformed into a tree.

Perhaps I ought just to turn myself into a tree, I thought, fleeing not from a god, but from an enraged Jean-Paul Monsi-gnac.

"You have good eyes," he had said, when he gave me the job. "Such an open, honest look. *Eh bien!* I like people who can look you straight in the eye."

My melancholy gaze wandered farther to the pretty little

windows with the white glazing bars and the double panes, where I used to look out over the roofs of the other houses and be able to see the spire of the Church of Saint-Germain and, on spring days, a patch of blue sky. I sighed deeply.

"Now don't get your knickers in a twist, André," the voice of Adam Goldberg rang out from far away. "We'll sort it out."

"We'll sort it out" was obviously his motto for life. But not mine. At least, not at this moment.

"Sam owes me a favor anyway," Adam continued, without noticing that I'd been struck dumb. "He's a good guy, and I'm sure he'll play along if I ask him. I'll ring him this evening and explain everything."

I wound the telephone cable round my finger without saying anything.

"What would be the best time?" asked Adam.

"Beginning of December," I muttered, staring at my cable-wound finger.

"So, then we've got more than two weeks!" said Adam happily, to my amazement.

To me, time was inexorable. To him it was an ally.

"I'll call as soon as I've reached my brother. Nothing to get worked up about," he said. And then my English friend ended our conversation with a little variation on his favorite phrase. "Don't worry. We'll sort it out in no time!"

The rest of the afternoon passed unspectacularly. I tried to work through the pile of manuscripts on my desk but wasn't really able to concentrate.

At one point Gabrielle Mercier dropped in to let me know, with a self-important expression, that after reading the novel by the Italian ice-cream parlor proprietor (beginning—middle—end), Monsieur Monsignac saw no hope of ever making a new

Donna Leon out of him. "An *ice-cream parlor proprietor* who writes, that's supposed to be extremely original or what?" Monsignac had said contemptuously. "If you ask me—it's junior high school prose. And not even exciting! Damn cheek asking so much money for it. *Ils sont fous, les Americains!*" Madame Mercier then came to the same conclusion—after all, she'd been agreeing with the boss for about twenty-five years—and so they'd happily agreed that the manuscript could be rejected.

About half past five Madame Petit came in with some letters and contracts that needed signing. Then she wished me good evening and departed with the news that today's mail was in the main office.

"Yes, yes," I said, nodding my acquiescence. On good days Madame Petit brought my mail in and personally put it on my desk. Usually she'd then ask if I wanted a nice cup of coffee. ("What would you say to a nice cup of coffee, Monsieur Chabanais?") When she was mad at me, like today, I was obviously not allowed to enjoy this double privilege. Madame Petit was not only a well-built secretary with a bosom that was, in Parisian terms, enormous. She was also a woman of principle.

Normally I came into the office at about ten and left at half past seven. The lunch break could be quite extensive, especially if I was lunching with an author—then it could last until three o'clock. *"Monsieur Chabanais est en rendez-vous,"* Madame Petit would then say busily, if anyone asked for me. After five it would finally get quieter in the offices of Éditions Opale—usually a hive of buzzing activity—and then you could get down to some real work. Time flew, and if I had a lot to do it sometimes happened that I looked at my watch to see that it was already almost nine. Today I decided to leave earlier. It had been a tiring day.

I turned off the old radiator beneath the window, shoved Mademoiselle Mirabeau's manuscript in my old briefcase, pulled on the brass chain that dangled from the dark green desk lamp and turned out the light.

"That's enough for today," I murmured, and pulled my office door shut behind me. But the eternal plan of divine providence had obviously decided that my day was not to end here.

"Excuse me," said the voice that had got totally on my nerves that afternoon. "But could you tell me where I can find Monsieur Chabanais?"

She stood before me as if she had just emerged from the ground. But it wasn't a crotchety eighty-year-old who was bothering me with her presumably missing letter. A slim young woman with a dark brown woolen coat and suede boots was the possessor of the voice. She had a knitted scarf slung carelessly around her neck. Her hair, longer than shoulder-length, swished and gleamed in the pale light of the lobby like spun gold as she now hesitantly took a step toward me.

She looked at me inquiringly out of dark green eyes.

It was Thursday evening, just before half past six, and I was suffering from déjà vu in a way that I could not immediately understand.

I didn't move, but stared at the shape with the dark blond hair as if it were an apparition.

"I'm looking for Monsieur Chabanais," she repeated earnestly. And then she smiled. It was as if a sunbeam were passing through the lobby. "You don't happen to know if he's still here?"

My God! I knew that smile! I'd seen it once before, about a

year and a half ago. It was this unbelievably enchanting smile that the story in my novel began with.

That's the thing about stories. Where do authors get their stories from? Are they just lying dormant within them to be brought to the surface by particular events? Do writers pluck them from the air? Do they follow the course of real people's lives?

What is true, and what invented? What really existed and what never existed? Does the imagination influence reality? Or does reality influence the imagination?

The illustrator and cartoonist David Shrigley once said: "When people ask me where I get my ideas from I tell them that I don't know. I think it's a stupid question. If you knew where your ideas came from they wouldn't be your ideas, they'd be someone else's, stolen by you. Ideas come from nowhere, put in your brain; maybe by God or evil spirits or something."

My theory is that people who write novels and tell stories to us fall into three main groups.

The first group always write only about themselves—many of them are among the literary greats.

The second group have an enviable talent for *inventing* stories. They sit in the train, look out the window, and suddenly they have an idea.

And then there are those who might be seen as the impressionists among writers. Their gift is finding stories.

They travel the world open-eyed and pluck situations, moods, and little scenes from the trees like cherries.

A gesture, a smile, the way someone brushes their hair back or ties their shoelaces. Snapshots behind which stories are hiding. Stories that become pictures.

They see a pair of lovers sauntering through the Bois de

Boulogne on a balmy summer evening and try and work out where life will take them. They sit in a café and observe two women friends chatting animatedly. They don't yet know that one of them will soon betray the other with her boyfriend. They wonder where the woman with the sad eyes who's sitting in the Metro with her head against the windowpane may be going.

They're standing at the cinema box office and chance to hear an extremely amusing discussion between the ticket seller and an ancient married couple who are asking whether there's a *student reduction*—you couldn't make it up! They see the light of the full moon pouring over the Seine like a sheet of silver and their heart fills with words.

I don't know if it's presumptuous of me to describe myself as an author. Well, anyway, I have just written a little novel. But if I did call myself one, I'd definitely put myself in the last category. I'm one of the people who *find* their stories.

And so I found the heroine of my novel that time in the little restaurant.

I still remember it exactly—I was strolling alone through Saint-Germain that spring evening—people were already sitting outside the restaurants and cafés—and for once went along a little street that I normally hardly ever use. My then girlfriend wanted a necklace for her birthday and had raved about a tiny jeweler's shop run by the Israeli designer Michal Negrin, which was on the Rue Princesse. I found the shop, left it a short time later with a brightly colored, old-style package, and then—without being prepared for it in any way—I found *her*!

She was standing behind the window of a restaurant that was about as big as the average living room, talking to a guest who was sitting with his back to me at one of the little tables with the red-and-white-checked cloths. The soft, yellowish light gleamed in her long, center-parted hair, and it was the way her hair flicked up with every movement that first caught my eye.

I stood still and absorbed every detail of that young woman. The simple, long, greenish dress of fine silk, which she wore as unconcernedly as a Roman goddess of spring, its broad straps leaving her arms and shoulders free. The hands with their long fingers moving charmingly as she spoke.

I saw how she touched her throat and played with a necklace of tiny, milky-white beads ending in a large antique cameo.

And then she looked up for a tiny moment and smiled.

It was that smile that enchanted me and filled me with joy even though it wasn't meant for me. I stood there looking in the window like a voyeur and hardly dared to breathe—so perfect did the moment seem.

Then the restaurant door opened, people came out onto the street laughing, the moment was over: The beautiful girl turned around and vanished, and I walked on.

I had never before eaten—nor did I later—in the snug little restaurant whose name I found so poetic that I couldn't help making my novel end there—in Le Temps des Cerises.

My girlfriend got her glitzy necklace. A short time later she left me.

But what remained was the smile of a stranger, which inspired me and gave my imagination wings. I called her Sophie and filled her with life. I put her through an adventurous story that I thought up.

And now she was suddenly standing in front of me, and I asked myself in all seriousness if it was possible for a character in a novel to become a human being of flesh and blood.

"Monsieur?" The voice assumed a note of concern, and I returned to the lobby of Éditions Opale, where I was still standing outside my closed office door.

"I'm sorry, mademoiselle," I said, making an effort to control my confusion. "I was lost in thought. What did you say?"

"I'd like to speak to Monsieur Chabanais if it's possible," she replied yet again.

"Well . . . you're speaking to him," I responded, and her surprised expression told me that she had expected the man who had slammed his phone down on her call in such an unfriendly way a few hours before to look somewhat different.

"Oh," she said, and her fine dark eyebrows shot up. "It's *you*!" Her smile vanished.

"Yes, it's me," I responded somewhat fatuously.

"Then we spoke on the telephone this afternoon," she said. "I'm Aurélie Bredin, do you remember? Who wrote a letter to your author . . . Monsieur Miller." Her dark green eyes looked at me reproachfully.

"Yes, actually, I do remember." She had damned lovely eyes.

"I'm sure you're surprised that I've just turned up like this?" she said.

What was I supposed to say to that? My level of surprise was about a thousand times more than she could possibly imagine. It was bordering on a miracle that Sophie, the heroine of my novel, should suddenly turn up here and ask me questions. That she was the woman from that afternoon who wanted the address of an author (who didn't exist!) because his book (that is, my book!) had apparently saved her life. But how could I have explained that? The whole thing was beyond my comprehension and I had the feeling that at any moment someone would jump out from round the corner on a wave of triumphant canned TV laughter and shout with overdone jollity: "Smile, you're on *Candid Camera,* hahaha!"

So I just went on staring at her and waited for my thoughts to sort themselves out.

"Well . . ." She cleared her throat. "After you were so . . ." She paused for effect. ". . . so impatient and frenetic on the phone this afternoon, I thought it might be better to come round in person and find out about my letter."

That was my cue to speak. Great, she'd only been here five minutes and she'd already started to talk like Maman! I immediately snapped out of my catatonic state.

"Listen, mademoiselle, I was up to my neck in work. But I was *not* frenetic or impatient."

She looked at me thoughtfully, and then she nodded. "You're right," she said. "To be honest, what you actually were was *unfriendly.* I've already asked myself if all editors are so unfriendly, or if it's just your specialty, Monsieur Chabanais."

I grinned. "By no means, we're just trying to do our job here, and unfortunately we sometimes get disturbed, Mademoiselle . . ." I'd forgotten her name again.

"Bredin. Aurélie Bredin." She held her hand out to me, and was smiling again.

I took it, and immediately wondered if there was any way I could manage to keep hold of the hand (and if possible more than the hand) longer than was absolutely necessary. Then I let go.

"Now, Mademoiselle Bredin, I'm really glad to have made your acquaintance. We don't meet such enthusiastic readers every day."

"Has my letter turned up?"

"Oh, yes! Of course," I lied, and nodded. "It's lying quite happily in my in-tray."

What could possibly happen? Either the letter was actually in my in-tray already, or it would be the next day or the day after. And even if the letter never turned up, the result would be the same: This wonderful reader's letter would never reach its addressee, but at best end up in my cabinet.

I gave a satisfied smile.

"Then you can forward it to Robert Miller," she said.

"But of course, Mademoiselle Bredin, don't worry. Your letter is already as good as in our author's hands. Still . . ."

"Still?" she repeated with concern.

"Still, if I were you I wouldn't expect too much. Robert Miller is an extremely reticent, not to say *difficult* man. Since his wife left him he lives like a recluse in his little cottage. His heart belongs totally to his little dog . . . Rocky," I said.

"Oh," she said. "How sad."

I nodded gravely.

"Yes, really very sad. Robert was always a bit peculiar, but now . . ." I sighed deeply and convincingly. "At this very moment we are trying to get him to come to Paris for an interview with *Le Figaro,* but I don't hold out much hope."

"Strange, I would never have thought that. His novel is so . . . so optimistic and humorous," she said. "Have you ever personally met Monsieur Miller?" She was looking at me with interest for the first time.

"Well . . ." I coughed self-importantly. "I think that I can say that I am one of the few people who really know Robert Miller. I certainly did a lot of work with him on his book, and he seems to have taken to me."

She looked impressed. "It really is a super book." And then she said: "Oh, I'd so love to meet this Miller. Don't you think there might be just a small chance that he might answer me?"

I shrugged. "What can I say, Mademoiselle Bredin? I think it's more likely that he won't, but I'm not God, after all."

She played with the fringes of her scarf. "You know . . . it's not a reader's letter in the *normal* sense. It would be going too far to explain everything to you, Monsieur Chabanais, and it's actually nothing to do with you, but Monsieur Miller helped me a lot when I was in a very difficult situation and I'd like to show my gratitude, you understand."

I nodded and could hardly wait to rush off to read what Mademoiselle Aurélie Bredin had to say to Monsieur Robert Miller.

"Hmm, let's wait and see," I said. "What's that nice English phrase? Let's wait and see, and have a cup of tea."

Mademoiselle Bredin made a moue of comic despair. "But I do so hate waiting," she explained.

"Who doesn't?" I countered magnanimously and had the pleasant feeling of holding all the strings in my hand. I would never have dreamt that only a few weeks later it would be me who would be waiting, anxious and desperate, for an all-decisive answer from an extremely wrathful woman with dark green eyes—an answer that would determine the final sentence of a novel. And at the same time determine my own life!

"Can I leave you my card?" said Mademoiselle Bredin, and pulled a small white visiting card with two red cherries on it out of her leather purse. "Just in case Robert Miller really does come to Paris. Perhaps you'd then be so kind as to let me know." She gave me a glance that was probably meant to be conspiratorial.

"Yes, let's keep in touch." I admit that at that moment there was nothing in the world I wanted more. Even if for readily comprehensible reasons I'd have liked to leave Robert Miller out of it. Honestly, I was beginning to hate the guy. I took the card and could hardly conceal my surprise. "Le Temps des Cerises," I read softly. "Oh . . . you *work* in that restaurant?"

"I *own* that restaurant," she replied. "Do you know it?"

"Eh . . . no . . . yes . . . not really," I stammered. I'd need to be careful what I said. "Isn't that . . . isn't that the restaurant in Miller's novel? Well, haha, what a coincidence!"

"*Is* it a coincidence?" She looked at me thoughtfully and I wondered in a moment of panic if she might know something. No, that was impossible! Totally impossible! No one but Adam and I knew that Robert Miller and André Chabanais were in reality one and the same person.

"*Au revoir,* Monsieur Chabanais." She smiled at me again as she turned to go. "Perhaps with your help I'll soon find out."

"*Au revoir,* Mademoiselle Bredin." I smiled too, and hoped that she'd never find out. And certainly not with my help.

Five

....

"Miller," said Bernadette. "Miller . . . Miller . . . Miller." She was leaning over her computer entering the name "Robert Miller." "Let's see what Google has to tell us."

It was Monday again and so much had been going on in the restaurant over the weekend that I'd had no time to devote to my new favorite activity—seeking and finding Robert Miller.

On Friday we'd had two large parties—a birthday where they'd sung and toasted each other a lot, and a group of even merrier businessmen who were obviously having their Christmas party in November and didn't seem to want to leave.

Jacquie had cursed and sweated because Paul, the sous-chef, was ill so that he had to take on all the grilling as well.

On top of that, none of the guests wanted the menu with the fish. They all ordered à la carte and Jacquie complained that I'd bought too much salmon, which he'd never get rid of now.

But my thoughts were far away, circling round a good-looking Englishman who was probably just as lonely as I was.

"Just imagine, his wife's left him and now all he's got is his little dog," I had told Bernadette when I called her on Sunday evening. I was lying on my sofa with Miller's book in my hand.

"No, *chérie!* That sounds like the Lonely Hearts' Ball! He was left, you were left. He loves French cuisine, you love French cuisine. And he wrote about your restaurant and perhaps even about you. All I can say to that is: *Bon appetit!*" she joked. "Has he been in touch with you then, your tragic Englishman?"

"Oh, really, Bernadette," I shot back, and stuffed a cushion behind my head. "Firstly, he's not *my* Englishman, secondly, I find all these *coincidences* really striking, and thirdly, he can hardly have received my letter yet." I thought again about the rather strange conversation I'd had a couple of days earlier in Éditions Opale. "I can only hope that that funny bearded man really does send my letter off."

"That funny bearded man" was, of course, Monsieur Chabanais, who with hindsight was beginning to seem ever more untrustworthy.

Bernadette laughed. "You worry too much, Aurélie! Give me one good reason why he should hold your letter back."

I contemplated the oil painting of Lake Baikal hanging on the opposite wall, which my father had bought from a Russian artist many years before on his adventurous journey to Ulan Bator with the Trans-Siberian Express. It was a bright, peaceful picture that I loved looking at. An old boat was bobbing on the water near the bank, the lake stretching out behind it. It was totally calm and clear, set against an early summer landscape, and shone out at me with its unfathomable blue. "You wouldn't think it," my father used to say. "It's one of the deepest lakes in Europe."

"I don't know," I replied, and gazed at the play of light and shade on the shimmering surface of the lake. "It's just a feeling

I have. Perhaps he's jealous and wants to protect his precious author from contact with other people. Or perhaps just with me."

"Oh, Aurélie—what are you saying! You're a silly old conspiracy theorist."

I sat up. "No, I'm not. That man *was* very strange. First he behaves like a Cerberus on the telephone. And then, when I spoke to him later in the publishing house he stared at me as if he was deranged. At first he didn't even react to my questions, just went on staring as if he had a screw loose."

Bernadette clicked her tongue impatiently. "Perhaps he was just surprised. Or he'd had a hard day. Good grief, Aurélie, what do you *expect*? He doesn't know you from Eve. You babble on at him on the telephone. Then you arrive at his office in the evening totally without warning, ambush the poor man, who's just leaving for home, and ask about a letter—which as far as he's concerned could be any old letter from any crazy autograph hunter throwing her weight around. So I find it astounding that he didn't just throw you straight out. Just imagine if every reader came storming into the office to make sure that their mail was being forwarded to various authors. For my part, I *hate* it when parents suddenly turn up unannounced after school and want to argue with me about why I've given their little prodigy extra work as a punishment."

I had to laugh. "Fair enough, fair enough. But I'm still glad that I got to talk with that editor personally."

"So you should be. Anyway, Monsieur Cerberus talked to you quite nicely in the end."

"Only to make it clear to me that there's no way the author will get in touch with me because he's sitting unsociable and embittered in his cottage and has no time for such nonsense," I threw in.

"And he's even going to let you know when Robert Miller comes to Paris," Bernadette carried on inexorably. "What more do you want, Mademoiselle I'm-never-satisfied?"

Yes, what more did I want?

I wanted to find out more about this Englishman who looked so attractive and wrote such wonderful things, and that was the reason why Bernadette was sitting at the search engine this Monday morning a week after everything had started.

"I'm so glad that you don't have to go in to school on Mondays so that we can get together," I said, and was flooded with a feeling of gratitude as I watched the look of concentration as she sought out all the Millers in the world for me.

"Hm . . . hm," said Bernadette, as she stuck a wisp of blond hair behind her ear and watched the screen, spellbound. "Rats! I've made a typo—No, I didn't mean Niller, but M-i-l-l-e-r!"

"Do you know, I can't really go out in the evenings because I have to go to the restaurant." I leaned over toward her so that I could make something out on the screen too. "Although . . . now Claude has gone it's obviously not bad to have something to do in the evenings," I went on. "These winter evenings can be really lonely."

"If you want, we could go to the movies this evening," said Bernadette. "Émile is going to be in so I can get away. Have you heard anything from Claude?" she asked without a pause.

I shook my head, thankful that this time she only said "Claude."

"I didn't expect anything better of the idiot," she growled, and wrinkled her forehead. "Unbelievable just to disappear like that." Then her voice became friendlier. "Do you miss him?"

"Well, yes," I said, and was a bit surprised myself how much my emotional state had improved since that unhappy day when

I'd wandered the streets of Paris. "At night it's strange lying alone in bed." I thought for a moment. "It's just a bit funny when there's suddenly no one to put an arm around you."

Bernadette had her great moment of empathy. "Yes, I can imagine it must be," without immediately adding that there was obviously a difference between having a nice man or an idiot putting his arm around you.

"But who knows what may turn up?" She looked at me and grinned. "In the meanwhile, you've found a wonderful distraction. And here we have him: Robert Miller—twelve million, two hundred thousand entries. So, what do you say?"

"Oh, no!" I looked at the screen in disbelief. "It's not possible!"

Bernadette clicked on a couple of entries at random. "Robert Miller—contemporary art." A rectangular picture made up of different colored stripes opened up. "Oh, really *very* contemporary!" She closed the page again. "And what have we here? Rob Miller, Rugby Union Player, pooh—sporty, sporty." She ran the cursor over the page. "Robert Talbot Miller, American agent, spied for the Soviet Union—it won't be him, he's already handed in his feeding pail." She laughed—the search was obviously turning out to be fun. "Boff!" she now cried. "Robert Miller, two hundred twenty-fourth richest person in the world! Are you sure you don't want to change your mind, Aurélie?"

"We're not going to get anywhere like that," I said. "You should put in 'Robert Miller author.'"

"Robert Miller author" only brought up 650,000 entries, which was still quite a challenge.

"Couldn't you find yourself an author with a more unusual name?" said Bernadette, clicking her way through the first page that opened. There was just about everything there—from a man who published books about horse training through a lecturer who'd written something about the English colonies for Oxford University Press, to a really terribly frightening-looking English author who'd produced a book on the Boer War.

Bernadette pointed to the photo. "It can't be him, can it?"

I shook my head violently. "For heaven's sake, no!" I cried.

"This is getting us nowhere," said Bernadette. "What was the title of the novel again?"

"The Smiles of Women."

"Good . . . good . . . good." She moved her fingers over the keyboard. "Aha," she said. "Here we have him: 'Robert Miller, *The Smiles of Women!*' " She smiled triumphantly, and I held my breath.

"Robert Miller in Éditions Opale . . . oh crap, all we get is the publisher's Web site . . . And this . . . is Amazon, but also only for the French edition . . . Strange, it should be possible to find the English original somewhere." She pressed another couple of keys and then shook her head. "Nothing doing," she said. "All there is is something about Henry Miller, *The Smile at the Foot of the Ladder*—a good book, by the way—but he's definitely not our man."

She tapped her lips thoughtfully with her index finger. "No reference to an Internet page, no Facebook—Mr. Miller remains a mystery, at least as far as the World Wide Web is concerned. Who knows, perhaps he's so old-fashioned that he rejects all modern technology. Still, it's very curious that I can't find the English version of the book." She closed her laptop and looked at me.

"I'm afraid I can't help you."

I leaned back, disappointed. I thought you were supposed to be able to find anything on the Internet these days.

"And what do we do now?" I asked.

"Now we make ourselves a little salad with goat's cheese—or rather, *you* make us a nice *salade au chèvre*. There must be some deeper purpose to having a chef as a friend, don't you think?"

I sighed. "Can't you think of anything else?"

"Yes," she said. "Why don't you call that Cerberus of a publisher and ask him if Robert Miller has a Web page and why you can't find the original English edition of his novel." She stood up from her desk and went into the kitchen.

"No, don't phone him," she called as she opened the door of the fridge. "Send the poor man an e-mail instead."

"I don't have his e-mail address," I answered reluctantly, and followed Bernadette into the kitchen. She shut the fridge and thrust an oak-leaf lettuce into my hand.

"My dear, that is really no problem at all."

I stared sullenly at the lettuce, which wasn't really to blame. Bernadette was right. Of course there was no problem finding the e-mail addresses of uninteresting people like André Chabanais, chief editor at Éditions Opale.

Six

"So, you find that strange," I murmured as I studied yet again the e-mail I'd printed out in the office that afternoon. "My dear Mademoiselle Aurélie, this whole business is more than strange."

With a sigh I put the e-mail aside and picked up the letter, which by now I knew by heart—I liked it much more than the unsolicited and not very charming inquiry.

Things were beginning to get complicated, and yet I couldn't help being surprised that one and the same person was capable of writing such different letters. I leaned back in my old leather chair, lit a cigarette, and dropped the book of matches from the Deux Magots on the coffee table.

I'd already tried to give up smoking several times—the last time had been after the book fair, when most of the stress seemed to be over and my life was returning to its pleasantly calm routine.

Carmencita, a hot-blooded young woman responsible for Portuguese licenses who had already been smoldering at me with her dark eyes during our meetings for three years, had this time invited me to dinner and then back to her hotel. The next morning I'd had to make it clear to her that my requirement for women to whom I could give necklaces was already fulfilled. When Carmencita finally left in a huff (not without extracting from me a promise to invite her to dinner next year), I thought that the greatest challenge for the rest of the year would be dealing with all the manuscripts I had requested in a fit of book-fair euphoria.

But since last Tuesday the little blue packs with the health-hazardous fire sticks had once more become my constant companions.

I smoked the first five cigarettes during the period when Adam failed to call me back. When he did finally call on the Thursday, I put the cigarettes in the top drawer of my desk and vowed to forget their existence. Then, as if falling from the sky, that girl with green eyes landed outside my office in the evening and my feelings were in a state of confusion I'd never experienced before. I found myself living in a dream that was simultaneously a nightmare. I had to shake off the obstinate Mademoiselle Bredin before she found out the truth about Robert Miller, and yet the thing I wanted most of all was to see the woman with the ravishing smile again.

After Mademoiselle Bredin disappeared at the end of the lobby I lit a cigarette. Then I rushed into the main office, where Madame Petit ruled by day, and rummaged through my green plastic in-tray until I found a long white envelope addressed to "The Author Robert Miller." I stuck my head hastily round the door and listened—making sure that Mademoiselle wasn't returning to find me opening her mail—and then I hurriedly tore the handwritten letter open without using a paper knife: the letter that had by now been in every part of my apartment and had been read over and over again.

Paris, November 2008

Dear Robert Miller!

You kept me awake all last night, and I'd like to say thank you! I have just read your book The Smiles of Women. Read? I devoured the book, which is so wonderful and which fell into my hands by pure chance only yesterday evening (as I was, in a way, fleeing the police) in a little Parisian bookstore. What I mean is that I was not looking for your book. My great passion is cooking, not reading. Normally. But your book blew me away, inspired me, made me laugh, and is at the same time so light and full of wisdom. In a word: Your book made me happy on a day when I was more unhappy than I had ever been (a broken heart, world weariness) and the fact that I found your book (or did your book find me?) at precisely that moment seems to me to have been destined by fate.

That may perhaps seem strange to you, but as soon as I'd read the very first sentence I sensed that this book was going to have a very special meaning for me. I don't believe in coincidences.

Dear Monsieur Miller, before you think you're dealing with a madwoman, you ought to know a couple of things.

Le Temps des Cerises, which appears in your book so often and which you describe so affectionately, is my restaurant. And your Sophie—that's me. At least, the similarity is striking, and when you look at the photograph I'm enclosing you'll understand what I mean. Admittedly, I don't know how these things all fit together, but I naturally wonder if we have met without my being able to remember it. You are a successful English author, I *am a French chef with a relatively unknown restaurant in Paris—how can our paths have crossed?*

You can perhaps imagine that all these "coincidences," which somehow just can't be coincidences, are bothering me.

I'm writing to you in the hope that you have an explanation for me. Unfortunately I don't have your address and can only reach you by going through your publisher. I would regard it as an honor to be able to invite the man who writes books like that and to whom I owe so much to a meal—prepared by me—in Le Temps des Cerises.

As I can see from your biography (and your novel), you love Paris, and I think that you must often come here. It would be so lovely if we could get to know each other personally. And perhaps many of my puzzles could then be solved.

I can imagine that, since your book appeared, you must receive many enthusiastic letters, and it is also clear to me that you do not have the time to answer every single one of your readers. But I am not "every" reader, you must believe me. For me The Smiles of Women *has been a very special, in fact fateful, book. And it is with a combination of deep gratitude, great admiration, and curious impatience that I send you this letter. I would be extremely delighted to receive an answer from you, and my greatest desire is that you will accept my invitation to dinner in Le Temps des Cerises.*

With the very best of wishes,

Yours,

Aurélie Bredin

PS: This is the first time I've ever written to an author. And it is not my usual custom to invite strange men to dinner, but I am sure that my letter will be safe in the hands of an English gentleman, as I assume you to be.

After reading this letter for the first time, I fell back into Madame Petit's office chair and smoked another cigarette.

I must admit that if I had been Robert Miller I would have felt I was the luckiest man alive. I wouldn't have wasted a second before replying to this letter, which was so much more than a normal love letter. Oh, I would have so gladly accepted the beautiful cook's invitation to a very private *dîner à deux* in her restaurant (the invitation sounded most tempting) and perhaps to other things as well (which in my imagination seemed even more tempting).

But stupidly enough I was just André Chabanais, a middle-of-the-road, run-of-the-mill chief editor pretending to be Robert Miller. That great, amusing, and yet deep-thinking author who wrote himself into the hearts of unhappy women.

I drew on my cigarette and studied the photo that Aurélie Bredin had enclosed with her letter very closely. In it she was wearing that green dress (obviously one of her favorites), her hair fell over her shoulders, and she was smiling lovingly into the camera.

Once more her smile was not for me. When the photo had been taken she had been smiling at someone, probably the guy who had later hurt her (broken heart, world weariness). And as she put the photo in the letter she had done it as a way of smiling at Robert Miller. If she had known that it would be me (and not her English gentleman) who would later secrete her picture in his wallet, she would not have smiled so delightfully, I was sure of that.

I stubbed out my cigarette, threw the butt into the wastepaper basket, and put the letter and its envelope into my briefcase.

As I was finally leaving the office after that eventful day, the Filipino cleaners who tidied the offices and took away the garbage were already coming in, laughing and chattering.

"Oooh, Missyu Zabanais, oways wokking sooo hahd!" they called cheerfully, nodding sympathetically. I nodded too, though absentmindedly rather than happily. High time to go home. It was cold but not raining as I walked down the Rue Bonaparte, wondering why it was that Mademoiselle Bredin had actually been fleeing the police. She didn't exactly look like the kind of person who'd steal T-shirts from Monoprix. And what did "in a way" mean in this context? Had the owner of Le Temps des Cerises committed tax fraud? Or was the policeman from whom she'd fled into the bookshop where she, thankfully, had found my book perhaps her ex, a brutal flatfoot whom she'd had a terrible row with and who was now stalking her?

However, I didn't ask myself the most important question until I was putting in the entry code that opened the door into the building in the Rue des Beaux-Arts where my apartment was.

How did you go about winning the heart of a woman who had got it into her head that she wanted to get to know a man she admired and whom she thought herself linked to by fate? A man who—how ironic fate is—didn't actually exist. The genie you could never get rid of, called up by two inventive sorcerer's apprentices who thought themselves very smart and worked in the business of selling dreams.

If I'd read this story in a novel, I would have found it highly amusing. If you yourself have to play the comic hero in the story, it's no longer quite so funny.

I pushed open the apartment door and switched on the light. What I needed was a stroke of genius, but unfortunately none was forthcoming. But I knew one thing for certain: Robert Miller, that perfect English gentleman who wrote so brilliantly and funnily, would never have dinner with Aurélie Bredin. Perhaps, however, if I got it right, that much nicer Frenchman André Chabanais with his rented apartment in the Rue des Beaux-Arts would.

A few minutes later that nice Frenchman was listening to his voice mail, including a reproachful message from his mother asking him if he'd finally pick up the phone.

"André? I know very well that you're in, *mon petit chou,* why don't you pick up the phone? Are you coming for lunch on Sunday? You could think about your poor old mother occasionally, I'm so bored, I can't spend all my time reading books," she said querulously, and I reached for the cigarette packet in my jacket pocket once again.

Then Adam's voice came on.

"Hi, Andy, it's me! So, everything okay? My brother's just gone to a Dental Congress in Sant'Angelo and won't be back until Sunday evening. Ha ha ha, they live the life of Riley, these dentists, don't they?"

He was laughing unconcernedly, and I wondered if he was aware that time was running out. Didn't his brother have a cell phone? Were there no telephones in this Sant'Angelo (wherever the hell that was)? What was going on?

"I thought it would probably be better to call Sam when he gets back and has less to think about," Adam immediately came in with the explanation. "Anyway, I'll call again when I've talked to Sam. Over the weekend we'll be with friends in Brighton, but you can get me on my mobile, as always."

I said, "Yes, yes, fine, on your mobile as always," and lit the next cigarette.

"Take care, then—and André?"

I raised my head.

"Don't get your knickers in a twist, my friend. We'll definitely get Sam to Paris."

I nodded my acquiescence and went into the kitchen to see what was in the fridge. The result wasn't too bad. I found a bag of fresh green beans, which I boiled a short time in salt water, and grilled myself a big steak to go with it: very rare, in the English fashion, of course.

When I'd eaten, I sat down at the round table in the living room with a sheet of paper and worked on my strategic ideas for the case of Aurélie Bredin = A.B. Two hours later, this is what I had down on paper:

1. Robert Miller ignores the letter and *doesn't* answer. ➤ A.B. will probably turn first to her contact at the publishers to find out what's happened to the author. André Chabanais = A.C. tells her that the author doesn't want to know and gives no further information. ➤ A.B. runs into a brick wall and at some stage loses interest ➤ she also has no more interest in A.C. as a possible go-between.

2. Robert Miller answers the letter, but A.C. offers his help ➤ thus endearing himself to A.B. However, A.B.'s thoughts are set in the wrong direction, that is toward the author not the editor. Can he ultimately help her? No, because Robert Miller doesn't exist. ➤ A.C. needs to gain time to show A.B. what a nice

guy he is. (And what a fool the Englishman really is—but only incidentally!)

3. Robert Miller writes a nice but rather vague letter back. ➙ The flame is kept alive. The author refers to his wonderful editor (A.C.) and hopes that he may be in Paris in the near future, but doesn't know if a meeting will be possible because he has so many appointments.

4. A.C. arranges something. Asks A.B. if she'd like to turn up at a meeting he has with Miller (for dinner?). ➙ She would, *and* is grateful. Of course, the author never appears, apparently canceling at the last moment. ➙ A.B. is peeved with the author. A.C. tells her that he is unfortunately always so unreliable. ➙ A.B. and A.C. spend a wonderful evening together and A.B. realizes that she very much prefers the likeable editor to the complicated author.

I nodded with satisfaction as I read item 4 once more. It wasn't too bad an idea as a beginning. Whether it was really a stroke of genius only time would tell. Nevertheless there were still a couple of unanswered questions:

1. Was Aurélie Bredin really worth all this fuss and effort? *Absolutely!*
2. Should she ever be told the truth? *Absolutely not!*
3. What would happen if Sam Goldberg actually did come to Paris in the guise of Robert Miller to give an interview or a reading and A.B. got to know about it?

At this late hour I couldn't, with the best will in the world, think of an answer to this last question. I stood up, emptied the ashtray (five cigarettes), and switched off the light. I was dog tired, and for the moment the more urgent question was rather what would happen if Robert Miller *didn't* come to Paris.

On Friday morning Monsieur Monsignac was already waiting for me in my office. "Ah, my dear André, there you are at last, *bonjour, bonjour!*" he caroled to me, swaying energetically back and forth in his brown leather shoes. "I've put a manuscript by a very young and very pretty author on your desk—she's the daughter of the last winner of the Prix Goncourt, who's a very good friend of mine and so as an unusual exception I'd like to ask you to take a *very quick* look at it."

I took off my scarf and nodded. In the whole time I'd been at Éditions Opale I couldn't remember a single occasion when Monsieur Monsignac hadn't wanted something dealt with quickly. I glanced at the Prix Goncourt winner's daughter's manuscript in its transparent folder. It bore the elegiac title *Confessions d'une Fille Triste* (Confessions of a Sad Girl). There were at most a hundred and fifty pages, and you'd probably only have to read five of them before being overcome with nausea at the habitual narcissistic navel-gazing that is so often passed off as meaningful literature these days.

"No problem, I'll let you know by lunchtime," I said, hanging my coat in the narrow cupboard beside the door.

Monsignac drummed his fingers on the chest of his blue-and-white-striped shirt. He wasn't really small, but still a couple of heads shorter than I and considerably stouter. In spite of his stature he knew how to dress. He hated ties, wore handmade shoes and paisley scarves, and in spite of his corpulence gave the impression that he was extremely agile and mobile.

"Great, André," he said. "You know, that's what I like about you—you're so totally unpretentious. You don't talk big, you don't ask unnecessary questions. You *make* things simple." He looked at me out of his shining blue eyes and clapped me on the shoulder. "You'll go far." Then he winked at me. "And if this thing here is garbage, just write a couple of encouraging sentences about the content. You know the kind of thing—there's a great deal of potential, we're looking forward to seeing what the writer produces next, and so on and so forth—and then gently reject it."

I nodded and choked down a grin. And then, as he was almost over the threshold, Monsignac turned once more and uttered the sentence I'd been waiting for the whole time.

"And? Everything okay with Robert Miller?"

"I'm in contact with his agent, Adam Goldberg. He's totally reliable." Old Monsieur Orban (the one who'd recently fallen out of the tree while picking cherries) had once given me a piece of advice. "If you're going to lie, keep as close to the truth as possible, son," he'd said when I'd played hooky one glorious summer day and was about to tell my mother a load of hair-raising lies, "then there's a chance that people will believe you."

"He says we'll get Miller to Paris," I went on heartily, and my pulse sped up. "It's basically just a matter of the . . . eh . . . fine tuning. I think I'll have more definite details on Monday."

"Fine . . . fine . . . fine." Jean-Paul Monsignac left the room with a satisfied expression and I scrabbled in my pocket. And after I'd taken a small dose of nicotine (three cigarettes) I gradually began to feel calmer. I threw open my window to let in the clear, cold air.

The manuscript was Françoise Sagan for dummies. Apart from the fact that a young woman who doesn't really know what she wants (and whose father is a famous writer) travels to a Caribbean island and lets us share her sexual experiences with a black islander (who is stoned the whole time), there was no recognizable plot. Every second section described the heroine's emotional state, which was of interest to no one, not even the Caribbean lover. At the end the young woman travels off, life lies before her like a great question mark, and she doesn't know why she is so sad.

For my part, I didn't know either. If as a young man I'd had the opportunity to spend eight unbelievable weeks on a dream island and enjoy myself with a Caribbean beauty on white sandy beaches in all possible positions, I wouldn't have been melancholic—I'd more likely have been inebriated with joy. Perhaps I lacked the necessary depth.

I formulated a careful rejection and made a copy for Monsieur Monsignac. At midday Madame Petit brought the mail and asked me suspiciously if I'd been smoking.

I looked at her with an innocent expression and raised my hands.

"You *have* been smoking, Monsieur Chabanais," she said, spying out the little ashtray behind the in-tray on my desk. "You've even been smoking in *my* office, I could smell it when I came in this morning." She shook her head in disapproval. "Don't start smoking again, Monsieur Chabanais, it's so unhealthy, as you are well aware."

Yes, yes, yes, I knew it all. Smoking was unhealthy. Eating was unhealthy. Drinking was unhealthy. Everything that was fun was in some way unhealthy or made you fat. Too much excitement was unhealthy. In essence the whole of life was a dangerous balancing act, and in the end you fell off a ladder while picking cherries or got run over by a car on the way to the baker like the concierge in the novel *The Elegance of the Hedgehog.*

I nodded dumbly. What could I say? She was right. I waited until Madame Petit had bustled out of the room and then thoughtfully took another cigarette out of the pack, leaned back, and a few seconds later was watching the way the little white smoke rings that I blew out slowly dissolved.

After Madame Petit caught me out smoking in the office there were further disturbing occurrences that regrettably got in the way of my leading a healthy existence. The healthiest—and probably the least exciting of these—was probably Sunday lunch with Maman in Neuilly, although I wouldn't want to claim that plates full of *choucroute,* fatty pork and sausages (my mother's mother came from Alsace, and so *choucroute* is a must for her), are the best thing to nourish your body with. And the fact that the "surprise" Maman had announced on the telephone turned out to be her permanently invalid sister and a talkative but rather hard-of-hearing (and for that reason rather loud) favorite cousin (not *my* favorite, by the way) whom she'd invited over for the occasion did not make that particular meal—eaten though it was off Alsatian china—much of a delight for me. The *choucroute* lay in my stomach like a stone and the three old ladies, who insisted on addressing a grown man of thirty-eight and over six foot as *mon petit boubou* or *mon petit chou* (my little cabbage!), drove me to distraction. Apart from that, everything was much as usual, only at three times the volume.

I was asked if I'd got thinner (No!), if I wasn't going to get married soon (when the right woman appeared), if Maman could still hope for a grandchild she could stuff with *choucroute* (but of course, I was looking forward to it already), if everything was going well at work (of course, everything was going very well). At the same time I was repeatedly asked if I'd like just a little bit more, or to tell them what news I had.

"What news have you got, André? Do tell!"

Three pairs of eyes were fixed expectantly on me and I felt like the Sunday radio. This question was always very tiring. I could hardly tell them the real news about my life (or would anyone at this table have understood that I was in a state of high nervous tension because I'd adopted a second identity as an English author, and the whole thing was threatening to blow up in my face?) and so I muttered something about the latest leak in the water pipes in my old flat, and that was fine, as the old ladies' attention span was somewhat limited (although that may have been because the things I was telling them were not interesting enough). Either way, I was soon interrupted by the deaf cousin with a loud "Who's died?" (she did however say the same thing five times in the course of the afternoon—I guess it was whenever she lost the thread of the conversation), and they turned to more interesting topics: inflammation of the veins, visits to the doctor, house decoration, lazy gardeners and sluttish cleaners, Christmas concerts, funerals, quiz programs, and what had happened to neighbors I didn't know or figures from the far distant past, until it was finally time for the cheese and fruit.

By this time both I and the capacity of my stomach were so exhausted that I excused myself for a moment and went into the garden for a smoke (three cigarettes).

That night I tossed and turned in my bed even though I'd taken three indigestion tablets (needed because of the goat's cheese and camembert), and had terrifying nightmares about Adam's brother, the good-looking English bestselling author, who was lying on a couch in his high-tech dental practice with a half-naked Mademoiselle Bredin, groaning with passion as he embraced her, while I sat incapable of motion (and also groaning) in a dentist's chair as his assistant pulled all my teeth out.

When I woke up, bathed in sweat, I was so messed up that I would gladly have had another smoke.

But all this was an innocent pleasure compared with the excitements that Monday held in store for me.

Early that morning Adam called me in the office with the news that his brother had initially been rather reluctant, but had now grasped the delicate nature of the whole Miller affair and was ready, just this once, to play along. ("He took it like a man" was Adam's laid-back comment.)

Nevertheless, Sam's knowledge of French naturally had limits, he was anything but a book person, and his knowledge of vintage cars was also quite restricted.

"Hmm, I'm afraid we'll have to get him well up to speed beforehand," Adam said. "For the reading you can prepare the relevant passages for him and he'll just have to practice them." Regarding shaving off the beard he, Adam, would have to put in a bit of persuasive effort.

I tugged nervously at my roll-neck sweater, which was suddenly threatening to strangle me. Of course it would be an advantage if *Robert Miller* looked like the Robert Miller in the photo, but I feared that the *dentist* would still look like a dentist. The whole thing was so damn complicated.

"Yes, you're right," said Adam. "I'll do what I can." And then he said something that had me reaching straight for my cigarettes.

"By the way, Sam would like to come over the Monday after next—or rather, that's the only time he *can* come."

I smoked as quickly as I could. "Are you crazy?" I shouted. "How's that supposed to work?"

The office door opened quietly, and Mademoiselle Mirabeau was standing on the threshold with an uncertain look and a transparent folder—waiting.

"Not now!" I shouted in annoyance, and waved her away with my hand. "Good grief, don't look so sheepish—you can *see* I'm on the phone!" I hissed at her.

She stared at me in fright. Then her lower lip began to tremble and the door shut as quietly as it had been opened.

"He's not coming *this very moment,*" said Adam in a soothing tone, and I turned my attention back to the phone. "That Monday would be perfect—I could travel over with Sam on the Sunday and we could discuss the whole thing at leisure."

"Perfect, perfect," I snorted. "That's only two weeks away! Things like this need to be set up. How are we going to manage that?"

"It's now or never," retorted Adam curtly. "You could at least be happy that it's happening at all."

"I'm delirious with delight," I said. "A good thing that it's not tomorrow!"

"What's the problem? *Le Figaro* is already on the starting blocks, as I understand it. And as far as the reading's concerned it's probably better if we keep it small. Or would you prefer a reading in Fnac?"

"No, of course not," I replied. The lower we kept our heads, the better. The whole thing needed to be got over with as unspectacularly as possible. Two weeks on Monday! I started to feel hot. With trembling hands I took a cigarette from the pack. "God, do I feel bad," I said.

"Why? Everything's hunky-dory," Adam countered. "You probably haven't had a proper breakfast again." I gnawed at my fist. "Toast, fried eggs, and bacon—that sets a man up for the day," my English friend lectured me. "What you lot eat for breakfast—that's only for wimps! Cookies and croissants! No one could seriously live on that!"

"Let's not start getting down to specifics, okay?" I answered. "Otherwise I'll start talking about English cuisine."

It wasn't the first time I'd argued with Adam about the advantages and disadvantages of our cuisine.

"No, please don't!" I could see Adam grinning. "Just tell me that everything's okay with that date before my brother changes his mind."

I took a deep breath. "*Bon.* I'll speak to our PR department immediately. Please make sure that your brother at least knows the main outline of the book when he gets here."

"Will do."

"Does he stammer?"

"Are you off your head? Why should he stammer? He speaks perfectly normally and has very nice teeth."

"That's reassuring. And Adam? One more thing."

"Yes?"

"It'd be good if your brother treated the whole business with absolute discretion. He mustn't tell anyone why he's going to Paris with you. His good old friends at the club, or his neighbors. And definitely not his wife. Stories like that spread quicker than you think, and it's a very small world."

"No worries, Andy. We Englishmen are *very discreet.*"

• • •

In spite of all misgivings Michelle Auteuil was over the moon when she heard that Robert Miller would be coming to Paris so soon.

"How did you manage to sort that out so quickly, Monsieur Chabanais?" she shrieked in surprise, and played a veritable drum roll on the table with her pencil. "The author seems not to be as difficult as you say! I'll talk to *Le Figaro* right away, and I've already put out feelers to a couple of small bookstores." She reached over to her Rolodex and leafed through the cards. "It's great that it's all worked out so well and . . . who knows?" She smiled at me, and her heart-shaped black earrings jiggled energetically against her slim neck. "Perhaps we could arrange a press trip to England in the spring—a visit to Robert Miller's cottage? What do you think of that?"

My stomach turned over. "Great," I said, and began to understand what a double agent must feel like.

I decided that good old Robert Miller would have to die as soon as he'd made his visit to Paris.

Over the edge of the road in his old Corvette. A broken neck. A tragedy—he wasn't that old. And now there was only the little dog. And he fortunately couldn't talk. Or write. Perhaps as Miller's loyal adviser and good-hearted editor I'd look after little Rocky myself.

You could see the cogs whirring behind Michelle Auteuil's pale forehead. "Is he still writing?" she asked.

"Oh, I think so," I said. "But he always takes a long time—not least because of his time-consuming hobbies. You know—he's always tinkering with his vintage cars." I pretended to be thinking. "I believe he took seven years over his first book. Yes. Almost like John Irving. But not as good."

I smiled happily and left Madame Auteuil in confusion in her office. The idea of making Miller die delighted me. It was going to rescue me.

But before I put an end to the English gentleman he was going to do me one last favor.

Aurélie Bredin's e-mail reached me at thirteen minutes past five. And up to that very moment I hadn't smoked a single cigarette since that morning. Strangely enough, I felt almost guilty as I clicked her e-mail open.

Well, I had read the letter that she had written in such confidence to Robert Miller and I was carrying her photo in my wallet without her being aware of it.

Of course those things were not right. But also not totally wrong. Because who, apart from myself, should have opened the author's mail?

The subject line made me vaguely uneasy.

Subject: Questions about Robert Miller!!!

I sighed. Three exclamation marks did not bode well. Without knowing what was in the rest of the message, I had the unpleasant feeling that I would not be able to answer Mademoiselle Bredin's questions to her satisfaction.

Dear Monsieur Chabanais,

Today is Monday and several days have passed since our encounter in the publishing house. I hope very much that you have in the meantime forwarded my letter to Robert Miller, and even if you tried not to raise my hopes, I am absolutely certain that I will receive a reply. I assume that it is part of an editor's duties to protect his authors from obstinate admirers, but perhaps you take this part of your job too seriously? However that may be, I would like to thank you for your efforts and ask a couple of questions I am sure you will be able to answer.

1. *Does Robert Miller have anything like a Web page? Unfortunately, I have been unable to find anything on the Internet.*
2. *I have also looked—in vain—for the original English edition and strangely could not find one. Who published Miller's novel in England? And what is the English title? If you enter the name "Robert Miller" in amazon.uk, the only entry is for the French edition. But the book is a translation from the English, isn't it? At least, the translator's name is listed there.*
3. *When we first spoke on the phone you mentioned that the author might possibly be coming to Paris for a reading. I would obviously really like to be there—has the date been fixed yet? If possible, I'd like to book two tickets.*

I hope I am not imposing too much on your valuable time, and would appreciate a swift response.
Best wishes,
Aurélie Bredin

I reached for my cigarettes and fell back in my chair. *Mon Dieu*, Aurélie Bredin really wanted to know it all. She was so damned obstinate! I would have to find some way to put a stop to her investigations—the last two paragraphs were definitely giving me indigestion.

I really didn't want to imagine what exactly might happen if

the enthusiastic Mademoiselle Bredin met up with a totally un-
prepared Robert Miller, a.k.a. Samuel Goldberg, and managed
to speak to him in person.

But the likelihood of the lovely chef hearing about the plans
for a reading was minimal. At least, there was no way I was going to inform her. And since the interview in *Le Figaro* could
only appear the day after at the earliest there wasn't much of
a threat from that direction. By then it would all be over, and if
she found the article or heard about the reading later on I would
surely be able to think up an explanation.

(The fact that Mademoiselle Bredin wanted two tickets was
not very encouraging. Why did she need two tickets? Surely
she hadn't already found a new admirer just after getting over
the pain of a broken heart. If she needed consoling at all, then I
was the one who should do it.)

I lit my next cigarette and thought on.

Point two, that is, the question about the original edition,
was very much more awkward, since there *was* no English edition, let alone an English publisher. I'd have to think up a satis-
factory answer. The last thing I wanted was for Mademoiselle
Bredin to get the idea of trying to find the (nonexistent) translator. She wouldn't find any information about that gentleman
on the Internet either. But what if she rang the office and stirred
up trouble? The best thing to do was to put the translator
straight on my death list as well. You could never underesti-
mate the energy of the delicate Mademoiselle Bredin. Being as
totally determined as she was, she'd end up going to see Monsieur Monsignac.

I printed out the e-mail so that I could take it home where I
could work out what to do without interruptions.

The paper crept out of the quietly rattling printer and I bent over and picked it up. Now I had two letters from Aurélie Bredin. But this one wasn't a very nice letter.

I scanned the printed lines once more trying to find a good word about André Chabanais. I couldn't find a single one. The young lady could be quite sharp-tongued. Between the lines you could clearly read what she thought of the editor she'd met in the lobby of the publishing house the week before: nothing! I had obviously not made any kind of impression on Aurélie Bredin.

I might have expected a bit more gratitude. Especially if you thought that it was actually me and my book that had made the mademoiselle happy again at her personal low point. It was *my* humor that had made her laugh. *My* ideas had enchanted her.

Yes, I must admit that I found it a bit hurtful that I had been dismissed in brief, almost unfriendly words and a simple "best wishes" when my alter ego had been wooed so charmingly and greeted so affectionately.

I took a furious pull on my cigarette. It was time to initiate Phase Two and redirect Mademoiselle Bredin's enthusiasm to the right person.

Of course, my performance in the lobby hadn't exactly been the kind of thing that would arouse a woman's fantasy. I'd been silent, stuttering, staring. And before that, on the phone, I'd been impatient—yes, even *unfriendly*. No wonder the girl with the green eyes hadn't deigned to give me even a glance.

Okay, I wasn't as smart a guy as the dentist in the author's photograph. But I'm not exactly bad-looking. I'm tall, well-built, and although I haven't played any sport in the last few years I'm quite physically fit. I have dark brown eyes, thick brown hair, a straight nose, and my ears don't stick out. And the only person who didn't like the well-trimmed beard that I've sported for the last few years was Maman. Every other woman found it "manly." At least, Mademoiselle Mirabeau had recently compared me to the publisher in *The Russia House*.

I ran my finger over the little bronze nude statue of Daphne that stood on my desk. What I needed, and soon, was a chance to present myself to Aurélie Bredin from my better side.

Two hours later I was in my flat circling my living room table where a handwritten letter and the printout of an e-mail were lying side by side in peaceful harmony. Outside an unfriendly wind was sweeping through the streets and it had begun to rain. I looked down at the street where an old woman was struggling with her umbrella as it threatened to turn inside out and two lovers had just taken hands to run and take refuge in a café.

I switched on the two lamps on the sideboard under the window and shoved a Paris Combo CD into the player. The first track began to play; a couple of rhythmic guitar chords and a soft female voice filled the room.

"On n'a pas besoin, non non non non, de chercher si loin . . . On trouve ce qu'on veut à coté de chez soi . . ." sang the vocalist, and I listened to her sweet words as if they were an epiphany: You didn't always have to look for things so far away, you'd find what you were seeking close to home.

Suddenly I knew what I had to do. I'd received two letters. I would write two letters. One as André Chabanais. And one as Robert Miller. Aurélie Bredin would find the reply to her e-mail to the editor in her mailbox that very evening, and I'd deliver

Robert Miller's letter to her house personally because the absentminded author had unfortunately thrown away the envelope with her return address and sent his answer to me so that I could pass it on.

I would bait two hooks, and the good thing about them was that in both cases I was the man with the rod in his hands. And if my plan succeeded, then on Friday evening Mademoiselle Bredin would be sitting in La Coupole having a very pleasant time with Monsieur Chabanais.

I got my laptop from the study and opened it. Then I entered Aurélie Bredin's e-mail address and put the printout down beside me.

Subject: Answers about Robert Miller!!!

Chère Mademoiselle Bredin,

To begin with your most urgent question, even if you did not mention it:

Of course I forwarded your letter to Robert Miller—I even put it in the mail with a "Priority" sticker on it so that your patience would not be excessively tried. Please do not think so badly of me! I cannot blame you if you think of me as being somewhat weird—the day when you turned up so unexpectedly in the publisher's office a number of unfortunate things had just happened and I am very sorry if you got the impression that I was somehow trying to prevent you making contact with Monsieur Miller. He is a wonderful author, and I hold him in very high regard, but he is also a quite eccentric man who prefers to live in isolation. I really am not as sure as you are that he will answer your letter, but I very much hope he will. One should not leave such a lovely letter unanswered.

I deleted that last sentence. I had no way of knowing if the letter was lovely or not. After all, I'd only forwarded it. I really needed to be careful not to give myself away. Instead I wrote:

If I were the author, I would definitely reply to you, but that is not of much use to you. A pity that Monsieur Miller cannot see what a beautiful reader is writing to him. You should have included a photo.

I couldn't help adding that little allusion.

But now for your other questions:

1. *Unfortunately Robert Miller doesn't have a Web page. He is, as I have already said, a very private person and is not interested in parading himself on the Net. We had enough trouble getting an author's photo from him. Unlike the majority of authors he does not like being suddenly addressed on the street. He hates nothing more than when someone suddenly stands in front of him and says, "Aren't you Robert Miller?"*

2. *There is in fact no English edition. The reason for this involves a long story which I won't bore you with. The main thing is that the agent who represents Robert Miller, also an Englishman, brought the manuscript directly to our company, and we had it translated. It has not yet found an English publisher. It could be that the story is not as suited for an English audience or that other things are more in demand on the English market at the moment.*

3. *It's not certain at the moment if Monsieur Miller will be available to meet the press in the near future. Just now that looks rather unlikely.*

That was a black lie—and yet it wasn't. In reality it was only a dentist who would be coming to Paris for the reading and answering a few questions and signing a few books in the persona of Miller.

It was quite a blow to him when his wife left him, and since then he's been a little reluctant to make decisions. However, if he does ever come to Paris for a reading, it will be a pleasure for me to reserve a ticket—or rather two tickets—for it.

I paused for a moment and scanned my e-mail. It all sounded very plausible and confident, I thought. And above all there was not a single trace of unfriendliness. And then I baited my first hook:

Dear Mademoiselle Bredin, I hope that this has answered your questions. I would really like to help you more, but you will understand that I cannot simply trample over the wishes (and rights) of our authors. Nevertheless (and if you promise me not to shout it from the rooftops), something a bit more informal might possibly be arranged.

As chance would have it, I'm meeting Robert Miller this coming Friday to discuss his new book. It was a completely spontaneous idea: He has things to do in Paris that day, and not much time, but we are going to meet for dinner. If you would like it, and if the time is possible, you could perhaps turn up as if by chance and have a drink with us—and in that way you'd have an opportunity to personally shake the hand of your favorite author at least once.

That is the best I can offer you at the moment, and I am

only making it so that you don't send me any more aggrieved e-mails.

Now—what do you say?

It was the best *immoral* proposition that I could make to her at that moment, and I was actually quite sure that Aurélie Bredin would bite. It was immoral above all because the person who was its main subject would ultimately fail to turn up for the meal. But of course Mademoiselle Bredin could not know that.

I sent the e-mail off, signing it "with very best wishes" and then walked decisively over to my desk to get a sheaf of paper and my ballpoint.

She *would* come—especially when she read Robert Miller's letter—the one I was now going to write. I sat down at the table, poured myself a glass of wine, and took a good swallow.

"Dear Miss Bredin," I wrote in a bold hand.

And then I wrote nothing for a long time. I sat in front of the blank sheet and suddenly had no idea how I should begin. All my skill at creating phrases seemed to have vanished. I drummed on the tabletop with my fingers and tried to think of England.

What would someone like Miller, sitting alone and abandoned in his cottage, write? And how would he react to the questions Mademoiselle Bredin was asking him? Was it pure chance that the heroine of his novel looked like the writer of the letter? Was it a mystery? Was he unable to explain it even to himself? Was it a long story that he would like to tell her sometime at leisure?

I took Aurélie Bredin's photo out of my wallet, let her smile at me, and lost myself in happy fantasies.

After a quarter of an hour I stood up. This was just a waste of time. "Mr. Miller, you're not very self-disciplined," I scolded.

It was just after ten, the cigarette packet was empty, and I urgently needed something to eat. I put on my coat and waved at the table.

"I'll be right back. And in the meanwhile, put your thinking cap on," I said. "Produce some ideas, you writer, you!"

It was still raining as I opened the very wet glass door of La Palette, which was quite full at this time of night. I was immediately surrounded by an animated hum of conversation, and at the back of the bistro, which was half in darkness, all the tables were occupied.

La Palette, with its simple scrubbed wooden tables and paintings on the wall, was very popular with artists, gallery owners, students, and even publishers. You came here for a meal or just for a coffee or a glass of wine. This old bar was only a stone's throw from my apartment. I came here often and nearly always met a couple of people I knew.

"*Salut, André! Ça va?*" Nicolas, one of the waiters, waved to me. "Lousy weather, isn't it?"

I shook off a few raindrops and nodded. "You can say that again!" I called back. I pushed through the crowd, sat at the bar, and ordered a *croque-monsieur* and a red wine.

The lively activity around me was, in a strange way, soothing. I drank my wine, took a bite of my toast, ordered more wine, and gazed around me. I could feel the chaos of this exciting day gradually falling away from me and began to relax. Sometimes you only need to take a step or two back from your problems and everything becomes simple. Writing the Robert Miller letter would be child's play. After all, it was only in the end a matter of keeping Aurélie Bredin's idée fixe burning until I'd succeeded in inserting myself between her and the author.

It might not always be an advantage to work in a profession that lives exclusively on words, stories, and ideas, and there were moments in my life when I would gladly have had something more tangible, more real, more solid, something you made with your hands—like building bookshelves or a bridge—just something that was more material and less intellectual.

Whenever I saw the Eiffel Tower thrusting so bold and indestructible into the Paris sky, I would think proudly of my great-grandfather, an engineer and prolific inventor who had been involved in the construction of that impressive monument of iron and steel.

I often thought what a glorious feeling it must have been to create something like that. But at this moment I would not have wanted to change places with my great-grandfather. Admittedly, I couldn't build an Eiffel Tower (and, to be totally honest, not even a bookshelf) but I could handle words. I could write letters and think up the right story to tell. Something that would lure a romantic woman who didn't believe in coincidences.

I ordered another glass of red wine and pictured my dinner with Aurélie Bredin, which, I was quite certain, would be followed by a much more intimate meal in Le Temps des Cerises. I just needed to set it craftily in motion. And one day, when Robert Miller was long forgotten, I might even tell her the whole truth. And we would laugh about it together.

That was my plan. But of course everything turned out differently.

I don't know why it is, but somehow people can't act any differently. They make plan after plan. And then they're surprised when the plans don't work.

And so there I was, sitting at the bar wallowing in my visions of the future, when someone tapped me on the shoulder. A laughing face swam into view, and I returned to the present.

There stood Silvestro, my old Italian teacher, from whom I'd taken lessons in the past few years to freshen up my rusty Italian.

"*Ciao,* André, good to see you," he said. "Do you want to come and join us at the table?" He pointed at a table behind us where two men and three women were sitting. One of them, a stunning redhead with freckles and a wide, soft mouth, looked over to us and smiled. Silvestro always had exceptionally pretty girls in tow.

"That's Giulia," said Silvestro, and winked at me. "A new pupil. Great-looking—and still available." He waved back to the redhead. "How about it? Are you coming?"

"That's very tempting," I replied with a smile, "but no thanks. I've still got things to do."

"Oh, forget about work for a while. You really do work far too hard." Silvestro gave a downward wave of his hand.

"No, no. This time it's something personal," I said dreamily.

"Aaaah, you mean you've got something on the go, eh?" Silvestro looked at me mischievously and grinned broadly.

"Yes, you could say that." I grinned back and thought of the white sheet of paper on my living room table, which was suddenly beginning to fill up with words and sentences. All at once I was in a hurry.

"*Pazzo,* why didn't you say so right away? Well, I won't get in the way of your good fortune!" Silvestro patted me benevolently on the shoulder a couple of times before going back to his table.

"My friends, he's got something on the go!" I heard him call—and the others waved and laughed.

As I headed for the exit, making my way through the customers who were chatting and drinking at the bar, I thought for a fraction of a second that I saw a slim figure with long dark blond hair sitting farther toward the back of the room with her back to the door, gesticulating energetically.

I shook my head. You're imagining things! At that moment Aurélie Bredin was in her own little restaurant in the Rue Princesse. And I was a little drunk.

Then the door flew open, a gust of cold wind blew in accompanied by a lanky guy with curly blond hair and a dark-haired girl in a crimson coat snuggled tight against him.

They looked very happy, and I stood aside to let them in. Then I went out myself, my hands deep in my pockets.

It was cold in Paris and it was raining, but if you were in love the weather didn't matter.

Seven

....

"When push comes to shove, you find the whole thing crazy, don't you? Admit it!"

I'd been sitting with Bernadette in La Palette for quite a while. It was full to bursting, but we'd managed to grab a table right against the back wall and our conversation had moved on from *Vicky Cristina Barcelona,* the film we'd seen that evening, to how realistic or unrealistic the expectations of a certain Aurélie Bredin actually were.

Bernadette sighed. "It's just that I think it might be better in the long run to invest your energy in more realistic projects— otherwise you'll end up disappointed again."

"Aha," I retorted. "But when that Cristina goes off with a totally unknown Spaniard who tells her that he wants to go to bed not only with her but also with her friends, you find that *realistic?*"

Our views of the heroines of the film were somewhat divided.

"That's not what I said. I just said that I can *understand* how it might happen. Anyway, the guy is at least totally honest. I like

that." She poured more wine into my glass. "Good grief, Aurélie, it's only a film, why are you getting so worked up? You find
the plot implausible, I find it plausible. You preferred Vicky, I
preferred Cristina. Do we have to quarrel about it?"

"No. It's just that it annoys me a bit when you apply a
double standard. It may well be that it's not very likely that the
guy will answer my letter, but it's *not* unrealistic," I said.

"Oh, Aurélie, that isn't the case at all. After all, I did actually help you to look for information about the author on the
Internet today. I find the whole thing amusing and exciting. I
just don't want you to go running down a blind alley again." She
took my hand and sighed. "You seem to have a penchant for
relationships that have no chance of success. First of all you're
with that weird designer who just vanishes every couple of
weeks and has several screws loose. And now all you talk about
is this mysterious author who—whatever you read into his
novel—definitely seems to be one thing at least: difficult."

"That's what that peculiar Cerberus at the publishing house
says. Do you know if it's true?" I stopped talking and pettishly
painted patterns on my napkin with my fork.

"No, I don't know that. Listen, I just want you to be happy.
And I sometimes just get the feeling that you set your heart on
things that will never work."

"But a pediatrician, that'd work, would it?" I replied. "That's
something realistic as well?"

"You'd do better to take a nice pediatrician instead of getting hung up on such unrealistic things" was what Bernadette
had said when, after the cinema, I'd wondered out loud how
long a letter would take to get from England to France.

"Okay, I shouldn't have said that about the pediatrician," she
now said. "Although Olivier is really nice."

"Yes. Nice—and boring." Bernadette had already introduced me to Dr. Olivier Christophle at her birthday party in the summer, when I was still with Claude, and since then had never given up the hope that we'd get together.

"Yes, yes, you're right." Bernadette waved dismissively. "He just isn't exciting enough." An almost imperceptible smile played on her lips. "Good. At the moment we are all agog to see how long the post office takes to carry a letter from England to Paris. And I want you to keep me in the loop about this affair, is that clear? And if the moment ever comes when a nice, boring doctor is called for, you can just let me know."

I crumpled my napkin and dropped it on my plate, which still showed the traces of a ham omelette.

"*D'accord!* That's what we'll do," I said, and reached for my purse. "It's my treat."

I noticed a slight draft in my back and shrugged my shoulders with a shiver.

"Do people always have to leave the door open so long?" I said, and reached for the saucer with the check.

Bernadette stared at me in surprise, and then her eyes narrowed.

"What is it? Have I said something wrong again?" I asked.

"No, no." She hastily lowered her gaze and at that moment I realized that it wasn't me she'd been staring at. "Let's have an espresso," she said, and I raised my eyebrows in astonishment.

"Since when do you drink coffee so late at night? You always say it stops you sleeping."

"But now I want to." She looked at me as if she was trying to hypnotize me, and smiled. "Here, look at this," she said, and took a leather folder out of her purse. "Have you seen these pictures of Marie? They were taken at home in Orange at my parents' place."

"No . . . Bernadette . . . what . . . what's all this about?" I noticed that her eyes were looking anxiously past me. "What do you keep looking at over there?"

Bernadette had the seat with a view of the bistro, while I was facing the oil painting on the wall. "Nothing. I'm just keeping an eye out for the waiter." She seemed tense, and I started to turn around.

"Don't look around!" hissed Bernadette, and grabbed my arm, but by then it was already too late.

In the middle of La Palette, right by the passage through to the back of the bistro where we were sitting, stood Claude, waiting for a table by the window where they were just paying the waiter. He had his arm lovingly around a young woman who, with her chin-length black hair and rosy cheeks, looked like a Mongolian princess. She was wearing a waisted coat of red felt with fringes around the sleeves and the hem. And she was unmistakably pregnant.

I cried all the way home. Bernadette sat beside me in the taxi, held me tight in her arms, and handed me one tissue after another.

"And do you know what the worst thing is?" I sobbed as Bernadette later sat down beside me on the bed holding out a mug of hot milk with honey. "That red coat . . . we'd recently seen it together in a shop window in the Rue du Bac, and I said I'd like it for my birthday."

It was the betrayal that hurt most. The lies. I counted off the months on my fingers and came to the conclusion that Claude had been deceiving me for half a year at least. Damn it, he'd looked so happy standing there with his Mongolian princess, who was pressing her hand to her little stomach.

We'd waited till they both took their seats by the window and then we'd gone out very quickly. But Claude would not have seen me anyway. He only had eyes for his little Snow White.

"Oh, Aurélie, I'm so sorry. And you were just starting to get over it. And now that! It's like a bad novel!"

"He shouldn't have given her that coat. It's . . . it's so heartless." I gave Bernadette a hurt look. "That woman stands there in *my* coat and is so . . . so happy! And my birthday's coming soon and I'm all alone and the coat has gone. It's so unfair!"

Bernadette stroked my hair gently. "Now, take a sip of your milk," she said. "Of course it's not fair. And bad. Such things really shouldn't happen, but things don't always go according to plan. And anyway, it's not really about Claude, is it?"

I shook my head and sipped my milk. Bernadette was right, this wasn't about Claude at all, but about something that ultimately always touches our souls: the love for someone we all long for, to whom we reach out our hands our whole life long, to touch them and hold them.

Bernadette looked thoughtful. "You know that I never thought much of Claude," she said. "But perhaps he did actually find the only woman for him. Perhaps he'd wanted to tell you for some time and was just waiting for the right moment, which of course never comes. And then your father dies, which made it all the more difficult, and he didn't want to leave you in that situation." She pursed her lips as she always did when she was thinking. "It could have been like that."

"But the coat," I insisted.

"Yes, the coat: that's unforgivable," she said. "We'll have to think of something." She bent over me and gave me a kiss. "Now, try and get some sleep, it's very late." She jabbed my duvet with her finger. "And you're not alone, d'you hear? Someone is always watching over you, even if it's only your old friend Bernadette."

I listened to her steps echoing slowly away into the distance. She had such a firm, reliable tread.

"Good night, Aurélie!" she shouted once more, and the floorboards in the front hall creaked. Then she put out the light and I heard the door closing quietly.

"Good night, Bernadette," I whispered. "I'm glad that you're there."

I don't know if it was because of the hot milk and honey, but I slept surprisingly well that night. When I woke up, the sun was shining into my bedroom for the first time in days. I stood up and opened the curtains. There was a clear blue sky over Paris—or at least the little rectangular patch that I could see from my balcony between the courtyard walls.

You never see more than a tiny segment, I thought as I prepared my breakfast. I would really have liked to see the whole thing.

The evening before, when I'd seen Claude with his pregnant girlfriend and the sight pierced me to the heart, I'd thought I was seeing the whole truth. But it was only *my* truth, my view of things. Claude's truth was different. And the woman in the red coat had another truth altogether.

Was it possible to understand the true depths of any other human being? What moved them, what drove them, what they really dreamed of?

I put the dishes in the sink and ran water over them.

Claude had lied to me, but perhaps I had let myself be lied to. I'd never asked. Sometimes you live better with a lie than with the truth.

Claude and I had never really spoken about the future. He'd never said to me, "I'd like to have a child with you." And I'd never said it either. We had kept each other company along a stretch of the road. There had been lovely moments, and some that were not lovely at all. And it was senseless to expect fairness in matters of the heart.

Love was what it was. No more and no less.

I dried my hands. Then I went to the bureau in the hall and opened the drawer. I took the photo of me and Claude out and looked at it once more. "I wish you happiness," I said, and then I took the picture and put it in the old cigar box where I keep my memories.

Before I left the house to do my shopping in the market and at the butcher's, I went over to the bedroom and stuck a new note on my wall of thought.

About love, when it's over.

Love, when it's over, is always sad.
It's rarely generous.
The one who leaves has a bad conscience.
The one who's left licks their wounds.
Breaking up hurts almost more than separation.
But at the end everyone is what they always were.
And sometimes a song remains, a sheet of paper with two hearts,
The tender reminder of a summer day.

Eight

....

When the call came I was in the process of making a groveling apology to a very upset Mademoiselle Mirabeau.

During the meeting I'd already noticed that the normally so charming assistant editor would not deign to grant me a single look. And even when I really got under way and described a book in such witty terms that even the snooty Michelle Auteuil almost fell off her chair laughing, the lovely blonde didn't react at all. All my attempts to get her to talk as I walked along the hall with her after the meeting failed. She said "Yes" and "No" and I couldn't get anything else out of her.

"Come into my office for a moment, please," I said as we reached the main office.

She nodded and followed me in silence.

"Please." I pointed to one of the chairs beside the little round conference table. "Take a seat."

Mademoiselle Mirabeau sat down like an affronted duchess. She folded her arms, crossed her legs, and I couldn't help noticing the sheer light silk stockings she was wearing under her short skirt.

"Now," I said jovially. "What's bugging you? Come on, tell me what's the matter."

"Nothing," she said, and studied the floor as if there was something really fascinating to be discovered there.

It was worse than I'd feared. When women insisted that it was "nothing," then they were really mad.

"Hm," I said. "Are you sure about that?"

"Yes," she said. She had obviously decided to speak to me only in one-word sentences.

"D'you know what, Mademoiselle Mirabeau?"

"No."

"I don't believe a word of it."

Florence Mirabeau just glanced at me before returning her attention to the floorboards.

"Come on, Mademoiselle Mirabeau, don't be so cruel. Tell old André Chabanais why you're so upset, otherwise I won't be able to sleep tonight."

I noticed that she was suppressing a smile.

"You're not that old," she retorted. "And if you can't sleep, it serves you right." She pulled at her skirt and I waited. "You said I shouldn't look so sheepish," she finally blurted.

"I said that to you? But that's . . . monstrous," I said.

"You did so." She looked at me for the first time. "You really went for me yesterday when you were on the phone. And I was only trying to bring you that report. You'd said it was urgent and I spent the whole weekend reading and I called off my date specially and I did it all as quickly as I could. And that was all the thanks I got!" That incandescent speech had given her red cheeks. "You really snapped at me."

Now that she said it, I remembered only too well that agitated telephone conversation with Adam Goldberg, which Mademoiselle Mirabeau had unluckily burst in on.

"*Oh, mon Dieu, mon Dieu,* I'm sorry." I looked at the little mimosa sitting in front of me with a reproachful expression. "I'm *really* sorry," I repeated emphatically. "I didn't really mean to get at you, you know, it's just that I was so worked up . . ."

"Even so," she said.

"No, no." I raised both hands. "That's not meant to be an excuse. I promise to improve. Really. Will you forgive me?"

I looked ruefully at her. She lowered her eyes and the corners of her mouth twitched as she jiggled her shapely leg.

"As an apology, I'll offer you . . ."—I leaned over thoughtfully in her direction—"a raspberry tart. How about it? Would you permit me to invite you to a raspberry tart in the Ladurée tomorrow lunchtime?"

She smiled. "You're in luck," she said. "I absolutely adore raspberry tarts."

"Can I take it from that that you're not mad at me anymore?"

"Yes, you can." Florence Mirabeau stood up. "Then I'll go and get the report," she said in a conciliatory tone.

"Yes, do that!" I said. "Wonderful! I can hardly wait!" I stood up to accompany her to the door.

"You don't have to exaggerate, Monsieur Chabanais. I'm just doing my job."

"And let me tell you something, Mademoiselle Mirabeau, you do your job extremely well."

"Oh," she said. "Thank you. It's nice of you to say that. Monsieur Chabanais, I . . ." She blushed again and stood hesitantly by the door as if she had something else to say.

"Yes?" I asked.

And then the telephone rang. I didn't want to be rude again, and so I stood still instead of shoving Florence Mirabeau out of the room and throwing myself at the desk.

After the third ring Mademoiselle Mirabeau said, "Do go and pick it up, perhaps it's important."

She smiled and disappeared through the door. Pity: Now I'd probably never find out what it was she had been going to say. But Florence Mirabeau had been right about one thing . . .

That call *was* important.

I recognized the voice at once. I would have recognized it among a thousand other voices. As she had the first time, she sounded a little breathless, like someone who had just run up a flight of stairs.

"Is that Monsieur André Chabanais?" she asked.

"It is," I replied, and leaned back in my seat with a broad grin. The fish had bitten.

Aurélie Bredin was enthusiastic about my offer to help her to meet Robert Miller "by chance," and questions one to three of her rather caustic e-mail to the *unfriendly* editor at Éditions Opale seemed to have been forgotten for the moment.

"What a fantastic idea!" she said.

I also found my idea fantastic, but I obviously kept that to myself. "Well, it's not all that fantastic but . . . it's not bad," I said.

"This is really incredibly nice of you, Monsieur Chabanais," Aurélie Bredin continued, and I basked in my sudden importance as a go-between.

"*Il n'y a pas de quoi*. You're welcome," I said. "I'm just glad to be of service."

She said nothing for a moment.

"And I thought you were a grumpy old editor who kept

everyone away from his author," she said apologetically. "I hope you'll forgive me."

Triumph, triumph! This was obviously the day for apologies.

Admittedly, I wasn't being offered raspberry tart, but I have to admit I'm not that keen on it. Aurélie Bredin's feelings of remorse tasted immeasurably sweeter.

"But my dear Mademoiselle Bredin, I couldn't possibly hold anything against you even if I wanted to. After all, I haven't exactly shown myself from my best side. Let us forget the whole unfortunate beginning and concentrate on our little plan." I rolled up to my desk on my office chair and opened my diary.

Two minutes later the matter had been arranged. Aurélie Bredin would turn up at half past seven on Friday evening in La Coupole, where I'd reserved a table in my name, and we'd have a drink together. At about eight Robert Miller (with whom I ostensibly had an appointment to discuss his new book) would also arrive, and there'd be plenty of opportunity to get to know one another.

I'd dithered a moment over the choice of restaurant.

A small intimate restaurant with cozy, red plush seats like Le Belier would obviously have been more suitable for my real purposes than the famous Coupole—that big, lively brasserie that was full every evening. But on the other hand it would have seemed a bit strange to be meeting an English author in a place that seemed to have been made just for lovers.

La Coupole was innocuous, and since the author was never going to turn up I thought I'd have a better chance of continuing the evening in the company of the capricious Mademoiselle Bredin if the restaurant was not too romantic.

"In La Coupole?" she asked, and I could hear immediately

that her enthusiasm was not unbounded. "Do you really want to go to that tourist trap?"

"Miller suggested it," I said. "He has something to do in Montparnasse beforehand, and anyway he loves La Coupole." (I would also have preferred Le Temps des Cerises, but I obviously couldn't say that.)

"He loves La Coupole?" Her irritation was audible.

"Yes, well, he is English," I said. "He thinks La Coupole is great. He says that that brasserie always makes him . . . cheerful because it is so lively and bright."

"Aha," was all that Mademoiselle Bredin had to say to that.

"He's also a great fan of the *fabuleux curry d'agneau des Indes*," I added, finding that I sounded most convincing.

"The famous Indian lamb curry?" Mademoiselle Bredin said. "I've never heard of that. Is it really that good?"

"No idea," I replied. "You as a chef will probably be better able to judge than most people. And Robert Miller found it absolutely superb the last time he was here. After every mouthful he said, 'Delicious, absolutely delicious.' But the English aren't exactly spoiled when it comes to cuisine—you know, fish and chips! I imagine they go totally overboard when someone puts some curry and some grated coconut in the food, hahaha." I wished Goldberg could have heard me at that moment.

Aurélie Bredin didn't laugh. "I thought Robert Miller loved *French* cuisine." She obviously felt that her honor as a chef was being impugned.

"Well, you can ask him all about that yourself," I replied, in order not to have to discuss our author's culinary predilections any further. I doodled a line of little triangles in my diary with a ballpoint.

"Has Monsieur Miller actually received your letter now?"

"I think so. But I haven't had an answer yet, if that's what you wanted to know." She sounded a little piqued.

"I'm sure he'll write to you," I said. "At the latest after he's met you in person on Friday."

"What do you mean by that?"

"That you are a totally enchanting young woman whose charm no man could resist for long—not even an unworldly English writer."

She laughed. "You're bad, Monsieur Chabanais, do you know that?"

"Yes, I know," I replied. "Worse than you think."

Nine

....

Post Nubila Phoebus. I softly whispered the inscription engraved
on the white boulder, and ran my fingers tenderly over the letters. "After the clouds, the sun."

It had been my father's motto—and he had been, something
you might not automatically expect in someone in his profession, a man with a humanist education who, unlike his daughter, had read a great deal. Rain is followed by sunshine—how
wise he had been!

I was standing in the Père Lachaise cemetery and above me
white clouds were scudding across the sky; when the sun finally
broke through it was actually quite warm. I hadn't been to Papa's grave since All Saints' Day, but today I had felt a very strong
urge to come here.

I took a step backward and laid the bright bouquet of asters
and chrysanthemums on the flat rectangular surface carved into
the ivy-covered grave for that very purpose.

"You can't imagine all that's happened, Papa," I said. "You'd
be amazed."

The week had begun so unhappily, and now I was standing here in the cemetery, in a strange way happy and excited. And above all I was looking forward impatiently to the following evening.

The sun that had shone so brightly into my room that Tuesday after all the recent dull and rainy weather had been a kind of harbinger. All at once everything had changed for the better.

After I'd unloaded my shopping in the restaurant that Tuesday, discussed three possible pre-Christmas menus with Jacquie, and then thought a couple of times about the red coat and its wearer, I'd gone home again and decided to fill this not exactly glorious day with an even less glorious activity before returning to the restaurant for the evening.

So I sat down at my computer and set to dealing with a pile of long-overdue bills by electronic transfer.

First, however, I glanced at my e-mails and found a friendly—you might even say totally charming—letter from André Chabanais, in which he not only answered all my questions but, to my great surprise, made a suggestion that immediately changed my mood to one of joyful anticipation.

I had the opportunity to meet Robert Miller, even if only for a short while, since Monsieur Chabanais was going to meet with the author and had invited me to come along as if by chance.

Of course I accepted his offer, and unlike my first telephone conversation with the bearded editor, this one was quite amusing and almost flirtatious, which, in the mood I was in, I found quite pleasant.

When I told Bernadette about it, she of course immediately began to pull my leg and said that she was starting to like this editor more and more and that if it ultimately turned out that the author was not quite as wonderful as his novel, I would have another option.

"You're impossible, Bernadette," I said. "You keep trying to set me up with one man or other. If I take anyone at all, it'll be the author—first of all, he looks better, and then he is after all the one who wrote the book, or have you forgotten that?"

"Is the guy as ugly as sin, then?" Bernadette wanted to know.

"How should I know?" I retorted. "No, probably not, I've never really looked. André Chabanais doesn't interest me at all. And he has a beard."

"What's so bad about that?"

"Come on, Bernadette! You know that men with beards just aren't my thing. I won't even give them a second glance."

"A mistake!" Bernadette threw in.

"And anyway, I'm not looking for a man. I'm not looking for a man, d'you hear? I just want an opportunity to talk to that author—for the reasons you are well aware of. And because I'm very grateful to him."

"Oh, divine providence, fateful entanglements wherever you look . . ." Bernadette sounded like the chorus in a Greek tragedy.

"Exactly," I said. "You'll see."

That same evening I told Jacquie that I would not be coming in to the restaurant on Friday. I'd called Juliette Meunier, a very good and very professional waitress who had previously been head waitress at the Lutetia and who had already stood in for me a couple of times. Now she was studying interior decoration and only took waiting jobs by the hour. Fortunately, she had nothing planned and accepted the offer.

Jacquie, of course, was not exactly delighted. "Do you have to? On a Friday? Especially now that Paul is ill," he grumbled, banging the pots and pans around as he cooked the meal for our little team.

We always used to eat together an hour before the restaurant opened: Jacquie, the chef and the oldest of us; Paul, the young sous-chef; the two kitchen hands, Claude and Marie; Suzette; and I. These meals, where we discussed all sorts of things, and not just restaurant business, had something of a family atmosphere. We talked, argued, laughed—and then everyone went to their posts refreshed.

"Sorry, Jacquie, but something very important has just cropped up," I said, and the chef gave me a piercing look.

"Seems to have cropped up very suddenly! This lunchtime when we were discussing the Christmas menus you knew nothing about it."

"I've already called Juliette," I said quickly to stop him probing any further. "She'll be happy to come, and for December we still need to decide whether we're going to need extra help in the kitchen. If Paul continues to be ill, I can help you in the kitchen and we can ask Juliette if she'll take my place in the restaurant on weekends."

"*Ah, non.* I don't like working with women in the kitchen," said Jacquie. "It takes balls to grill properly, and women just can't do it."

"Now don't be so cheeky," I said. "I certainly can do it. And you're an old chauvinist, Jacquie."

Jacquie grinned. "Always have been, always have been."

He chopped up two large onions on a wooden chopping board at lightning speed and scraped the pieces into a large pan with the knife. "And anyway, you're not really much good with sauces." He waited till the onion was golden yellow in the butter, poured some white wine over it, and turned down the gas a little.

"What on earth are you saying, Jacquie?" I was enraged! "You taught me how to make most of the sauces yourself, and you've always said that my fillet steak in pepper sauce is absolutely delicious."

He smirked. "Yes, your pepper sauce is wonderful, but that's only because you know your papa's secret recipe." He threw a handful of fries into the fryer and my protest was drowned by the hissing of the hot fat.

When Jacquie worked at the range he became a juggler. He loved to keep several balls in the air at once, and was breathtaking to watch.

"But you do make very good desserts, I'll grant you that," Jacquie went on, unimpressed, and shook the pan. "Well, let's hope that Paul's back in the saddle on Saturday." He looked at me over the fryer and lowered an eyelid. "Something very important, eh? Who's the lucky guy, then?"

The lucky guy was Robert Miller, even though he had no inkling of his good fortune. He didn't know that on Friday he'd be going on a blind date in La Coupole. And I wasn't sure if he'd be so madly delighted if an uninvited guest disturbed his conversation with André Chabanais.

But then came Thursday, and with it a letter, which filled me with certainty that I had done everything right and that it was sometimes good to follow your feelings, no matter how absurd it seemed to other people.

I took a letter out of the mailbox. It had nothing on it but my name. Someone had stuck a note on the envelope that read:

Dear Mademoiselle Bredin, this letter arrived at the office yester-
day, congratulations! Robert Miller accidentally destroyed the
envelope with your address and so he sent it to us. I hope it's in
order to deliver it directly to you. See you tomorrow evening.
Bonne lecture! *André Chabanais.*

I smiled. It was so typical of Chabanais to congratulate me
as if I'd won a bet and wish me enjoyable reading. It had probably surprised him that his author had answered me in spite of
everything.

Not for a single moment did the question enter my mind:
Where had André Chabanais actually got hold of my private
address?

I couldn't wait but sat down in my coat on the cold stone
steps in the stairway and tore the letter open. Then I read the
sentences that had been literally jabbed into the paper in a spiky
hand in blue ballpoint.

Dear Miss Aurélie Bredin,
I have been very happy to receive your nice letter. Unfortu-
nately my small dog Rocky also licked the letter, especially the
envelope. When I realized that, it was too late, and Rocky, this
greedy small monster, had already swallowed the envelope with
the address. I must apologies for mine dog, he is still very young
and I send my answer to my trustful editor André Chabanais,
who will give it to you, hopefully. I would like to say you, dear
Mademoiselle Bredin, that I have received much fan mail but
never one so lovely and exciting.
I am really glad that my little Paris novel did help you in a
time when you were so unhappy. Thus it has been of use and

that is more than you can speak of most books. (I hope also that you in the long run could escape from the police!) I think I could understand you well. I was also been long unhappy and feel with you from my deep heart.

I am not the man kind who is liking to be in public, I prefer to stay incognito and I fear I am a bit boring because I really like to be in my cottage, to walk in the nature, and to repair old cars, but if that does not scare you I accept the charming invitation to your little restaurant when I will come back to Paris.

My next time is only very short and stuffed full of appointments, but I would like to come with more time so that we can talk nice and calmly. Yes I know your restaurant, I falled in love with it at the first look, especially the red-and-white-check tableclothes.

Thank you very much a lot for the lovely photo what you sent me. Dare I say without being intruding that you are very sexy?

And of course you are right—the sameness between Sophie and you, dear Aurélie, is astonishing—and I think I owe you an explication of my small mystery! Just one thing: Never in my boldest expectations did I thought receiving mail from my heroine from my book—it is like a dream that is becoming truth.

I hope so very much that you feel yourself better now and are freed of your unhappiness. I really look forward so much to seeing you in the flesh.

Forgive me, my French is not very good! But I wish you was still pleased that I writed back to you.

I can not wait to sit in your lovely restaurant and in the end to speak to you about ALL.

Friendly wishes and à tout bientôt!

Yours faithfully,

Robert Miller

· · ·

"Do you have a watering can, mademoiselle?" said a croaking voice behind me.

I gave a start and turned around.

There in front of me was a little old woman in a black Persian lamb coat with a matching cap. She had bright red lipstick and was inspecting me curiously.

"A *watering can!*" she repeated impatiently.

I shook my head. "No, I'm afraid not, madame."

"That's bad, very bad." She shook her head and pursed her red lips crossly.

I wondered what the old lady wanted a watering can for. It had after all rained so much in recent weeks that the ground was definitely damp enough.

"Someone's stolen my watering can," the old lady explained. "I know exactly that I hid it behind that gravestone"—she pointed at a nearby grave standing under the gnarled branches of an old tree—"and now it's disappeared. Things get stolen everywhere these days—even in a cemetery, and what do they do about it?"

She rummaged in her big black handbag and finally pulled out a pack of Gauloises. I was quite taken aback. She lit a cigarette, inhaled deeply, and blew the smoke up into the blue sky.

Then she held out the pack to me. "Here, do you want one too?"

I shook my head. I sometimes smoked in cafés, but never in cemeteries.

"Go on, take one, my child." She waved the pack around in front of my face. "We'll never be as young as this again." She giggled, and I covered my mouth with my hand, smiling in amazement.

"All right. Thanks very much," I said. She gave me a light.

"There you are," she said. "Oh, let's forget the stupid watering can. It leaked anyway. Isn't it lovely that the sun is shining after all that rain?"

I nodded. Yes, it was lovely. The sun was shining, and life was full of surprises.

And that's how it came about that on that Thursday I was standing in the Père Lachaise with a bizarre old lady who seemed to have sprung straight out of a Fellini film, puffing a cigarette. We were surrounded by serene silence, and I felt as if we were the only people in the whole gigantic cemetery.

In the distance towered the Muse Euterpe, symbol of jollity, who has been watching over Frédéric Chopin's grave for a long time now. At the foot of the stone tomb there were a lot of vases full of flowers, and bunches of roses had been stuck in the iron railings. I looked around. Some graves still had the flowers that had been put there on All Saints' Day. Some had been ravaged by time: Nature had reconquered her territory and weeds and wild plants were growing in profusion over the stone monuments. These dead had been forgotten. And there were more than a few of them.

"I've been watching you," said the old lady, and twinkled at me out of her knowing brown eyes, which were surrounded by hundreds of tiny wrinkles. "You looked as if you were thinking about something very beautiful."

I took a pull at the cigarette. "I was, actually," I replied. "I was thinking about tomorrow. Tomorrow evening I'm going to La Coupole, you know."

"What a coincidence," said the old lady, and shook her head delightedly. "I'll be in La Coupole tomorrow as well. I'm celebrating my eighty-fifth birthday, my child. I *love* La Coupole—I go there every year on my birthday. I always have the oysters, they're very good."

I suddenly imagined the Fellini lady, surrounded by her children and grandchildren, sitting at a long table in the brasserie, celebrating.

"Then I wish you a pleasant celebration in advance," I said.

She shook her head regretfully. "No, it will only be a very small party this time," she said. "Very small *indeed*, to be honest. Just me and the waiters, but they are always lovely." She smiled happily. "My goodness, what parties we've had in La Coupole. Wild parties. Henry, my husband, was a conductor at the opera, you know. And after premieres the champagne flowed: By the end we were all so gloriously drunk." She giggled. "Well, that was long ago . . . And George only comes to Paris with the children at Christmas. He lives in South America . . ." I assumed that George was her son. "*Eh bien,* and since my old friend Auguste went"—she paused for a moment and looked over at the gravestone where the watering can should have been—"there's unfortunately no one left to celebrate with me."

"Oh," I said. "I'm sorry."

"No need for you to be sorry, my child, that's life. Everything to its own time. Sometimes I lie in bed at night and count all my dear departed ones."

She gave me a conspiratorial look and lowered her voice. "There are *thirty-seven* already." She took a last puff of her cigarette and threw the butt carelessly to the ground. "Well, I'm still here, what do you say to that? And let me tell you something, my child. I enjoy every goddamn day. My mother lived to be a hundred and two and was cheerful to the end."

"Impressive," I said.

She stretched her little hand, clothed in a black leather glove, forcefully toward me. "Elisabeth Dinsmore," she said. "But you're welcome to call me Liz."

I dropped my cigarette end and shook her hand.

"Aurélie Bredin," I introduced myself. "Do you know what, Liz? You're the first person whose acquaintance I've ever made in a cemetery."

"Oh, I've got to know a lot of people in the cemetery," Mrs. Dinsmore said, smiling broadly with her red lips. "They certainly weren't the worst."

"Dinsmore . . . that doesn't sound very French," I said. I had noticed before that the old lady's pronunciation had a slight accent to it, but had put it down to her age.

"That's because it isn't," Mrs. Dinsmore replied. "I'm American. But I've lived in Paris for ages. And you, my child? What will you be doing in La Coupole?" she asked without any transition.

"Oh, I . . . ." I responded, noticing how I was blushing. "I'm going there to meet . . . someone."

"Aaaah," she said. "And . . . is he nice?" One of the advantages of age was obviously that you could get down to essentials without wasting any time.

I laughed and bit my lower lip. "Yes . . . I think so. He's a writer."

"My goodness, a writer!" cried Elisabeth Dinsmore. "How *exciting!*"

"Yes," I said, without going into any more detail. "I *am* quite excited."

After I had taken my leave of Mrs. Dinsmore—Liz—who had invited me to join her for a glass of champagne at her table the following evening ("But you'll probably have better things to do than quaff champagne with an old biddy, my child," she had added with a twinkle), I stood beside the white boulder for a moment longer.

"*Au revoir,* Papa," I said quietly. "Somehow I have the feeling that tomorrow's going to be a quite unusual day."

And—in some ways—I turned out to be right.

I was standing in a line that reached right up to the big glass door. Even if La Coupole wasn't exactly my favorite restaurant, it was still a favorite meeting place for both young and old. It wasn't only tourists who streamed into the legendary brasserie on the busy Boulevard Montparnasse with its red canopy— and, so it was said, the largest dining room in Paris. Businessmen and people who live in Paris also liked to come here to eat and to celebrate. A few years before they had held salsa evenings every Wednesday in the dance hall beneath the brasserie, but since then the salsa craze had probably calmed down; at least, I couldn't see any posters advertising such a spectacle.

I moved forward a bit with the line and went inside La Coupole. I was immediately engulfed by a lively buzz of conversation. Waiters carrying silver trays hurried between the long rows of white-covered tables under the vast arch of the great hall. Even if you would search in vain for a real cupola, the hall with its green pillars and the art deco lamps under the ceiling was nevertheless most impressive. The restaurant vibrated with life—the motto of the place was *se donner en spectacle* and the guests here seemed to be heeding it. I hadn't been here for a long time and observed the lively activity with amusement.

A friendly maître d' was distributing little red cards to the people who didn't have reservations and sending them to the bar to wait. On the cards were the names of famous composers, and every few minutes you would hear a young waiter, who obviously found it extremely amusing, walking around in the bar shouting at the top of his voice like a circus ringmaster: *"Bach, deux personnes, s'il vous plait"* or *"Tchaikovsky, quatre personnes, s'il vous plait"* or *"Debussy, six personnes, s'il vous plait."* At that, some of those who were waiting would get up to be led to their tables.

"Bonsoir, mademoiselle, vous avez une réservation? Do you have a reservation?" the maître d' asked me briskly when it was my turn, and a young woman took my coat and pressed a cloakroom ticket into my hand.

I nodded. *"J'ai un rendez-vous avec Monsieur André Chabanais,"* I said.

The maître d' glanced at his long list. *"Ah, oui,* here it is," he said. "A table for three. One moment, please!" He waved a waiter over. The waiter, an elderly man with short gray hair, smiled at me agreeably.

"Follow me, please, mademoiselle."

I nodded, and could feel my heart beginning to pound. In half an hour I would finally be meeting Robert Miller, who was, as his letter had said, so looking forward to seeing me "in the flesh."

I smoothed down my dress. It was the green silk dress, the dress in the book, the dress I was wearing in the photo I'd sent to Robert Miller. I'd left nothing to chance.

The friendly waiter stopped suddenly in front of one of the wood-paneled niches. *"Et voilà,"* he said. "Here you are."

André Chabanais jumped up from the bench immediately to welcome me. He was wearing a suit and a white shirt with an elegant dark blue tie. "Mademoiselle Bredin," he said. "How lovely to see you . . . please take a seat." He pointed to his place on the bench and went to stand by one of the chairs on the opposite side of the table.

"Thank you." The waiter moved the table with its white cloth set with glasses a little and I went past him and sat down on the leather-upholstered seat.

André Chabanais sat down too.

"What would you like to drink? Champagne—to celebrate the *great* day?" He grinned at me.

I could feel myself turning red and was annoyed with myself because I could see that he noticed it too. "Don't be impertinent," I replied, and held my purse tight in my lap. "But yes, champagne would be very nice."

His gaze slid over my bare arms, then he looked up at me again. "My compliments," he said. "You look enchanting, if I may be so bold as to say so. The dress suits you superbly. It emphasizes the color of your eyes."

"Thank you," I said, and smiled. "You don't look too bad yourself this evening."

"Oh . . ." André Chabanais waved to the waiter. "I'm only playing a very small bit part this evening, you know." He turned round. "Champagne for two, please!"

"I thought I was the bit player this evening," I retorted. "After all, I was only passing here by chance."

"Well, we'll see," declared Monsieur Chabanais. "And anyway, you might as well put down your purse. Your author won't be here for a quarter of an hour at least."

"Your author, you mean," I said, and put my purse down beside me.

Monsieur Chabanais smiled. "Let's just say *our* author."

The waiter came and served the champagne. Then he handed us the menus. "Thanks, but we're waiting for someone else," said Monsieur Chabanais, and put the menus aside.

He took his glass and toasted me, and we briefly clinked glasses. The champagne was ice cold. I took three great gulps and could feel my nervousness giving way to relaxed anticipation.

"Thanks once again for arranging things," I said. "To be honest, I'm as tense as a bowstring." I put the champagne flute down.

André Chabanais nodded. "I can understand that very well." He leaned back in his seat. "For example, I'm a great Woody Allen fan. I even began to learn the clarinet once, just because he plays clarinet." He laughed. "Unfortunately my new passion was not born under a lucky star. The neighbors kept banging on the ceiling whenever I practiced."

He took a sip and stroked the white tablecloth. "Well, anyway, then Woody Allen came to Paris and gave a concert with his funny old-time jazz band. The hall, which was normally used for classical concerts by great orchestras, was sold out, and I'd managed to get hold of a seat in the fifth row. Like everyone else, I wasn't really there for the music. I mean, to be honest, Woody Allen played no better than any old jazz musician in any old bar in Montmartre. But to see this old guy that I knew from so many films close up, to hear him speaking in person—that was something incredibly special and very exciting."

He leaned forward, resting his chin in his hand. "There's one thing that annoys me to this very day."

He paused for a moment, and I emptied my glass and leaned forward too. Chabanais was a good storyteller. But he was also very attentive. When he saw that my glass was empty, he made a sign to the waiter, who immediately brought two more glasses of champagne. *"À la vôtre,"* said André Chabanais, and I raised my glass without protest.

"So there's something that annoys you to this very day," I repeated eagerly.

"Yes," he said, dabbing at his mouth with his napkin. "This is what happened: When the concert was over, there was a massive burst of applause. People stood up or stamped their feet to honor that slight old man who was standing there in his sweater and corduroys looking as unassuming and confused as he does in his films. He'd already left the stage five times, returning to his fans' thunderous applause, when all of a sudden a great hulk of a guy in a black suit leapt onto the stage. He had slicked-down, gelled hair and looked at first glance like a theater official or a tenor. Anyway, he shook the startled Allen's hand and then gave him a pen and a ticket to get him to sign his autograph. And Woody did it, too, and then finally vanished from the stage."

Monsieur Chabanais downed his champagne. "I wish I'd had the chutzpah to simply jump onto the stage like that. Just imagine: I could have shown that autograph to my children later on." He sighed. "Now good old Woody is back in America, I rush to see all his films, and it's hardly likely that I'll ever come face-to-face with him again in this life."

He looked at me, and this time I could discern no trace of mockery in his brown eyes.

"You know, Mademoiselle Bredin, when all is said and done I admire your determination. If you want something, you really have to *want* it."

A quiet ringtone interrupted his tribute to my willpower.

"Excuse me, please. That's mine." André Chabanais took his cell phone from his jacket and turned to one side. *"Oui?"*

I glanced at my watch and was astonished to see that it was already a quarter past eight. Time had flown, and Robert Miller would appear any minute.

"Oh dear, how silly, I'm so sorry," I heard Monsieur Chabanais say. "No, no. No problem at all. I'm sitting here quite comfortably. Don't let it stress you." He laughed. "Good. See you later, then. *Salut.*" He put the phone back in his pocket.

"That was Robert Miller," he said. "He's been held up and won't be here for another half hour." He looked at me with puppy-dog eyes. "It's just too bad that you've got to wait."

I shrugged. "The main thing is that he comes at all," I said, and wondered what was holding Robert Miller up. What did he actually do when he wasn't writing books? I was just about to ask when André Chabanais said:

"À propos—you haven't told me anything about Miller's letter. What did it say?"

I smiled at him and wound a strand of hair around my finger.

"Do you know what, Monsieur Chabanais, chief editor at Éditions Opale?" I said, and paused significantly. "That's absolutely none of your business."

"Oh," he said. "Oh, come on, be a little indiscreet, Mademoiselle Bredin. After all, I did bring the letter to you."

"Never," I said. "You're just pulling my leg again."

He put on an innocent expression.

"No, no, no," I said. "How did you get hold of my address anyway?"

For a brief moment he seemed to be irritated, then he laughed. "A professional secret. If you won't reveal anything to me, I won't reveal anything to you. Although I might have expected a little bit of gratitude."

"No chance!" I insisted, and took another sip of my champagne. Until I knew what it was that was linking me and Robert Miller I wouldn't say a single word. After all, Miller had mentioned a "little secret."

The champagne was beginning to go to my head. "At any rate, I don't think that *our author*," another significant pause, "would be too annoyed to find me sitting here. His answer was very nice."

"Astonishing," replied Monsieur Chabanais. "Your letter must have been irresistible."

"How well do you actually know Miller?" I asked, passing over the "irresistible."

"Oh, *quite* well." Could I see a hint of irony in Monsieur Chabanais's smile, or was I just imagining it? "We're not exactly the closest of friends, and in many respects I find him a bit eccentric, but I would claim to be able to see right into the most convoluted twists of his brain."

"Interesting," I said. "And for his part he seems to think a lot of his 'trustful' editor."

"I should hope so." André Chabanais looked at his watch. "Do you know what? This is getting a bit ridiculous. I'm so hungry I could eat a horse. What do you think, should we order something to eat?"

"I don't know," I said, "I wasn't actually expected . . ." By now it was half past eight, and I noticed that I was also beginning to get hungry.

"Then I'll decide," declared André Chabanais, and to the waiter once more: "I'd like to order now," he said. "We'll have two—no, three—*curry d'agneau des Indes,* and with it we'll drink"—he pointed to the wine list—"this Château Lafite-Rothschild."

"Very good, sir." The waiter took the menus back and put a basket of bread on the table.

"And since you're here, you ought to try the famous lamb curry," said Monsieur Chabanais, whose mood seemed to be getting better all the time, and pointed to the Indian waiters, dressed like maharajas, who kept going up and down between the tables with their little trolleys, serving the lamb curry. "I'd be interested in your professional opinion."

When André Chabanais's cell phone rang for the second time shortly after nine and Robert Miller finally canceled their date at La Coupole, it was too late to leave, although I did briefly think about doing so.

We'd already drunk a glass of the superb, silky red wine, and the fabulous lamb curry—which in my opinion wasn't all that fabulous and could have done with a bit more banana, apple, and grated coconut—was steaming on our plates.

Monsieur Chabanais probably noticed my slight hesitation as he told me the news with a sympathetic expression and I, in my profound disappointment, grabbed my big, rounded redwine glass.

"What a shame!" he said finally. "I'm afraid we're going to have to eat the curry up all by ourselves." He looked at me in comic desperation. "You wouldn't leave me sitting here alone with two pounds of lamb and a whole bottle of red wine, would you? Tell me you're not serious."

I shook my head. "No, of course not. You're not in the least to blame. Oh well, I suppose there's nothing else we can do . . ." I took a sip of the wine and forced myself to smile.

My coming here had been totally in vain. I'd taken the evening off in vain. I'd bathed and done my hair and put on the green dress totally in vain. I'd stood in front of the mirror thinking of the things I wanted to say to Robert Miller totally in vain. I'd come so close. Why couldn't something work out for once?

"Oh dear, oh dear, now you're terribly disappointed," said Chabanais. Then he wrinkled his forehead. "Sometimes I could send Miller off to the moon. This is not the first time he's canceled an appointment at the last moment, you know."

He looked at me with his brown eyes and smiled. "And now you're sitting here with that stupid editor and thinking that you've wasted your time coming here and the curry isn't as good as it's cracked up to be . . ." He sighed. "That's a real blow. But the wine is excellent, you must admit!"

I nodded. "Yes, I do." André Chabanais was making every effort to console me, which was kind of nice in spite of everything.

"Oh, come on, Mademoiselle Bredin, don't be so sad," he now said. "You'll get to meet our author somehow—it's only a matter of time. He did at least write to you, and that's got to mean something, hasn't it?" He spread his arms quizzically.

"Yes," I said, and ran my index finger thoughtfully over my lips. Chabanais was right. Nothing had been lost. And in the end it would probably even be better to meet Robert Miller alone. In my own restaurant.

Chabanais leaned forward. "I know I'm a poor substitute for the great Mr. Miller, but I will do everything in my power to make sure that you don't have bad memories of this evening— and perhaps even give me just a teeny-weeny smile."

He patted my hand and held it a moment longer than was

necessary. "You have such a strong belief in fate, Mademoiselle Bredin. What do you think—might there perhaps be a deeper meaning to our sitting here now holding hands?"

He grinned at me, and I had to smile, before I pulled my hand away and rapped him on the fingers.

"When you give some people your little finger they immediately try to take the whole hand. There *can't* be that much fate, Monsieur Chabanais—just give me a bit more wine."

Ten

....

The evening went better than I had expected. Aurélie Bredin was visibly nervous but euphoric as she arrived in La Coupole— five minutes too early and in the green dress, I noted with a smile.

She looked stunning, and it took all my self-control not to keep staring at her. I cracked a few jokes to pass the time, and Aurélie proved, in her state of joyful expectation, to be rather more approachable than I'd thought she would be.

Then, as arranged, Silvestro rang me on my cell phone. He'd taken on the assignment without asking too many questions.

"So, how's it going?" he asked, and I said, "Oh dear, how silly, I'm so sorry."

"That sounds good," he said, and I answered, "No, no. No problem at all. I'm sitting here quite comfortably. Don't let it stress you."

"Then have fun—I'll call again later," he said, and I ended the call.

Aurélie Bredin swallowed the delay and I ordered us some champagne. We drank and chatted, and once I almost broke out in a sweat when she suddenly asked me how I'd got her home address. But I managed to get out of it quite cleverly. Anyway, she refused to tell me any of her little secrets. Not a word about the letter I'd written. And she didn't tell me that she'd invited Robert Miller to her lovely restaurant either.

At a quarter past nine we were eating our lamb curry and Mademoiselle Bredin was just explaining to me why she didn't believe in coincidence when Silvestro called again, saying, "So, have you got off with her yet?"

I groaned into the phone and ran my fingers theatrically through my hair. "No, I don't *believe* it . . . oh, that's so annoying!"

He laughed and said, "Then keep at it, my lad!"

And I responded, "I'm extremely sorry about that, Mr. Miller. But couldn't you just look in anyway—for a moment at least?"

From the corner of my eye I could see that she had put down her knife and fork nervously, and was looking across at me. "Well, we . . . eh, I mean . . . *I've* ordered something to eat, and perhaps you could still make it?" I wasn't letting go.

"Perhaps you could still make it!" repeated Silvestro with an audible smirk. "You should just hear yourself. That's what I call making an effort. But no, I'm not coming. I wish you a successful evening with your little one."

"At least two more hours . . . aha . . . totally exhausted . . . hm . . . hm . . . well, I suppose nothing can be done about it then . . . yes . . . a *great* pity . . . okay . . . you'll call when you get home." In a sinking tone I echoed the words that Miller never uttered.

"Now bring this to an end—that's quite enough," said Silvestro. *"Ciao ciao!"* He ended the call.

"Okay . . . No, I do understand . . . okay . . . No problem . . . Good-bye, Mr. Miller." I put my phone down beside my plate and looked Mademoiselle Bredin straight in the eye.

"Miller's just canceled," I said, taking a deep breath. "There are problems. It'll take at least two more hours before his meeting is over, perhaps even longer, he says, and he's totally exhausted and there would be no point arranging another meeting because he has to leave for home early tomorrow morning."

I saw her swallow, and reach for her wineglass like a safety anchor, and for a moment I was afraid that she'd just get up and leave.

"I'm really sorry," I said. "Perhaps the whole thing wasn't such a good idea after all."

And when she then shook her head and didn't get up and told me that I wasn't in the least to blame, I somehow had a bad conscience. But what could I do? I couldn't actually conjure up Robert Miller. After all, I was already there.

And so I devoted myself to consoling Mademoiselle Bredin and teasing her with a couple of jokes about her belief in fate. For one sweet moment I even held her hand, but she pulled it away and rapped me on the fingers as if I were a naughty schoolboy.

Then she asked me what Robert Miller actually did when he wasn't writing books, and what kind of a meeting it had been, and I said I didn't know exactly, but he was an engineer and was probably working as a consultant for the motor company.

After that I patiently listened to what she found so great about Robert Miller's book, how incredible it was that she'd found the book at exactly the right moment, and what passages had made her laugh or moved her. I felt flattered as I listened to her kind words and watched her dark green eyes getting quite soft.

More than once I was overcome with the temptation to tell her that it was me and only me who had saved her soul. But the fear of losing her before I'd even had the chance to win her for myself was too great.

And so I pretended to be surprised as she told me—hesitantly but with growing trust—about what I knew all too well already: the close correspondence of the restaurant and the heroine of the book.

"Don't you understand now why I *have* to meet that man?" she said, and I nodded. After all, I was the only one who held the key to the "fateful mystery." The secret that was probably even easier to explain than Aurélie Bredin thought, even if it was no less fateful.

If I'd published the book under *my own* name with *my own* photo, the girl with the green eyes and the enchanting smile whom I'd seen through a restaurant window and chosen as the heroine of my fantasy would have seen in *me* the man that fate had sent her. And all would have been well.

But as things were I was condemned to lie and to compete with a fictitious writer. Well, not *so* fictitious, as I painfully realized with Aurélie Bredin's next question.

"I wonder why that woman left Miller," she said, picking at the remains of the lamb curry on her plate with her fork. "He's a successful engineer, he must be a warmhearted man with a sense of humor, otherwise he couldn't write a book like that. And apart from that, I think he looks fantastic. I mean, he could be an actor, don't you think? How could anyone leave such an attractive man?"

She emptied her wineglass, and I shrugged and refilled it. If she thought that the dentist looked *fantastic,* it would be hard for me. It was good that she'd never meet Sam Goldberg in person. Not if I could prevent it!

"What is it? You're looking so grim all of a sudden." She looked at me in amusement. "Have I said something wrong?"

"Good God, no!" I decided that it was time to bring the superhero down a peg or two.

"Well, you can never see what's going on behind the façade, can you?" I said. "And good looks aren't everything. For my part I believe that his wife didn't have a very easy time with him, no matter how much I respect Miller as an author."

Mademoiselle Bredin looked rattled. "What do you mean by that—didn't have a very easy time with him?"

"Oh, nothing at all, I'm talking nonsense—just forget what I said." I laughed a bit too loudly as if I wanted to cover up the fact that I'd said more than I wanted to. And then I decided to change the subject. "Do we really want to spend the whole evening talking about Robert Miller? I know he's the reason we're both here, but he did stand us up." I took the bottle and refilled my glass. "I'm more interested in why such an enchanting woman as you isn't married yet. Do you have that many faults?"

Aurélie blushed. "Aha," she said. "And you?"

"Do you mean why such an enchanting man as me isn't married yet? Or what faults do I have?"

Aurélie took a sip of red wine and a smile crossed her face. She leaned her elbow on the table and looked at me over her clasped hands. "The faults," she said.

"Hm," I replied. "That's what I feared. Let me think." I took her hand and counted on her fingers. "Eating, drinking, smoking, leading beautiful women astray . . . is that enough for a start?"

She took her hand away from me and gave an amused laugh. She nodded, and I looked at her mouth, wondering what it would be like to kiss it.

And then at last we were no longer talking about Robert Miller, but about us, and this rather conspiratorial meeting became something like a real date. When the waiter came to the table to ask, "Can I get you anything else?" I ordered another bottle of wine. I was just beginning to feel in seventh heaven when something happened that was not foreseen on my romantic menu.

Even today I still ask myself if the mysterious author would not have sunk into obscurity with me taking his place if that absurd old woman hadn't suddenly sat down at our table.

"*Un, deux, trois—ça c'est Paris!*" A dozen good-natured waiters had gathered to one side of the hall in a semicircle. They bellowed those words at the top of their voices. It sounded like a battle cry, and rang out at La Coupole every evening (sometimes several times). Because among the crowd of guests there's always one whose birthday it is.

Half the room looked up as the waiters marched across in a line to the table where the birthday girl was sitting. They were carrying a gigantic cake on which a whole lot of sparklers were spraying out light like a little fireworks display. It was a table two rows behind us, and Aurélie Bredin, who was facing in that direction, craned her neck to get a better look.

And then she suddenly stood up and waved.

I turned around in astonishment and saw a gleeful old woman in a garish purple dress sitting alone at a table with a massive dish of oysters in front of her. She shook every waiter's hand.

And then she looked in our direction and waved delightedly back.

"Do you know that lady?" I asked Aurélie Bredin.

"Yes, of course!" she cried enthusiastically, and waved once more. "That's Mrs. Dinsmore. We met yesterday, at the cemetery—isn't that *terribly* funny?"

I nodded and smiled. I didn't find it all that terribly funny. It was half past ten, and I had the uncomfortable (but justified) feeling that the pleasant twosome at our table was now at an end.

A few minutes later I made the acquaintance of Mrs. Dinsmore, an eighty-five-year-old American, who floated over to us in a cloud of Opium. She was the widow of a conductor, mother of a bridge-building engineer son in South America, grandmother of three blond-curled grandchildren, and muse to numerous artists who all had one thing in common: They had all celebrated wild parties in La Coupole with Mrs. Dinsmore. And they were all already pushing up daisies.

There are some people who sit down at a table and take over the conversation straightaway. Gradually the others stop talking, every other theme gutters out like a dying candle, and after five minutes at the latest everyone else is listening spellbound to the stories and anecdotes of these powerful personalities, who operate with broad gestures and are undeniably of great entertainment value—but who can hardly ever be stopped.

I'm afraid Mrs. Dinsmore was someone like that.

After the eighty-five-year-old with her silver-gray waves and her bright red lips sat down between us exclaiming, "What a delightful surprise, child—let's drink a Bollinger to that!" I no longer had even the slightest opportunity to attract Aurélie Bredin's attention.

The champagne was immediately brought over to our table in a silver cooler brimming with ice cubes, and it was impossible to ignore the fact that Mrs. Dinsmore was the absolute darling of Alain, Pierre, Michel, Igor, and whatever the other waiters' names were. Suddenly our table was the center of attention for the serving staff of La Coupole. And our peace was at an end.

After two glasses of champagne I abandoned myself to the charisma of the old lady, who was talking uninterruptedly, and watched with fascination the feathers on her little purple cap, which bobbed up and down with her every movement. Aurélie Bredin, who hung on Mrs. Dinsmore's every word and seemed to be enjoying herself a great deal, glanced over at me every time we both started laughing at the comic experiences of the extraordinary old lady. The more we drank, the funnier it got, and after a while I was having as much fun as everyone else.

Occasionally Mrs. Dinsmore interrupted her amusing monologue to point out other guests in the hall (for an old lady she had astonishingly good eyesight) and to ask us if we had ever celebrated a birthday in La Coupole ("You must definitely do it sometime, it's always great fun!"). Then she wanted to know when our birthdays were (and at least in that way I found out that Aurélie Bredin's birthday was coming up soon, on December sixteenth) and clapped her tiny hands in delight.

"April the second and December the sixteenth," she repeated. "Aries and Sagittarius. Two fire signs—they go together wonderfully!"

I didn't know particularly much about astrology, but in this matter I was obviously glad to admit that she was right. Mrs. Dinsmore herself had been born on the last day of Scorpio. And Scorpio women were quick-witted and dangerous in equal measure.

La Coupole was gradually emptying—it was only at our table that the partying, drinking, and laughter carried on: Mrs. Dinsmore was obviously enjoying one of her more sparkling moments.

"It was at this very table—or was it that one over there, well, it doesn't matter—that I used to sit with Eugène to celebrate my birthday," gushed Mrs. Dinsmore as one of the waiters poured us more champagne.

"Eugène who?" I inquired.

"Ionesco, of course. Who else?" she answered impatiently. "Oh, he was sometimes indescribably funny—not only in his plays! And now he's there in Montparnasse, poor thing! But I visit him from time to time." She giggled dreamily. "I can still remember precisely—this evening I've forgotten exactly which birthday it was—it happened twice, can you imagine it? Twice . . . !"

She looked at us with her dark little eyes that shone like two buttons. ". . . that a clumsy waiter spilt red wine over Eugène's light gray jacket. And do you know what he said? He said, 'Now I think of it, I never really liked the color of that jacket.'" Mrs. Dinsmore threw her head back and gave a high-pitched laugh, the little feathers on her head bobbing as if she were about to take off and fly away.

After this little excursion into the private life of Eugène Ionesco, which would surely not be found in any biography, Mrs. Dinsmore turned back to me.

"And you, young man? What do you write? Aurélie told me you were a *writer*! A wonderful profession," she added without waiting for my reply. "I must say I always found writers a bit more interesting than actors or painters." Then she leaned over to Aurélie, put her red lips quite close to Mademoiselle Bredin's delicate ear, which, as I noticed only then, stuck out a little, and said, "My child, he is definitely the right one for you."

Aurélie laughed aloud, putting her hand in front of her mouth, and her outburst of hilarity bewildered me, as did the old lady's assumption that I was a writer—damn it, I *was* a writer, even if not a writer of great literature, and anyway I was definitely the right one. And so I relaxed and joined in the two ladies' laughter.

Mrs. Dinsmore raised her glass. "Do you know what? I like you, my boy," she declared, and patted my trouser leg with her hand, on which she wore rings with strikingly large stones. "Just call me Liz."

And when "Liz," Mademoiselle Bredin, and I left La Coupole half an hour later than all the other diners—all the waiters bidding us a hearty farewell—to share a taxi that—Mrs. Dinsmore decided ("It's my birthday, and I'll pay for a taxi, that would be so much nicer!")—dropped off first Mademoiselle Bredin, who, like Mrs. Dinsmore, sat next to me in the taxi (I was between the two ladies) and occasionally let her head with its sweet-smelling hair fall against my shoulder, then me, and finally the birthday girl, who lived somewhere in the Marais, I had to admit that the evening had turned out differently from what I had hoped.

But it was without question the most fun evening I had ever had.

A week later I was sitting on Sunday afternoon with Adam Goldberg on the red leather seats of the Café des Éditeurs, telling him about Aurélie Bredin and all the strange turns that my life had taken in the past few weeks.

We were actually waiting for Sam, who had arrived with Adam but had gone off to the Champ de Mars to buy light-up models of the Eiffel Tower for his children.

"Oh boy," said Adam when I told him about my evening in La Coupole and Silvestro's faked phone calls. "You're skating on thin ice, I hope you realize. Couldn't you lie a little less?"

"Says who?" I retorted. "Let me just remind you once more—this whole business with the pseudonym and the author's photo was your idea." I wasn't used to seeing my otherwise so imperturbable friend looking worried.

"Hey, Adam, what's up?" I asked. "You normally take every chance to tell me not to get my knickers in a twist, and now you're banging the big moral drum."

Adam made a placatory gesture. "Fair enough, fair enough. But before it was just a professional matter. Now the whole thing's getting personal, and I don't like it." He drummed his fingers on the arm of his chair. "I think it's dangerous, my friend. I mean, she's a woman, André. She has feelings. What do you think would happen if she found out that you've been leading her by the nose? That you've deliberately deceived her? She'll make a hell of a fuss, come into the office and weep and wail to Monsieur Monsignac—and then you really can pack your things."

I shook my head. "My plan's absolutely watertight," I said. "Aurélie will never find out the truth—unless you tell her."

Since my evening in La Coupole I'd had enough time to think about what I was going to do next. And I'd decided that Mademoiselle Bredin would, in the not too distant future, receive another letter from Robert Miller in which he would suggest a date for them to dine together in Le Temps des Cerises.

I also knew exactly when that date would be: Aurélie Bredin's birthday.

But this time the letter would have to come directly from England. And that's why I'd asked Adam to take it with him after the reading and put it in the mail in London. I still hadn't thought of a reason why Robert Miller would then fail to turn up again in the end. I just knew that I would be there that evening—for some reason I would have to invent. And no matter what, it was clear that this latest cancelation, which would happen at very short notice, could not be passed on by me this time.

That would look just a bit too suspicious.

As I now sat with Robert Miller's English agent in the café-restaurant where editors and publishers like to meet to talk about high—and not so high—literature under the bookshelves on the walls, an idea shot into my mind that began to appeal to me more and more. But it would need to be refined a bit more to get Adam to play along. So I held my tongue and listened to my friend's objections.

"What if she finds out about the reading and comes to it? We can't bring my brother into the loop of your mendacious amorous intrigues. Sam had enough of a problem not telling his wife the real reason for his trip to Paris." He looked at me. "And before you ask—no, he hasn't removed his beard. That's because my sister-in-law thinks the beard is very nice. She might have thought that he'd found a mistress, and Sam was not prepared to risk that."

I nodded. "Okay, granted. Anyway there's nothing wrong with an author growing a beard, is there? But he mustn't blab. He hasn't got a wife. Because he lives alone with his little dog, Rocky—you remember?—in his silly bloody cottage."

(Adam had been particularly proud of inventing Rocky when we'd been writing the author's biography. "Such a sweet little dog is always a draw," he had said. "Women will flock to read about it!")

"You can tell him all about that yourself soon enough," responded Adam, and looked at the clock. "Where's he got to anyway?"

We both automatically looked at the door, but Sam Goldberg was taking his time. Adam sipped his Scotch and leaned back on the red leather cushions.

"It's also a pain that you can't smoke anywhere here anymore," he said. "I wouldn't have expected you French to give in that easily. *Liberté toujours,* eh?"

"Yeah, it's a real shame," I responded. "Does your brother know what's in the novel?"

Adam nodded. "So"—he returned to the cause of his apprehension—"what will you do if Mademoiselle Bredin gets wind of the reading?"

I laughed condescendingly. "Adam," I said. "She's a cook. She has only ever read one book, and that chanced to be my book. She's not the kind of person who normally goes to readings, *tu vois?* And anyway, the whole thing's taking place in a small bookshop on the Île Saint-Louis. That's not her normal stomping ground. And even if she reads the interview in *Le Figaro,* it can't appear until the day after at the earliest and by then— *voilà!*—it will all be over."

For the first time in my publishing career I was glad that the marketing in this case had been "suboptimal," as Michelle Auteuil had put it. "But the better-situated bookstores were already all booked, and although Robert Miller is admittedly not totally unknown he isn't a crowd-puller that the bookstores would fight to get hold of—at least, not yet." She looked regretfully through her black-framed glasses. "Given the circumstances we can count ourselves lucky to get the Librairie Capricorne. The bookseller is a charming old gentleman who keeps reordering batches of the novel, and he has his regular customers. The bookstore will be really full."

I also felt that we could be very satisfied.

Adam was not totally convinced. *"Et voilà!"* he repeated, which sounded quite funny in his English accent. "Let's hope you're right, Andy. But I still wonder if it mightn't be better to put an end to this whole Mademoiselle Bredin thing. From what you've told me, she seems to be very highly strung. A rather strange girl. Can't you just keep your hands off her?"

"Non," I said.

"Okay," said Adam.

And then we fell silent for a while.

"You must understand, Adam," I said finally, "she's not just any woman, she's *the* woman! The one and only. And she's not strange at all—she's just got a lively imagination and believes in higher powers. Kismet." I stirred three spoonfuls of sugar into my espresso and sipped the hot, sweet brew.

"Kismet," repeated Adam, and sighed.

"Well, what's so odd about that? And anyway I'm going to kill Robert Miller off very soon. As soon as the meal in Le Temps des Cerises is over, good old Miller will make his final exit from the stage."

"Does that mean you're not going to write anymore?" Adam sat up in alarm.

"Yes," I said. "It does mean that. This double life is far too stressful for me. After all, I'm no James Bond!"

"Are you off your head?" Adam said excitedly. "Now, when the novel is actually starting to sell, you want to throw in the towel? How many have you sold so far? Fifty thousand? Just think logically for a moment. You write very well, and you'd be a dope not to profit from it. This has great potential. Foreign publishers are also beginning to wake up. On my desk there are initial inquiries from Germany, Holland, and Spain. Believe me, there's a lot more running in this book. And we'll pitch the second novel a bit higher straightaway. We'll make a best seller of it."

"For God's sake," I said. "You sound just like Monsignac."

"Don't you want a best seller?" Adam asked in astonishment.

"Not under these circumstances," I said. "I want some peace. You've just been telling me that all these lying games are so dangerous, and now you want to sail gaily on?"

Adam smiled genteelly. "I am a professional, of course," he said, quite the English gentleman.

"You're a megalomaniac," I said. "And how do you imagine this continuing in the future? Will the author be writing his novels somewhere at the end of the world? In New Zealand or at the North Pole? Or will we fly your brother in every time?"

"If all goes really well, we can tell the truth later." Adam leaned back coolly. "When the time is ripe we'll make a great story of it. You need to understand how the business works, André: If you're successful, you're always right. So I think that Robert Miller should definitely carry on writing."

"Over my dead body," I said. "To my mind the only good author is a dead author."

"Hi, fellows. Are you spikking about me by any chance?" said a voice behind me in mangled French.

Sam Goldberg had come in through the door unnoticed and had probably heard the last bit of our heated discussion. So: There stood my alter ego in a dark blue duffle coat and a tartan cap, carrying little plastic bags full of Eiffel Towers and pastel-colored boxes from the Confiserie Ladurée.

I looked at him curiously. He had short blond hair and blue eyes like his brother. Unfortunately he looked as good as he did in the photo. And although he must have been around forty, he had that boyish air that some men never lose no matter how old they get. The beard made no difference to that, especially when, as now, he put on that mischievous Brad Pitt smile.

"Hi, Sam, where have you been all this time?" Adam stood up and greeted his brother with a friendly clap on the shoulder. "We were beginning to think you'd run away."

Sam grinned, and a row of gleaming white teeth came into view. He was clearly someone who would make a very trust-worthy impression in his profession; I could only hope that he would be just as convincing as an author.

"Shopping," he explained, and I noticed that his voice was very like his brother's. "I had to premise to bring something back for the family. Oh dear, and the line in that Ladurée shop was so long! I felt completely in a home." He laughed. "So many Japanese personages who all wanted to buy cakes and these gaudy things." He pointed to the boxes of macaroons. "Do they really taste that well?"

"This is André," Adam introduced me, and Sam shook my hand. "Nice to see you," he said, beaming at me. "I've horde so much abut you." He had a powerful handshake.

"Only good, I hope," I answered somewhat tensely. All the old clichés. "Thanks for coming to Paris, Sam. You're really helping us out of a mess."

"Oh, yes!" He grinned and nodded. "Out of a moss," he repeated. "Yes, yes. Adam has said me everything. You two have pulled off a great stunt, haven't you? I must say, I was very surprised to hear I'd wrote a book." He winked at me. "Fortunately I have a good sense of humor."

I nodded in relief. Adam had obviously done his work well. Even if his brother had been a bit unnerved when this unexpected project was first presented to him—at this moment he seemed very relaxed.

"So now we're something like . . . like—what do you call it? . . . Blood brooders?" he continued. "Well, I hope everything works out with our little pot."

All three of us laughed. Then we sat down and my blood brother ordered a tea with milk and an apple tart and looked around at the Café des Éditeurs. "Lovely place," he said appreciatively.

Over the next two hours, which we spent coaching Sam Goldberg in his new identity, it became clear that Adam's brother was a real sentimentalist whose basically positive character found expression in two words above all: "lovely" and "sexy."

"Lovely" was used for the city of Paris, the light-up golden plastic Eiffel Towers for his children, the *tarte aux pommes* he was eating with his tea, cutting it into fine slices, and my book, of which he had admittedly only read the first chapter, although Adam had given him the content of the whole book *en détail*.

"Sexy" was used for the waitresses in des Éditeurs, the bookshelves on the wall, Adam's offer to show him the Moulin Rouge that evening, the old black Bakelite telephone at the reception desk in his hotel and—astonishingly—my ancient Rolex watch (it had been my father's and was made in a time when Rolex

watches still had leather straps and were somewhat more restrained in design than they are today).

I noticed with some relief that Sam's French was better than
I had expected. Because typically English people speak English
and nothing else. However, the two Goldberg brothers had
spent a lot of their summer holidays with an uncle in Canada
and so they had learned some French. Because of his professional interests Adam spoke fluent French, whereas his brother
mangled the language, although his vocabulary was quite large
and he had no problems speaking in public. He was used to
giving papers on prophylaxis and the treatment of periodonto-
sis at dental conferences.

We talked through the interview with *Le Figaro,* which was
to take place the next morning, and then the passages from the
book that he was to read out in the bookstore the same evening. I explained how the reading would run and advised him
urgently to practice his new signature as "Robert Miller" a few
more times so that he would make no mistake when signing
autographs.

"I must troy that straightaway," he said, took a pen and a sheet
of paper, and inscribed his new name in a round, looping hand.

"Robert Miller," he said, looking contentedly at the signature. "That looks really sexy, don't you think?"

After the reading, which was to begin at eight o'clock and
go on for no more than an hour and a half, there was to be a
dinner for just a few people ("Relaxed and intimate," Monsieur
Monsignac had emphasized): the author, the bookseller (who
had definitely read the book), Jean-Paul Monsignac (who only
knew the beginning, middle, and end of the book), Michelle
Auteuil (who had scanned through the book when it was in
proof), Adam Goldberg (who knew the whole book), and my

humble self. I must admit that I was a little apprehensive about this intimate, relaxed evening.

Readings in a bookstore all somehow run along the same track: a welcome from the bookseller, a welcome from the publisher (in this case, I was to do this job, as I was going to present the whole thing), the author says a few words about how glad he is to be there and so on and then reads a couple of extracts. Then applause; has anybody any questions for the author? Always the same questions: How did you come to write this book? In your book there's a little boy who grows up without a father, are you that boy? Did you always want to be a writer? Are you writing another book? What's it about? Is it set in Paris again? And sometimes, though more rarely, there are questions like: When do you write (morning, afternoon, evening, night)? Where do you write (looking out into the fields, only with a white wall in front of me, in a café, in a monastery)? And of course the clincher: Where do you get your ideas from?

But often people just aren't that interested, or are too shy to ask a question, and in such cases the bookseller, editor, or chairman then says something like: Then I have a question (to round the whole thing off). Or he says: If there are no more questions, then I would like to thank you all for coming; and of course many thanks to our author, who will now gladly sign your books. Renewed applause. Then the audience come forward to buy the book and have it autographed. And at the end they take a few photos.

A reading by an author is a pleasant and well-ordered event, as far as I'm concerned.

When it's a select dinner, on the other hand, there are rather more imponderables, especially if you have something to hide. My ability to foresee possibilities was not so great as to be capable of preempting all the possible and impossible subjects that might come up on such an occasion. I could see Monsieur Monsignac suddenly asking the supposedly Francophile Englishman, "Do you like snails?" and the latter pulling a face in disgust. I hoped they wouldn't talk about books too much, as Sam Goldberg was not very well up on the bestseller lists, and we could not exclude the possibility that he'd think Marc Levy was an actor or Anna Gavalda an opera singer.

Still, Sam Goldberg would be sandwiched between Adam and me like bodyguards. And as long as the dentist showed a little presence of mind the evening would no doubt run passably smoothly.

I advised Sam to retreat into his "insufficient knowledge of French" if awkward questions cropped up at the reading or the dinner. "Oh, sorry. I didn't quite understand: What exactly did you mean?" he should ask ingenuously, and then one of us would leap into the breach.

The important thing was that he should know the following points, which we went over again and again, by heart: He lived alone in his cottage. The location we'd decided on was picturesque Tunbridge Wells. ("Lovely place," said Sam and: "What a pity I'm not allowed a family.")

His dog, Rocky, was a Yorkshire terrier and not a golden retriever, as Sam initially wrongly claimed, and was being looked after by a neighbor.

To the question of whether his book had autobiographical elements, he should answer, "Well, you know, every book is autobiographical to a certain extent. Of course there are things in it that I've experienced myself, and some that I've heard about—or simply made up."

He had often visited Paris earlier when he was working for the automobile firm, but at the moment he needed peace and countryside and loved his isolated cottage.

For him, the idea of journalists visiting his home was a nightmare. (This just as a precaution, in case he fell into the hands of Michelle Auteuil.)

He was not a party animal.

He loved French cuisine.

He had a second Paris novel in mind, but that would take quite a while and he would not give any (!) definite details about the content.

His hobby was old cars.

The danger of a writer getting involved in a conversation about old cars in France was relatively limited, but just in case I pressed an illustrated book about old-timers into Sam's hands as we parted.

"See you tomorrow evening, then," I said as the three of us stood outside the café with Sam Goldberg swinging his carrier bags in anticipation of the evening's adventures.

The two brothers wanted to return to their hotel before painting Paris red that evening, and I just wanted to get home. "It would be good if you could get there half an hour early." I breathed in deeply. "Don't want to risk things going wrong, do we?"

"It'll all be fine," said Adam. "We'll be very punctual."

"Yes, we'll pull it off okay," said Sam.

And then our ways parted.

Major catastrophes are always preceded by omens, but quite often people fail to see them. When I was shaving in the bathroom the next morning, I heard a loud crash. I ran into the darkened hall in my bare feet and stepped on a shard of glass before I could see what had happened.

The heavy old mirror that hung beside the coat stand had fallen down, the dark root-wood frame had broken, and there were shards and splinters of glass all over the place. Cursing, I pulled the shard of glass out of my bleeding foot and hobbled into the kitchen to get a Band-Aid.

"A bomb wouldn't move it," my friend Michel had said as he put up the mirror I'd bought at the Marché aux Puces, the flea market by the Porte de Clignancourt, a few weeks before, first bringing it into town on the subway and then carrying it up to my apartment.

Superstitious people say that a mirror that falls off a wall and breaks brings bad luck. But I'm not superstitious, thank God, and so I contented myself with sweeping up the fragments to the accompaniment of a litany of curses and then set off for the office.

That lunchtime I met with Hélène Bonvin, the author with the writing block. We sat on the first floor of the Café de Flore, ate the *assiette de fromages dégustation*, and after I'd managed to convince her that I thought what she'd written so far was good ("You're not just saying that to put my mind at rest, are you, Monsieur Chabanais?"), and given her a couple of ideas for the further course of the novel to send her on her way, I rushed back to my desk in the office.

Seconds later Madame Petit was in my office to tell me that my mother had called and wanted me to ring back urgently.

"It sounded *really* urgent," Madame Petit assured me when I looked at her with a raised eyebrow, and I said, "Oh, yes— *everything*'s urgent with my mother, there's probably a neighbor who's fallen off a ladder again. I've got a reading this evening, Madame Petit, there's nothing I can do now."

Half an hour later I was sitting in a taxi on my way to the hospital. This time it hadn't been a neighbor.

Maman had chosen that very Monday to spontaneously decide to take a little trip to Paris, and had fallen down the escalator in the Galeries Lafayette, together with all her purchases.

Now she was stuck in Ward IV with a broken leg and smiling somewhat hesitantly at me over her splint. She looked very small lying there under the bedclothes, and for a moment my heart shrank.

"Maman, what on earth have you been up to?" I asked, giving her a kiss.

"*Oh, mon petit boubou,*" she sighed. "I knew you'd come right away."

I nodded shamefacedly. When Maman had called a second time after an hour to give the address of the hospital, Madame Petit had been enough of a friend to act as if I'd just walked in the door. Then she looked at me and said, reproachfully, "I told you so, Monsieur Chabanais. Now off you go at once!"

I took Maman's hand and swore to myself that from now on I'd always call her back, even if only briefly. I looked at her leg in its thick splint lying on top of the bedclothes. "Does it hurt?"

She shook her head. "It's all right now. I've been given painkillers, but they're making me very sleepy."

"How did it happen?" I asked.

"Oh, you know, in December there are always such wonderful decorations in Lafayette." She looked at me with shining eyes. "And so I thought, I'll go and look at it all, have a little snack, and do a bit of Christmas shopping. And then I somehow got into a tangle on the escalator with all my bags and fell over backward. It all went very quickly."

"My goodness," I said. "Who knows what might have happened!"

She nodded. "I have a good guardian angel."

My gaze fell on a pair of brown sling-back shoes with slim and not too low heels standing beside the little cupboard beside her bed. "You weren't wearing *those* shoes by any chance, were you?" I asked.

Maman said nothing.

"Maman, it's winter. Any sensible person would put on tough shoes, and you go Christmas shopping in *high heels*? On an escalator?"

She looked up guiltily from under the covers. We'd quite frequently had this debate about sturdy and, as I said, suitable shoes for her age, but she just would not listen.

"Good grief, Maman, you're an old lady. You ought to be more careful, you know."

"I just don't like those old granny shoes," she grumbled. "I may be old, but I still have nice legs, don't I?"

I smiled and shook my head. Maman had always been incredibly proud of her well-shaped legs. And even though she was seventy-four, she was still rather vain.

"Yes, of course you do," I said. "But if they're broken, they'll be no use to you at all."

I stayed with Maman for two hours, bought her some fruit, some juice, a couple of magazines, and some emergency toiletries, and then returned to Éditions Opale to get my papers.

It was already half past five and there was no point going home. So I decided to go directly from the office to the bookstore. Madame Petit had already gone when I returned, but at the very last moment, just as I was about to turn out the light, I noticed a little note from her stuck to my reading lamp.

How is your mother? said the note. And beneath that: *Someone called Aurélie Bredin would like you to call her back.*

Today I still ask myself if I shouldn't have heard the alarm bells ringing at that moment at the latest. But I didn't see the signs.

The little bookstore in the Rue Saint-Louis was sold out to the very last seat. I stood with Pascal Fermier, the gray-haired proprietor of the Librairie Capricorne, in a kind of kitchen annex, peeping through the gray curtain that divided the back room from the rest of the store. Next to me on the floor were heaps of catalogs from just about every publisher under the sun, and there were a couple of coffee mugs and plates in a cupboard above the sink. Cartons were piled up to the ceiling and a refrigerator hummed nearby.

Robert Miller, alias Sam Goldberg, was standing beside me clutching a glass of white wine.

"How lovely!" he'd exclaimed when he entered Monsieur Fermier's enchanting bookstore an hour previously. But now he was a bit nervous and said hardly a word. Again and again he opened the book at the passages I'd marked for him with little red Post-its.

"My compliments." I turned to the old bookseller. "The bookstore is packed!"

Fermier nodded, and his kindly face beamed. "I've sold a lot of copies of Monsieur Miller's book from the very beginning," he said, "and when I hung the poster for the reading in my window last week, a lot of people from the neighborhood were interested and immediately bought tickets. But even I did not expect so many people to turn up."

He turned to Sam, who was staring fixedly to the front. "You obviously have a lot of fans, Mr. Miller," he said. "It's really good that you could come."

He stepped out through the curtain, smiled at the full rows of seats, and went over to a little wooden table that stood slightly higher on another level at the back of the room. On the table there was a microphone, and beside it a carafe of water and a glass. Behind it was a chair.

"Here we go," I said to Sam. "No panic, I'm sitting very near you." I pointed to a second chair at the side of the rostrum.

Sam coughed. "I hope I don't miss up."

"It'll be fine," I said as Pascal Fermier tapped the microphone, and squeezed his arm briefly. "And thanks again!"

Then I also stepped out in front of the curtain and positioned myself next to Monsieur Fermier, who now picked up the microphone. The bookseller waited until the whispers and scraping of chairs died down and then he heartily welcomed all those present in very few words and handed the microphone over to me. I thanked him, and looked out over the audience.

Half our publishing house was sitting in the front row; even Madame Petit, imperious and unmissable, was there, and was just saying something to Adam Goldberg. Jean-Paul Monsignac, wearing a bow tie, was seated next to Florence Mirabeau, who looked at least as nervous as Sam Goldberg. It was probably the first time she'd been part of the team at a reading.

And right on the edge, queening it, sat an extremely satisfied Michelle Auteuil, in black as ever, next to the photographer. "He's really sweet, your Miller, everything went very well with the journalists," she had said quickly to me as I came into the bookstore.

"Ladies and gentlemen," I began, "this evening I would like to introduce to you an author who has chosen our beautiful city as the setting for his wonderful novel. He could actually be sitting comfortably by the fireplace in his English cottage at this moment, but he has spared no effort to be here to read to us this evening. The title of his novel is *The Smiles of Women,* but it could just as well be called 'An Englishman in Paris,' since it is all about what happens when an Englishman tries to establish a well-known English automobile manufacturer in Paris, and even more about what happens when an Englishman falls in love with a French woman. Please welcome—Robert Miller!"

The audience clapped and looked expectantly at the slim, agile man in shirt and vest who gave a little bow and went to take his place behind the table.

"Well," said Robert Miller, leaning back in his chair, smiling, "it's very nice in my cottage, but I must say that I found it very comfortable here too." Those were his first words.

A few friendly laughs came from the packed rows.

"No, really." Encouraged by this, Robert Miller went on. "This booksellers is like my . . . er . . . living room, except that I don't have so much books." He looked around. "Wow," he said, "this is really sexy."

I wasn't aware of what might be thought sexy about a bookstore—was that English humor?—but the audience liked it anyway.

"Still. I'd like to thank you for coming. Unfortunately I don't say French so good as you, but perhaps it's not too bad for an Anglishman."

Renewed laughter.

"Right," said Robert Miller, and opened my book. "Then we'll begin."

It turned out to be a very entertaining reading. Fired up by the reaction of his fans, Adam's brother hit top form. He read, he mispronounced words amusingly, he told his little jokes; the audience was delighted. I must admit that I couldn't have done it better myself.

At the end there was thunderous applause. I looked over to Adam, who nodded conspiratorially and raised his thumb. Monsieur Monsignac clapped with a satisfied expression and then said something to Mademoiselle Mirabeau, who had hung on the author's words throughout the reading. Then came the first questions from the audience, which our author dealt with masterfully. However, when an attractive blonde in the fifth row asked him about his new novel, he began to deviate from our plan.

"Oh yes! *Of course* there will be a new novel. It's as good as finished," he said self-satisfiedly, probably forgetting for a moment that he wasn't a real author at all.

"What's your new novel about, Monsieur Miller? Is it set in Paris again?"

The author nodded. "Yes, of course! I love this beautiful city. And these time my hero is an Anglish dentist who falls in love at a conference with a dancer from the Moulin Rouge," he invented spontaneously.

I gave a warning cough. His excursion into the night life of Paris the previous evening had obviously given him new inspiration.

Miller looked over to me. "Well, I cannot betray all, or my editor will be cross with me and nobody buys my new book," he said quick-wittedly.

Monsieur Monsignac laughed aloud, as did many others. I squirmed on my seat and tried to smile as well. So far everything had gone well, but now it was time for the dentist to bring things to a close. I stood up.

"Why have you grown a beard, Mr. Miller? Have you got something to hide?" called a precocious young girl with a ponytail from the very back, and then giggled with her friends.

Miller stroked his thick blond beard. "Now, you're very young, mademoiselle," he replied. "Otherwise you would know that no man likes to show too much of his cards. But . . . ," he paused for effect, ". . . if you mean, am I in the Secret Service, I'm afraid I must disappoint you. The explanation is actually much simpler . . . I have a wonderful . . ." He stopped, and I held my breath. Surely he wasn't going to talk about his wife? ". . . a wonderful razor," he continued. "And one day that was broke."

Everyone laughed, and I went over to Miller and shook his hand.

"That was great. Many thanks, Robert Miller," I said loudly, and turned to the audience, who were applauding frenetically. "If no one has any more questions, our author would be glad to move on to signing your books."

The applause ebbed away, and the first members of the audience were getting up from their seats when a clear, somewhat breathless voice rang out over the rows of chairs.

"I have another question, please," said the voice, and my heart missed a beat.

On the left, close to the entrance, stood Mademoiselle Aurélie Bredin.

In my lifetime I've chaired many a reading—in much bigger

and more important bookstores and with much more famous authors than Robert Miller.

But none of them made me sweat blood and water as much as that Mónday evening at the little Librairie Capricorne.

Aurélie Bredin was standing there as if she'd sprung out of the ground, and doom began to approach inexorably in a dark red silk dress and bouffant hair.

"Mr. Miller, did you really fall in love with a Parisienne—like the hero of your novel?" she asked, her lips forming a delicate smile.

Robert Miller looked at me anxiously for a moment, and I closed my eyes and abandoned myself into the hands of God.

"Well . . . er . . ." I could feel the dentist losing the plot as he looked over at the woman in the red silk dress once more. "How shall I say . . . the women in Paris are simply . . . so . . . incredibly . . . attractive . . . and it is so hard to resist . . ." He was obviously regaining control and put on his "I'm-just-a-little-boy-who-can't-help-it" smile, before ending his sentence. "But I'm afraid I cannot tell anything—I am a gentleman, you know?"

He sketched a little bow and the audience broke out in applause once more as Monsieur Monsignac leapt forward to congratulate Robert Miller and then be photographed with his author.

"Come over here, André," he called to me, and waved. "You should be in the photo too!"

I stumbled over to the side of the delighted publisher, who then put an arm around both Robert Miller and me, and whispered to me, "*Il est ravissant, cet Anglais!* This Englishman is delightful."

I nodded, and forced myself to smile for the picture while

anxiously watching the audience forming a line to get their books signed. And the woman in the red silk dress stationed herself at the end of that line.

Robert Miller sat down again and began the signing, while I pulled Adam aside. "Mayday, Mayday," I whispered anxiously.

He looked at me in astonishment. "But it's all gone very well."

"Adam, that's not what I mean: She's here," I said softly, and noticed how my voice was threatening to crack. *"She!"*

Adam got it at once. "Good heavens!" he cried. "Not the one and only?"

"Exactly: her!" I said, and grabbed his arm. "It's the woman in the red silk dress, standing at the end of the line, there—do you see her? And she's going to get her book signed any moment now. Adam, she is not—under any circumstances—to get any chance to talk to your brother, do you hear? We've got to prevent that!"

"Okay," said Adam. "Then let us move to our posts."

When Aurélie Bredin finally stepped forward—the last in the line—and put her book down on the table, behind which Robert Miller, flanked by me and Adam, was sitting, my heart began to race.

She turned her head to one side for a moment and looked at me coolly with raised eyebrows. I murmured a *"Bonsoir"* but she didn't deign to speak a word to me. Without any doubt she was angry with me, and her little pearl drop earrings shook aggressively on her earlobes as she turned away again. Then she bent over to Robert Miller and her expression brightened.

"I'm Aurélie Bredin," she said, and I groaned softly.

The dentist gave her a friendly smile, obviously not understanding.

"Have you any particular wishes?" he asked, as if he was an old hand at this.

"No." She shook her head and smiled. And then she gave him a meaningful look.

Robert Miller, a.k.a. Sam Goldberg, smiled too. It was obvious that he was enjoying the attention being paid him by the pretty woman with the bouffant hair. He pulled the open book over and thought for a moment.

"Well, then, let's write, 'To Aurélie Bredin with very best wishes from Robert Miller'—that okay?" He leaned forward and concentrated totally on his signature. "There you are," he said, and looked up.

Aurélie Bredin smiled again and clapped the book shut without looking inside.

Sam's gaze lingered on her mouth for a moment, and then he said: "May I give you a compliment, mademoiselle? You have really *wonderful* teeth." He nodded appreciatively.

She blushed and laughed. "I've never had a compliment like that before," she said in surprise. And then she said something that had my heart sinking into my boots.

"Such a pity you weren't at La Coupole, because I was there too, you know."

Now it was Sam Goldberg's turn to be surprised. You could see his brain rattling. I'm not sure if our dentist didn't think at first that La Coupole was the kind of establishment where long-legged dancers with bunches of feathers on their behinds strutted their stuff, but either way he stared at Aurélie Bredin with a glazed look as if he were trying to remember something, and then said carefully:

"Oh, yes. La Coupole! I really must go there. Lovely place, very lovely!"

You could see that Aurélie Bredin was irritated: The rosy red of her cheeks went a shade darker, but she made another attempt.

"I got your letter last week, Mr. Miller," she said softly, and bit her lower lip. "I was so glad that you wrote back to me." She looked at him expectantly.

That wasn't in our script. A red flush broke out on Sam Goldberg's forehead and I began to sweat. I was incapable of uttering a single word, and listened helplessly as the dentist stuttered with embarrassment, "Well . . . I . . . I was really glad to do that . . . really glad . . . you know . . . I . . . I . . ." He was searching for words that he had no way of finding.

I shot Adam an imploring glance. He looked at his watch, and leaned down to his brother. "Sorry, Mr. Miller, but we really have to go now," he said. "We have the dinner to go to."

"Yes," I interrupted, and my petrifaction yielded to the panicked desire to prize the dentist away from Aurélie Bredin. "We're *already* late for that."

I grabbed Sam Goldberg by the arm and literally dragged him from his seat. "I'm very sorry, but we must go." I nodded apologetically to Aurélie Bredin. "Everyone's waiting for us."

"Oh, Monsieur Chabanais." As if she was seeing me for the very first time that moment. "Thanks very much for the invitation to the reading." Her green eyes flashed as she took a step back to let us pass.

"It was nice to see you, Mr. Miller"—she shook the surprised Sam by the hand—"I hope you won't forget our rendezvous."

She smiled again and smoothed back a strand of dark blond hair that had escaped from her hair clip. Sam looked at her, speechless. Then he said, *"Au revoir, mademoiselle,"* and before he could say anything else we shoved him through the crowd of onlookers who were putting on their coats and chatting.

"Who . . . who *is* that woman?" he asked softly, and kept turning his head back to look at Aurélie Bredin, who was standing at the table with the book, and following him with her gaze until we had left the bookstore.

Eleven

....

It was long past midnight when I asked Bernadette to call me a taxi. After that remarkable reading in the Librairie Capricorne we had gone back to her place for a glass of wine—which I really needed.

I must admit that I was in a state of great confusion as I followed Robert Miller with my eyes. He too continually looked back over his shoulder before stumbling out of the bookstore in the company of André Chabanais and another man in a light brown suit.

"Do you know what I don't understand?" Bernadette said to me when we'd taken off our shoes and were sitting opposite each other on her big sofa. "You wrote a letter, he wrote a letter, and then he stares at you as if you were an apparition, doesn't react, and behaves as if he'd never heard your name. I find that rather strange."

I nodded. "I can't explain that either," I responded, and tried to call to mind all the details of my short conversation with Robert Miller. "You know, he seemed so . . . so baffled. Almost spaced out. As if he couldn't understand anything. Perhaps he hadn't expected me to come to his reading."

Bernadette sipped her wine and took a handful of macadamia nuts from the dish.

"Hm," she said, chewing thoughtfully. "But he wasn't drunk, was he? And why should he be baffled? Let's be honest: He is an author, after all, and so he can't possibly be totally floored when a woman who thinks his book so great that she's even invited him to dinner actually turns up at his reading."

I said nothing, and silently added: someone who had even sent him a photo of herself. But Bernadette knew nothing about that, and I had no intention of telling her.

"When I mentioned our rendezvous, he also just stared very strangely." I suddenly had a thought. "Or do you think he was embarrassed because the other people from the publishers were there as well?"

"I don't think that's very likely . . . he wasn't exactly shy before that. Just consider how he dealt with the questions!"

Bernadette pulled the clip out of her hair and shook it loose. The light blond strands shone in the light of the standard lamp beside the sofa. I watched her running her hands through her hair.

"Do you think I look very different when I have my hair up?" I asked.

Bernadette looked at me. "Well, I'd always recognize you." She laughed. "Why do you ask? Because the woman in the book who looks like you wears her hair down?" She shrugged and leaned back. "Did he mention the reading in his letter, then?" she asked.

I shook my head. "No, but it could have overlapped. He probably didn't know anything definite about the reading when he wrote me the letter, that's possible." I also fished a handful of nuts from the dish. "What I really find too much, however, is that that Chabanais never said a word about it." I crunched a nut. "And he looked quite guilty when I suddenly turned up."

"Perhaps he just forgot."

"Oh, forgot!" I retorted. "After that totally crazy evening we spent together in La Coupole? When he invited me there *specially* because of Miller? I mean, he *knew* it was important to me."

I leaned back against the armrest of the sofa. If it hadn't been for Bernadette I wouldn't have heard about Robert Miller being in Paris. But since my friend lived on the Île Saint-Louis, she often bought books from that nice Monsieur Chagall, who in reality was called Pascal Fermier, and so she had seen the poster by chance one morning in his store window.

We'd arranged to go for a walk in the Tuileries that cold, sunny Monday morning, and the first thing Bernadette asked me was if I was going to Robert Miller's reading that evening and if she could come along as well.

"I do want to see the wonder author after all that's happened," she had said, linking arms with me.

And I had shouted, "I don't believe it. Why didn't that dumbbell from the publishers tell me about it?"

And then I'd gone to the Librairie Capricorne that afternoon to buy two tickets for the reading. Just lucky that the restaurant's closed today, I thought, as I climbed the steps in the subway station.

A few minutes later I pushed open the door of the little bookstore I had entered for the first time a few weeks earlier, fleeing from a concerned policeman.

"We meet again," said Monsieur Chagall, when I went up

to him at the cash desk. At least he had recognized me immediately.

"Yes," I answered. "I really liked that novel."

I'd regarded it as a good omen that Robert Miller's reading would take place in the very bookshop where I'd found his book.

"Are you better now?" the old bookseller asked. "You looked so lost the last time."

"I was!" I answered. "But in the meantime a lot has happened. A lot of nice things," I added. "And it all began with that book."

I looked thoughtfully into the red wine as it washed around my glass. "Do you know, Bernadette, I think that Chabanais is just totally unpredictable and moody," I said. "Sometimes he can be really charming, then he goes over the top—you should have seen him in La Coupole—and then he's unfriendly and grumpy again. Or he gets them to say he's not there."

That afternoon I had rung the publishing house to complain to André Chabanais and to inform him that I'd already bought my own tickets, but unfortunately there was only a secretary at the other end of the line who fobbed me off and answered my question about when the chief editor would be coming back rather brusquely, saying that Monsieur Chabanais had no time at all that day.

"He does at least look quite pleasant," remarked Bernadette.

"Yes, that's true," I said, seeing in my mind's eye the Englishman's light blue eyes as they looked at me so helplessly when I mentioned the broken appointment at La Coupole. "Although he does have a beard now."

Bernadette burst out laughing. "I actually meant Chabanais." I threw a cushion at her and she ducked quickly. "But the Englishman also looks nice. And I found him very witty, I must admit."

"Yes, wasn't he?" I sat up. "The reading was very funny. But he makes unusual compliments." I snuggled down in the sofa cushions. "'You have wonderful teeth,' he said. What do you think of that? If he'd said eyes, now, or 'You have a beautiful mouth.'" I shook my head. "You just don't tell a woman she has wonderful *teeth*."

"Perhaps Englishmen are different," countered Bernadette. "But I do find his behavior toward you strange. Either the man has a memory like a sieve or—I don't know—his wife was around and he has something to hide."

"He lives alone, you must have heard that," I said. "And anyway, Chabanais told me his wife had left him."

Bernadette looked at me with her big dark blue eyes and wrinkled her forehead. "There's something fishy about this business," she said. "Perhaps there is a really simple explanation, though."

I sighed.

"Think hard, Aurélie. What *exactly* did Miller say at the end?" asked Bernadette.

"Yes, well, at the end everything was in a rush because Chabanais and that other guy were pressing him to leave. They shielded him like a politician's bodyguards." I paused for thought. "He sort of stuttered that he was glad he'd written the letter and then he said *Au revoir*. Good-bye."

"That's at least something," said Bernadette, and polished off her red wine.

• • •

As I sat in the taxi a little later, driving along the brightly lit Boulevard Saint-Germain, I opened the book where Miller had written his dedication for me:

To Aurélie Bredin with very best wishes from Robert Miller

I stroked the signature and stared a long while at the looping letters as if they were the key to Miller's secret.

And so they were. Except that I didn't at that moment realize how.

Twelve

....

I was always deeply impressed by a scene from the old black-and-white film *Les enfants du paradis*. It's the last shot, where the despairing Baptiste is running after his great love Garance and finally loses her in the commotion of a street carnival. He's overwhelmed, he can't get through, he's surrounded and shoved by the laughing, dancing crowd he's stumbling through. An unhappy, confused man among joyful people who are exuberantly celebrating—that's an image you don't easily forget, and which I remembered when I was sitting after the reading with Sam Goldberg and the others in an Alsatian restaurant near the bookstore.

The fat proprietor sat us at a big table against the back wall of the restaurant and cheerfully clattered cutlery and glasses down in front of us. Everyone seemed to be in the best of moods; there was drinking, jokes, celebration; the dentist played the role of Everybody's Darling, and finally all were happily united in the spirit of wine—apart from me, the unhappy Baptiste, sitting there in the middle like an alien because things had not gone so wonderfully for him.

"Man, was she mad!" Adam whispered to me as we left the Librairie Capricorne with his brother asking over and over again who the lovely woman in the red dress had been.

Adam explained to him that it was quite possible at a reading for enthusiastic fans to make eyes at an author.

"Wow!" the dentist shouted, adding that he was enjoying being an author more and more. "Perhaps I should really write a book, what do you think?"

"For heaven's sake, don't you dare!" Adam said.

I remained dumb, and in the course of the evening became ever dumber.

However you looked at it, I'd blown it with Aurélie Bredin— as nice chief editor André Chabanais, who was always on the spot to help. And now even the fabulous Robert Miller had put his foot right in it.

After our not-actually-an-author had put on such an embarrassing performance, I was not even sure that the Englishman's attractiveness had not also suffered a serious downturn. "Oh yes, La Coupole. Lovely place, very lovely!" She must have thought he was soft in the head. And the business with the teeth! I could only hope that would not change her mind about inviting Robert Miller to her restaurant, because then I no longer had any chance at all.

I stared at my plate and heard the others as if from far off.

Then even Jean-Paul Monsignac, who was having a great time with our author, noticed. He raised his glass to me and asked, "What's the matter, André? You're not saying a word."

I said I had a headache as an excuse.

I would really have liked to go home straightaway, but I had the feeling I ought to keep an eye on Robert Miller.

Adam, the only one I would have liked to talk to, was sitting at the other end of the table. He occasionally threw me an encouraging glance, and as we all left for home hours later he promised to drop in briefly at my place the next morning before he left for London.

"But alone," I said. "We need to talk."

I was just tearing up my new letter from Robert Miller to Aurélie Bredin when the doorbell rang. I threw the envelope in the wastepaper basket and pressed the door opener. I had actually intended to give this letter, which contained Miller's definite acceptance of the invitation to Le Temps des Cerises, to Adam, but after the previous day's events, the content was out of date. I'd lain awake half the night thinking about what I should do now. And I had an idea.

When Adam entered, he looked at the chaos in the hallway where the shattered mirror was still lying together with the heap of shards I'd swept up hastily the day before.

"Oh, what's happened here?" he said. "Did you have a fit of rage?"

"No. The mirror fell off yesterday morning. Just what I needed!" I explained.

"Seven years' bad luck," said Adam, grinning.

I took my winter coat off the hook and opened the door.

"I hope not," I said. "Come on, let's go and get breakfast somewhere, I've got nothing in the house."

We walked the few steps to Au Vieux Colombier and went past the counter to the very back, where there are wooden benches and big tables. How often I'd been here with Adam before, and we'd discussed book projects and talked about the changes in our lives.

"Adam, you're my friend," I said, as the waiter brought our breakfast.

"Okay," said Adam. "Tell me what it is you want. Is this about the letter to Mademoiselle Bredin that I'm supposed to mail? No problem. Now that I've seen the girl, I can at least understand why you're so hung up on her."

"No," I said. "The letter's not a good idea, not after yesterday evening. And anyway, that would take too long for me. I want to cut straight to the chase."

"Aha," said Adam, biting into his ham baguette. "And what can I do to help?" he asked as he chewed.

"You've got to call her," I said. "As Robert Miller."

Adam nearly choked. "You're crazy, man," he said.

"No, I'm not crazy." I shook my head. "You and Sam have very similar voices and if you mangle the language a bit it shouldn't be too hard. Please, Adam, you must do me this favor."

And then I explained my new plan to him. Adam should call Le Temps des Cerises from England in the evening. He should apologize to Aurélie Bredin and say that he'd been totally overcome when he first saw her, and then there'd been so many people standing around and he didn't want to say the wrong thing.

"Spin her some kind of yarn, beguile her with your gentlemanly charm—just make sure that Robert Miller is rehabilitated. You can do it." I drank my espresso. "What's important is that you nail the date fast. Tell her that you're looking forward to a dinner à deux. Suggest the sixteenth of December because you have business in Paris then and will have the whole evening free for her."

The sixteenth of December was perfect in two respects. Firstly, it was Aurélie Bredin's birthday, and secondly, I'd discovered that the restaurant—as on every Monday—would be closed. Would *normally* be closed.

This increased the likelihood that I would find myself alone with Aurélie Bredin in Le Temps des Cerises.

"Oh, and one other thing, Adam. Make it obvious that she should keep the arrangement to herself. Say that that editor is likely to butt in if he hears his author is in the city. That will ultimately make the thing more credible."

If it did actually come to a rendezvous on the sixteenth of December (which I optimistically presumed would be the case), Adam would ring again that evening.

But this time as Adam Goldberg calling off the date on Miller's behalf.

The reason for the cancelation was an idea of genius—for which I congratulated myself when it struck me at half past two in the morning—because it would strike at Aurélie Bredin's pride and make it impossible for her ever to want to contact Robert Miller again. And another thing that was not so bad was that the savior who would console her in her loneliness and pain would already be standing in the starting blocks—that is, outside the restaurant.

"*Mon ami,* you're really taking on a lot—that sounds like a bad American B movie. You are aware that things like that never work out, aren't you?" Adam laughed.

I leaned forward and gave him a piercing look. "Adam, I'm really serious about this. If there's anything I want in life, then it's this woman. All I need is an undisturbed evening with her.

I need a *real* chance, do you see? And if, in order to achieve this, I have to embroider the truth a little, then I'll do it. I don't give a damn about any mixed-up Americans—we French call it *corriger la fortune.*"

I leaned back and looked out through the dark green iron window frames of the café into the Parisian dawn. "Sometimes you just have to give fortune a push in the right direction."

Thirteen

....

"Mademoiselle Bredin, Mademoiselle Bredin," someone called out behind me as I left the house and entered the stone passageway that led to the Boulevard Saint-Germain. I turned round and saw a tall man with a dark winter coat and a red scarf looming up out of the darkness.

It was late afternoon, and I was on the way to the restaurant. And the man was André Chabanais.

"What are you doing here?" I asked in astonishment.

"As chance would have it—I'm just coming from a meeting." He pointed to the Procope and smiled. "My office is getting so full of manuscripts and books that I can't meet more than one person there." He waved his leather briefcase. "Well, this is a pleasant surprise." He looked around. "You live in a really lovely area."

I nodded and marched on without reacting. My joy at seeing the chief editor was not unbounded.

He walked beside me. "Can I accompany you for a while?"

"You already are," I snapped, and increased my pace.

"Oh dear, you're still mad at me because of yesterday evening, aren't you?"

"So far I haven't received any apology," I said, and turned into the boulevard. "First you invite me to La Coupole. Then you don't even inform me about Miller's reading. What do you think you're playing at, Monsieur Chabanais?"

We walked silently down the street side by side.

"Listen, Mademoiselle Bredin, I'm really sorry. The business with the reading happened very quickly and of course I *intended* to let you know about it . . . But then something always got in the way and in the end I simply forgot about it."

"You're trying to tell me that you didn't have the thirty seconds it takes to say, 'Mademoiselle Bredin, Miller's reading is at eight o'clock on Monday evening'? And in the end you forgot? What sort of apology is that? People don't forget things that are important to them." I walked on angrily. "And then you got them to say you weren't there when I called your office."

He reached for my arm. "No, that's not true! They informed me that you'd called, but I really was not there."

I shook his hand away. "I don't believe a word of it, Monsieur Chabanais. You told me yourself in La Coupole how you get your secretary to get rid of unwanted callers, how you stand there and make signals to her . . . and that's all I am to you, isn't it? An unwanted caller!"

I have no idea why I was so angry. Perhaps it was because the reading the evening before had ended in disappointment and I was blaming the chief editor for that even though strictly speaking it wasn't his fault.

"My mother had an accident yesterday and I was in the hospital the whole afternoon," said André Chabanais. "That's the truth; and you are anything but an unwanted caller to me, Mademoiselle Bredin."

I stopped. "Oh my goodness," I said, taken aback. "I'm . . . I'm very sorry."

"Do you believe me now?" he asked, looking me straight in the eye.

"Yes." I nodded, finally looking away in embarrassment. "I hope everything's all right . . . with your mother," I said.

"She'll be okay. She fell down an escalator and broke a leg." He shook his head. "Yesterday was not exactly my lucky day, you know."

"That makes two of us," I said.

He smiled. "Nevertheless, it is of course unforgivable that I didn't let you know." We walked on past the lights of the store windows on the boulevard, giving way to a group of Japanese who were being led through the city by a guide with a red umbrella. "How did you actually hear about the reading?"

"A friend of mine lives on the Île Saint-Louis," I said. "She saw the poster. And fortunately Monday is my day off."

"Thank goodness for that," he said.

I stopped at a traffic light. "So," I said. "This is the parting of our ways." I pointed toward the Rue Bonaparte. "I have to cross here."

"Are you going to the restaurant?" André Chabanais stopped too.

"You guessed it."

"Sometime I must visit Le Temps des Cerises," he said. "It's really a very romantic little spot."

"You do that," I responded. "Perhaps you could bring your mother when she gets out of the hospital."

He pulled a face. "You won't let me have any fun, will you?"

I grinned, and the light turned green. "I must go, Monsieur Chabanais," I said, and turned away.

"Wait a moment. Tell me, is there anything I can do to make up for my negligence?" he shouted as I stepped into the crossing.

"Try and think of something!" I called back. Then I ran across the street and waved to him once more before turning into the street leading to the Rue Princesse.

"What are you doing at Christmas?" Jacquie asked as I helped him to prepare the *boeuf bourguignon* that was on the day's menu. Paul, the sous-chef, was actually well again, but he would be arriving a bit later that day.

We'd browned the chunks of meat in two pans, and now I put it in the big sauté pan and shook a little flour over it.

"No idea," I said. It was only at that moment that I realized that this would be the first Christmas I would really be alone. A strange idea. The restaurant would also close down on the twenty-third of December, not reopening until the second week in January. I stirred the pot with a wooden spoon, waiting for the fat to bind with the flour. Then I poured the Burgundy over it. The wine hissed briefly, the smell of the liquid rose to my nostrils, and the pieces of meat bubbled in the dark sauce.

Jacquie came over with the sliced carrots and mushrooms and swept the vegetables off the big wooden chopping board into the pot.

"You could always come to Normandy with me," he said. "I'll be at my sister's: She's got a big family and at Christmas it's always very lively, good friends drop in, and neighbors . . ."

"That's very sweet of you, Jacquie, but I don't know . . . I haven't actually thought about it at all. And everything is different this year . . ."

I suddenly felt a lump in my throat, and coughed. Just don't go all sentimental now, I told myself, that won't achieve anything. "I'll sort things out somehow. I'm not a little girl anymore, after all," I said, and in my imagination saw myself sitting alone in front of my *Bûche de Noël,* that delicious chocolate cake that is always served at Christmas—my father always used to bring it to the table with a great fanfare when everyone was already saying that they were about to burst after eating Christmas dinner.

"For me you'll always be a little girl," said Jacquie, and put his meaty arm round my shoulder. "Somehow, I'd feel a lot better if you came to the seaside with me, Aurélie. What will you do all alone here in Paris where it does nothing but rain? It's not nice to be all alone at Christmas."

He shook his head worriedly and his white chef's hat wobbled threateningly. "A couple of days in that lovely fresh air and a few walks on the beach would do you good. And I've promised to cook and could really do with your help." He looked at me. "Promise me that you will at least think about it, Aurélie . . . okay?"

Moved, I gave a little nod. "I promise," I replied with a catch in my voice. Good old Jacquie!

"And do you know what the best thing is when you're there?" he asked, and I joined in with a laugh as he said, "You can see far out to sea!"

I tasted the sauce in the big wooden spoon. "That could definitely do with more red wine," I said, and poured in more Burgundy. "Now, into the oven with it!" I looked at my watch. "Oh, I've got to set the tables." I took off my apron, then my headscarf, and shook my hair loose. Then I went over to the little mirror on the wall near the kitchen door and freshened my lipstick.

"Won't make you any prettier," said Jacquie as I went into the dining room. A few minutes later, Suzette arrived and together we put wineglasses and water glasses on the tables and folded the white linen napkins. I glanced at the reservation book. We were going to have a lot to do in the next couple of weeks and I urgently needed to take on a new server.

December was a really busy month and our little restaurant was actually fully booked almost every evening.

"We've got a Christmas party coming in this evening— sixteen of them," I said to Suzette, "but it shouldn't be a problem, they're all having the set menu."

Suzette nodded and shoved the tables next to the wall together.

"When it's time for dessert we must make sure that they all get their crêpes suzette at the same time. Jacquie can come out from the kitchen and flambé them on the dessert wagon."

For the chef to make a personal appearance to flambé the crêpes suzette at the table in a large copper pan, and fillet the oranges with flamboyant gestures, cutting them into slices, then strew almonds over them and pour Grand Marnier over them, was always a special attraction, and half the restaurant would watch as the bluish flames flared up for a few seconds.

I was just checking the cutlery when the telephone rang. "You get it, Suzette," I said. "Don't take any more reservations for this evening."

Suzette went to the telephone, which was at the back of the restaurant near the till. *"Le Temps des Cerises, bonsoir,"* she trilled, her *"bonsoir"* stretching out to include a questioning tone. *"Oui, monsieur,* one moment, please." She waved to me. "It's for you, Aurélie." She handed me the phone.

"Hello?" I said, not expecting what was coming.

"Er . . . Bong soir—do I spik to Mademoiselle Aurélie Bredin?" said a voice with an unmistakable English accent.

"Yes." I could feel the blood rushing to my head. "Yes, this is Aurélie Bredin." I turned to the counter where the reservation book lay open.

"Oh, Mademoiselle Bredin, I am so heppy that I reach you. This is Robert Miller, I could only find the number out of the restaurant. Am I disturbing you?"

"No," I said, and my heart shot into my mouth. "No, no, you're not disturbing me at all, the restaurant doesn't open for another half hour. Are you . . . are you still in Paris?"

"Oh, no, I'm afraid not," he replied. "I had to get back to Angland early the next morning. Listen, Mademoiselle Bredin . . ."

"Yes?" I blurted, pressing the phone to my ear.

"I'm really terribly sorry about yesterday evening," he said. "I . . . my goodness! . . . I was thunderstruck when you were suddenly there, standing in front of me as if you had fallen from the heavens. I could only look at you, you were so lovely in your red dress—like from a different galaxy . . ."

I took a deep breath and bit my lip. "And I thought you wouldn't even remember me," I said with relief.

"No, no!" he cried. "No, you must not thought that! I remind everything—your lovely letter, the picture! I just could not believe at that first moment that it were really you, Aurélie. And I was so confused by all those many people who all wanted something from me and my editor and my agent who kept on looking and listened to everything we spoke. And I suddenly was unsure what I must say." He sighed. "And now I have such fear that you hold me for a great idiot . . ."

"But no," I answered, my ears going red. "Everything is all right."

"My goodness, I have been stupid. Please, you must forgave me. I am not so good with so much people, you know," he said abjectly. "Be not angry with me."

Mon Dieu, was he sweet! "Of course I'm not angry with you, Mr. Miller," I hurriedly said.

I heard a noise behind me and saw Suzette, who was following our conversation with increasing interest. I decided to ignore her, and leaned over the reservation book.

Robert Miller made a sound of relief. "That is so nice of you, Aurélie—could I say Aurélie?"

"Yes, of course." I nodded—I could have gone on with this conversation forever.

"Aurélie . . . could I then still hope for eating with you? Or will you no more invite me to your little sweet restaurant?"

"Yes, of course I will, I will!" I almost shouted, and turned to see the question mark in Suzette's eyes as she busied herself behind me. "You only have to say when you can make it."

Robert Miller was silent for a moment and I could hear the rustle of paper. "How about the sixteenth of December?" he said. "I've got business near Paris all day, but the evening belongs to you."

I closed my eyes and smiled. The sixteenth of December was my birthday. And it was a Monday. It looked as if everything that was important in my life just then was on a Monday.

It was on a Monday that I'd found Miller's book in the little bookstore. It was on a Monday that I'd encountered the faithless Claude and his pregnant girlfriend in La Palette. It was on a

Monday that I'd seen Robert Miller for the first time at a reading I'd only heard about just in time. And it would be on a Monday that also happened to be my birthday that a little private dinner with a most interesting writer would take place. If things went on like this, I'd probably marry on a Monday, too, and die on a Monday, and Mrs. Dinsmore would water my grave with her little watering can.

I smiled again.

"Hello, Mademoiselle Aurélie? Are you still there?" Miller's voice sounded worried. "If the Monday is not a good day then we will seek another day. But the eating must take place, I insist."

"The meal *will* take place." I laughed happily. "On Monday the sixteenth of December at eight o'clock. I'm looking forward to seeing you, Monsieur Miller!"

"As much as I am looking forward could you not look forward," he said.

Then he added hesitantly, "Could I also ask you a little favor, Mademoiselle Aurélie? Please don't say nothing about our meeting to André Chabanais. He's very nice, but he is some of the times a bit, how do you say . . . business obsessed. If he knows I am in Paris he will also want to see me and then we won't have enough time for us . . ."

"Don't worry, Mr. Miller. I'll be as silent as the grave."

When I hung up, Suzette looked at me wide-eyed.

"*Mon Dieu,* who *was* that man?" she asked. "Did he proposition you, or what?"

I smiled. "That was the man who'll be my dinner guest here on the sixteenth of December," I said. "And my *only* guest, at that!"

And with those cryptic words I left the astonished Suzette standing and unlocked the restaurant door.

The meeting with Robert Miller would remain my little secret.

Paris is not called the City of Light for nothing. And to my mind Paris particularly deserves the name in December.

No matter how gray November had been with its rain and those days when you had the feeling that it would never be bright again—in December Paris was transformed as it was every year into a sea of sparkling light. You really got the feeling that a fairy had flown through the streets and sprinkled the houses with stardust. And if you drove through Paris in the afternoon or evening, the city with its Christmas decorations shone like a fairyland in silver and white.

The gnarled trees on the Champs-Élysées were adorned with thousands of little lights; children and even adults stood in amazement at the window displays in Galeries Lafayette, Printemps, or the smaller but very up-market department store Bon Marché, admiring the glittering decorations; in the little streets and great boulevards you could see people with the beribboned paper bags that held their Christmas gifts; there were no long lines outside the museums anymore—even in the Louvre you could get through to the *Mona Lisa* with no trouble in those last weekends before Christmas and wonder at her enigmatic smile to your heart's content. And over everything else the Eiffel Tower shone out—that powerful and yet delicately filigreed symbol of the city, a magnet for all lovers visiting the city for the first time.

I'd been skating there twice with little Marie, Bernadette's daughter. *Patiner sur la Tour Eiffel*, announced the sky blue poster that showed a white Eiffel Tower with a pair of old-fashioned skaters in front of it. Marie had insisted on going up to the first level of the tower on foot. I hadn't been up the tower for ages, and as we climbed up kept stopping to look down between the iron supports, which from really close up looked gigantic. The cold air and the climb took my breath away, but then we were at the platform, circling the ice on our skates, flying with reddened cheeks and shining eyes above the sparkling, glittering city, and for a few moments I actually felt like a child once more myself.

There's something about Christmas that always throws us back upon ourselves, on our memories and wishes, our childhood self, which is always standing wide-eyed with amazement outside the great door behind which the wonder is waiting.

Rustling paper, whispered words, burning candles, decorated windows, the smell of cinnamon and cloves, wishes that are written on paper or spoken to the heavens and that may perhaps come true—Christmas wakens, whether you want it or not, that eternal desire for the wonderful. And the wonderful is not something you can possess or hold on to, it doesn't *belong* to you and yet it is always there like something that is gifted to us.

I leaned my head happily against the window of the taxi as it crossed the Seine and looked down on the river glistening in the sunlight. On my lap, wrapped in tissue paper, lay the red coat. Bernadette, who had invited me to breakfast that morning, had given it to me for my birthday.

All in all this sixteenth of December had begun very promisingly—it had actually begun the night before as we all, after the last guests left at about half past twelve, drank a champagne toast to my thirty-third birthday: Jacquie, Paul, Claude, Marie, and Pierre, our new kitchen boy, who at sixteen was the youngest of us all; Suzette, who had spent the whole evening hinting that there was yet another surprise awaiting me; and

Juliette Meunier, who had been helping out almost every evening since the first week in December.

Jacquie had baked a delicious chocolate cake with raspberries, and we all ate a slice. He also presented me with a big bouquet of flowers on behalf of them all. There were brightly wrapped packages for me—a thick scarf with matching knitted gloves from Suzette, a little notebook with an oriental pattern from Paul, and from Jacquie a satin bag of shells containing a train ticket.

It was a lovely, almost family moment as we all stood in the empty restaurant and rang in my new year with champagne. And when I pulled the covers up about two o'clock, I fell asleep to the thought that I was about to have an exciting rendezvous with a good-looking writer whom I didn't really know, though I thought I did.

The taxi driver drove over a bump in the road and the paper the coat was wrapped in rustled.

"You're crazy!" I'd cried out as I opened the big package that was lying on the breakfast table. "The red coat! You're really crazy, Bernadette, it's far too expensive!"

"It's to bring you luck," Bernadette had answered as I hugged her tight with tears in my eyes. "This evening . . . and always, whenever you wear it."

And so it came about that in the early afternoon of the sixteenth of December I was standing in a carmine red coat outside Le Temps des Cerises, which was actually closed on Mondays—an adventurer wrapped in the scent of Heliotrop and the color of happiness.

Half an hour later I was standing in the kitchen preparing the meal. It was my birthday dinner, but more than that it was the menu with which I wished to show my gratitude for the fact that a terribly unhappy November day had ended with a happy smile—a smile that would prepare the way for something new.

And last but not least it was also, of course, my first dinner with Robert Miller.

I had thought for a long time about what culinary delights I would impress the English writer with—but had still ended up with the *menu d'amour* my father had left me.

It was certainly not the most refined menu French cuisine had to offer, but it had two unbeatable advantages: It was easy, and I could cook it perfectly, so that I could give my undivided attention during the meal to the man whose arrival I was—I have to admit it—awaiting with delicious anxiety.

I put on my white apron and unpacked the bags I'd filled at the market at midday: fresh field salad; two heads of celery; oranges; macadamia nuts; little white mushrooms; a bunch of carrots; red onions; shiny, almost black eggplants and two gleaming red pomegranates; lamb; and bacon fat. There was always a supply of potatoes, cream, tomatoes, herbs, and baguettes in the kitchen, and I'd prepared the blood orange parfait with cinnamon that, together with the *gâteaux au chocolat,* formed the crowning glorious finale to the *menu d'amour,* the evening before.

The hors d'oeuvre was to be field salad with fresh mushrooms, avocados, macadamia nuts, and little cubes of crisp-fried bacon. Over this I would pour—and that was the really special ingredient—Papa's delicious potato vinaigrette.

But first I needed to get on with the lamb ragout, because the longer it was braised in the oven at low temperature, the more tender the meat would be.

I washed the pink lamb meat and dabbed it carefully dry with a kitchen towel before I cut it into cubes, browned it in olive oil, and set it aside. Then I blanched the tomatoes in boiling water, skinned them, and took out the flesh.

The tomatoes would be put into the pot only at the very end, together with the white wine, so that their strong flavor wouldn't dominate the other vegetables too much. I got a glass and poured myself some of the pinot blanc I was intending to use in cooking.

Humming softly, I cut open the pomegranates and picked out the seeds with a fork. They rolled toward me like shimmering red freshwater pearls. I was used to cooking quickly, but when, as on that day, I took plenty of time in the preparation of the dishes, cooking almost became a poetic activity in which I could totally lose myself. With every action my initial tension relaxed more and more, and if at the beginning I had been imagining how the evening with Robert Miller would pan out, and thinking of the questions I wanted to ask him, after a while I was just there with my cheeks red from the heat of cooking, feeling totally at ease.

The delicious aroma of the lamb ragout filled the kitchen. It smelled of thyme and garlic. The little leaves of the field salad had been washed and were lying in a big, stainless-steel sieve; the mushrooms had been finely sliced, and the avocados cubed. I tasted the potato vinaigrette and put the little *gâteaux au chocolat,* which were waiting for their final bake, on the metal oven shelf. Then I took off my apron and hung it on its hook. It was just after half past six and everything was prepared. The bottle of champagne had been in the refrigerator for hours. All I had to do now was wait.

I went over into the dining room, where I'd set a table in a niche by the window. The lower third of the window was hung with a white net curtain to conceal my guest and me from inquisitive looks from outside. A silver candlestick with a candle was standing on the table, and a CD with French chansons was loaded ready in the sound system.

I took the bottle of pinot blanc and poured myself a little more wine. Then I went over to the table with my glass and looked out into the night.

The street stood lonely and dark. The few little shops that were on it had already closed. In the window I could see my reflection. I saw an expectant young woman in a sleeveless green silk dress who now slowly raised her arm to loosen the band that held her hair back. I smiled, and the woman in the window smiled back. It might well have been childish to put the silk dress on again, but I had felt that it was the only dress I wanted to wear that evening.

I raised my glass and toasted the woman in the window with her shimmering hair.

"Very best wishes for your birthday, Aurélie," I said softly. "Let's drink to today being a very special one!" And I caught myself thinking: I wonder how far this evening might go.

Half an hour later—I was just standing in front of the stove with two big oven gloves and shoving the hot shelf with the lamb ragout back in—I heard someone knocking loudly on the restaurant window. Surprised, I pulled off the gloves and left the kitchen. Could Robert Miller have arrived for our rendezvous an hour early?

At first I could only see a gigantic bouquet of champagne-colored roses outside the window. Then I saw the man behind it, who was waving to me happily. But the man was not Robert Miller.

Fourteen

....

Since Aurélie Bredin had run waving over the zebra crossing two weeks before, to disappear a couple of seconds later down the street on the opposite side, I had both longed for and dreaded this moment. I don't know how many times I had run the evening of the sixteenth of December in my mind's eye.

I had thought of this evening as I visited Maman in the hospital; I had thought of it as I sat in the editorial meeting and doodled little stick men in my notepad; I had thought of it as I rushed beneath the city on the Metro, as I leafed through the superb illustrated books in my favorite bookstore, Assouline, and as I met my friends in La Palette. And as I lay in bed at night, I thought about it anyway.

Wherever I was, wherever I went, the thought of this evening accompanied me, and I anticipated it as nervously as an actor does the premiere of his new play.

More than once I had held the telephone in my hand with the thought of hearing Aurélie Bredin's voice and, on the off chance, asking her out for a coffee, but I'd always hung up for fear of getting the brush-off. And anyway, she hadn't been in touch with me since the day I had met her outside her house "by chance"; the day my friend Adam had rung her pretending to be Robert Miller to arrange the date in her restaurant.

As I made my way to Le Temps des Cerises with my bouquet and a bottle of Crémant, I was more nervous than I had almost ever been before. And now I was standing at the window trying my damnedest to put on a relaxed and not too solemn expression. My idea, to drop in at the restaurant totally spontaneously after work to wish Aurélie Bredin (briefly) a happy birthday (having remembered the date purely by chance), was supposed to look as natural as possible.

So I knocked quite loudly on the windowpane, knowing full well that I would find the beauteous cook alone in the restaurant, and my heart was knocking at least as loudly.

I saw her surprised expression, and a few seconds later the door of Le Temps des Cerises opened and Aurélie Bredin gave me a questioning look. "Monsieur Chabanais, what are *you* doing here?"

"Wishing you a happy birthday," I said, holding out the bouquet to her. "I wish you all the very best—and hope that all your wishes come true."

"Oh, thank you very much, that is really very kind of you, Monsieur Chabanais." She took the bouquet in both hands and I used the opportunity to push past her into the restaurant.

"May I come in for a moment?" A swift glance established the fact that a table was set in the niche near the window, and I sat down on one of the wooden chairs near the entrance. "Do you know, when I looked at the calendar today, I suddenly thought . . . the sixteenth of December, that means something, that definitely means something. And then I remembered. And then I thought you might be pleased if I brought you a bunch of flowers." I smiled winningly and put the bottle of Crémant on the table beside me. "I did threaten you that I'd visit your restaurant one day, do you remember?" I stretched my arms out. "*Et voilà*—here I am."

"Yes . . . here you are." Her expression showed that she was not exactly over the moon at my sudden appearance. She looked embarrassedly at the sumptuous roses, and sniffed them. "This is . . . a wonderful bouquet, Monsieur Chabanais . . . it's just that . . . the restaurant is actually closed today."

I slapped my forehead. "Well there's a thing, I'd completely forgotten that. Then it's very lucky that I found you here at all." I sat up. "But what are you doing here then? On your birthday? You're not working secretly, are you?" I laughed.

She turned and got a glass vase out from under the bar.

"No, of course not." I could see a light shade of pink coloring her face as she went into the kitchen to fill the vase with water. She came back and stood the vase of roses on the counter near the cash register and the telephone.

"Well then . . . thank you very much, Monsieur Chabanais," she said.

I stood up. "Does that mean you're throwing me out before I even have the chance to drink a birthday toast with you? That's hard."

She smiled. "I'm afraid there's hardly time for that. You really have arrived at an awkward moment, Monsieur Chabanais. I'm sorry," she added with a regretful expression, and clasped her hands.

I pretended to see the table that was set by the window for

the first time. "Oh," I said. "*Oh là là!* You're *expecting* someone. That looks like a romantic evening."

I looked at her. Her green eyes shone.

"Well, whoever it is can count himself lucky. You look particularly lovely tonight, Aurélie." I stroked the bottle, which was still on the table. "When does your guest arrive?"

"At eight o'clock," she said, pushing her hair back.

I looked at my watch. A quarter past seven. In a few minutes Adam would ring. "Oh, come along, Mademoiselle Bredin, a quick glass to toast your birthday!" I pleaded. "It's only a quarter past seven. In ten minutes I'll disappear. I'll just open the bottle."

She smiled, and I knew that she wouldn't say no.

"All right," she sighed. "Ten minutes."

I rummaged in my trouser pocket for a corkscrew. "See," I said, "I've even brought the right tools with me." I pulled the cork out, and it left the neck of the bottle with a soft pop.

I poured the sparkling wine into two glasses that Aurélie fetched from the cupboard. "Then once more, very best wishes. I feel honored," I said, and we clinked glasses. I drank the Crémant in great gulps and tried to remain calm even though my heart was hammering so wildly that I was afraid she might hear it. The countdown was running. The telephone would ring very soon, and then we'd see if I was really condemned to leave. I looked deep into my glass, and then once more at Aurélie's lovely face. Just to have something to say, I remarked, "You can't be left out of one's sight for two weeks, can you? I just turn my back once—and you already have a new admirer."

She blushed and shook her head.

"What?" I said. "Do I know him by any chance?"

"No," she said.

And then the phone rang. We both looked at it on the counter, but Aurélie Bredin made no move to pick it up.

"Probably someone who wants to make a reservation," she said. "I don't need to pick it up, the answering machine is switched on."

We heard a click, and then the restaurant's message. And then Adam's voice rang out.

"Oh, good evening, this is Adam Goldberg with a message for Aurélie Bredin," he said without beating about the bush. "I'm Robert Miller's agent, and I'm calling on his behalf," continued Adam, and I saw how Aurélie turned pale. "I would have preferred to tell you personally, but Miller has asked me to cancel your meeting this evening. I am to tell you that he's very sorry." Adam's words fell into the room like stones. "He . . . how should I put it? . . . He's totally rattled. Yesterday evening his wife turned up unexpectedly and . . . well . . . she's still there and it looks as if she's there to stay. They have a lot to talk about, I should think." Adam paused for a moment. "I find it very embarrassing to have to tell you about these private matters, but Robert Miller felt that it was important that you know that he . . . well . . . that he's calling off for a very important reason. He wants me to tell you that he's very sorry and hopes that you'll understand." Adam listened for a couple of seconds and then he said good-bye and hung up.

I looked at Aurélie Bredin, who was standing there frozen to the spot and clasping her wineglass so tightly that I was afraid it would shatter.

She stared at me, and I stared at her, and for a long while neither of us said a word.

Then she opened her mouth as if she wanted to say something, but she didn't say anything. Instead, she emptied her glass in a single gulp and pressed it to her breast. She looked down at the ground. "Well . . ." she said, her voice trembling revealingly.

I put my glass down, and at that moment I felt like a total rotter. But then I thought, *Le roi est mort, vive le roi* and decided to act.

"You were going to meet *Miller*?" I asked in bewilderment. "Alone in your restaurant? On your *birthday*?" I said nothing for a moment. "Wasn't that going a bit over the top? I mean, you hardly *know* him."

She looked at me without saying a word and I saw the tears welling up in her eyes. Then she quickly turned away from me and stared out of the window.

"Oh my goodness, Aurélie, I . . . I don't know what to say. This is simply . . . awful, completely awful." I went and stood behind her. She was weeping softly. I put my hands very carefully on her shaking shoulders.

"I'm sorry. My God, I'm so sorry, Aurélie," I said, noting to my surprise that I actually meant it. Her hair smelled faintly of vanilla, and I would have loved to push it to one side and kiss the nape of her neck. Instead, I stroked her shoulders reassuringly. "Please, Aurélie, don't cry," I said gently. "Yes, I know, I know . . . it hurts when you're let down like that . . . it's all right . . . it's all right . . ."

"But Miller called me. He just had to see me and said such nice things on the phone . . ." She sobbed. "And then I . . . get everything ready here, keep the evening free . . . After the letter I thought I meant something special to him . . . He gave such hints, you understand?" She suddenly turned round and looked at me with tear-stained eyes. "And now his wife suddenly returns and I feel . . . I feel . . . I feel terrible!"

She covered her face with her hands, and I took her in my arms.

It took quite a while until Aurélie calmed down again. I was so glad to be with her to console her, handing her tissue after tissue and hoping devotedly that she would never find out why I had been there at the precise moment that the answering machine in Le Temps des Cerises clicked on and catapulted Robert Miller into the unattainable distance.

At some stage—by then we were sitting opposite each other—she looked at me and said, "Have you got a cigarette for me? I think I could do with one now."

"Yes, of course." I took out a pack of Gauloises, and she took a cigarette and looked at it thoughtfully. "The last time I smoked a Gauloise was with Mrs. Dinsmore—in the *cemetery!*" She smiled and said, more to herself than me, "I wonder if I will ever find out what the novel is really about."

I held out a burning match for her. "Quite possibly," I answered vaguely. And looked at her mouth, which suddenly seemed very close to my face. "But not this evening."

She leaned back and blew the smoke into the air. "No," she said. "And I can probably forget dinner with the author too."

I nodded sympathetically, and thought that her chances of dinner with the author were actually quite good—even if he wasn't called Miller. "Do you know what? Forget about that Miller chap for now: He obviously doesn't know what it is that he wants. Look at it this way: It's the book that is really important. That novel helped you to forget your sorrows—it fell from the heavens, so to speak, to save you. And I think that's great."

She smiled hesitantly. "Yes, perhaps you're right." She sat upright and gazed at me for a long time in silence and then said,

"Somehow I'm very glad that you're here at this moment, Monsieur Chabanais."

I took her hand. "My dear Aurélie, you can't possibly imagine how glad I am that I'm here now," I replied in an emotional voice. Then I stood up. "And now we're going to celebrate your birthday. There's no way you're going to sit here wallowing in misery. Not as long as I can prevent it." I poured us the rest of the Crémant and Aurélie emptied her glass in one single gulp and put it down determinedly.

"This is how it should be done," I said, and pulled her up from her chair. "May I lead you to our table, Mademoiselle Bredin? If you reveal where you keep your delicacies, I'll get the drinks and the food."

Of course Aurélie refused to let anyone else put the final touches to the dishes she had prepared, but at least I was allowed to enter the kitchen, where she instructed me to open the red wine and put the salad in a big stoneware dish while she browned the bacon lardons in a little pan. I had never been in a restaurant kitchen before, and was amazed at the stove with its eight burners and the numerous pots, pans, and ladles that all stood or hung within reach.

We drank the first glass of red wine before we left the kitchen, and the second glass at the table.

"It tastes delicious," I cried out, dipping my fork into the tender leaves that gleamed under the lardons, and when Aurélie then brought the whole casserole with the lamb ragout from the kitchen and put it on our table I went over to the little stereo system behind the bar and switched the music on.

Georges Brassens sang *"Je M'Suis Fait Tout Petit"* in his seductive voice, and I thought that every man meets once in his life a woman he would gladly allow to tame him.

The lamb melted in our mouths and I said, "Pure poetry!" Then Aurélie told me that the recipe, not to mention the whole menu, had been created by her father, who had died in October, far too early.

"He cooked it for the first time when he . . . when he . . ." She became tongue-tied and suddenly blushed. "Anyway, many, many years ago," she ended the sentence, and reached for her red-wine glass.

While we ate the lamb ragout she told me about Claude, who had deceived her so atrociously, and the story of the red coat that she had been given for her birthday by her best friend, Bernadette, "The blond woman who was there at the reading with me, do you remember, Monsieur Chabanais?"

I looked into her green eyes and could not remember anything, but I nodded enthusiastically and said, "It must be lovely to have such a good friend. Let's drink a glass to Bernadette!"

So we downed a glass to Bernadette and then, at my insistence, another to Aurélie's beautiful eyes.

She giggled, and said, "Now you're getting silly, Monsieur Chabanais."

"No, not in the slightest," I countered. "I have never seen eyes like them, you know. Because they are not simply green, they are like . . . like two precious opals, and now in the candlelight I can see the gentle shimmering of a broad sea in your eyes . . ."

"My goodness," she said, impressed. "That's the loveliest thing I have ever heard about my eyes." And then she told me about Jacquie, the boisterous chef with the heart of gold who missed the broad seas of Normandy.

"I've got a heart of gold too," I said, then took her hand and placed it on my chest. "Can you feel it?"

She smiled. "Yes, Monsieur Chabanais, I believe you really

do," she said earnestly, and left her hand on my beating heart for a moment. Then she leaped up and shook her hair back. "And now, *mon cher ami,* let's fetch the *gâteaux au chocolat.* That's my specialty. And Jacquie always says that a *gâteau au chocolat* is as sweet as love." She ran laughing into the kitchen.

"I believe he's absolutely right." I took the heavy casserole and followed her out. I was intoxicated with the wine, with Aurélie's nearness, with this whole wonderful evening that I just wished would never end.

Aurélie put the plates on the sideboard and opened the stainless steel refrigerator to get out the blood orange parfait, which she assured me was a work of genius in combination with the warm little chocolate cakes (*"C'est tout à fait génial!"* she said)— that irresistible combination of sweet chocolate and the slightly bitter taste of the blood oranges. I listened to her descriptions reverently and was enchanted by the sound of her voice. She was definitely right in what she said, but I believe that I simply found everything irresistible at that moment.

From the dining room I could hear *"La Fée Clochette"* playing, a song that I really liked, and I hummed softly along as the singer went on about how many whiskies he'd drink and how many cigarettes he'd smoke to get that girl, whom he was still searching for, into his bed.

I had found my *fée clochette!* She was standing just a few inches away from me, holding forth passionately about little chocolate cakes.

Aurélie closed the fridge door and turned to me. I was standing so close behind her that we bumped into each other.

"Oops," she said. And then she looked me straight in the eye. "Can I ask you something, Monsieur Chabanais?" she inquired conspiratorially.

"You can ask me anything," I responded, whispering like her.

"When I'm going downstairs at night, I never turn round because I'm afraid that there's something there behind me." Her eyes were opened wide and I fell head over heels into that soft, green sea. "Do you find that funny?" she asked.

"No," I murmured softly, and leaned my head down toward her. "No, I don't find it funny at all. Everyone knows that you shouldn't turn round on the stairs in the dark."

And then I kissed her.

The kiss lasted a long time. At some point, when our lips separated for a brief moment, Aurélie said softly: "I'm afraid the blood orange parfait will be melting."

I kissed her on the shoulder, on the neck, I bit her earlobes tenderly until she sighed softly, and before returning to her mouth I whispered: "I fear we'll just have to live with that."

And then neither of us said anything for a long, *long* time.

Fifteen

....

My birthday ended in a *nuit blanche,* a white night, a night that never wanted to end.

Midnight was long past when André helped me into my red coat and we dreamily found our way through the silent streets in a close embrace. Every few meters we'd stop for a kiss, and it took ages before we were finally standing at my apartment door. But time had no meaning in that night, which had neither day nor hour.

As I leaned forward to unlock the door, André kissed the nape of my neck. As I took him by the hand and drew him along the hall he put his arm round me from behind and reached for my breast. When we were standing in my bedroom, André slipped the straps of my dress from my shoulders and took my head in his hands with an infinitely tender gesture.

"Aurélie," he said, and suddenly kissed me so urgently that I almost swooned. "My lovely, lovely fairy."

Our clothes fell to the parquet floor with a soft rustle, and as we sank into my bed and lost ourselves in it for hours, my last thought was André Chabanais was the right Mr. Wrong.

There was not a single moment in that night that we untwined from each other. Everything was all touching, everything had to be discovered. Was there a single place on our bodies that was overlooked, that was not treated with tenderness, conquered with pleasure? I don't think so.

When I woke up, he was lying next to me, his head supported by his hand, and smiling at me.

"You look so lovely when you're asleep," he said.

I looked at him, and tried to imprint this morning when we both woke up together on my memory. His broad smile, his brown eyes with their black lashes, the dark wavy hair that had become totally disheveled, his beard, which still showed enough of his face and was far softer than I'd imagined, the light scar over his right eyebrow where he'd fallen into a barbed-wire fence as a little boy—and behind him the balcony door with the half-drawn curtains, a quiet morning in the courtyard, the branches of the big chestnut tree, a patch of sky. I smiled and closed my eyes for a moment.

He ran his finger tenderly over my lips. "What are you thinking?" he asked.

"I was just thinking that I'd like to preserve this moment," I said, and held his fingers against my lips to kiss them. "I'm just so happy," I said. "So absolutely, totally happy."

"That's lovely," he said, and took me in his arms. "Because I am too, Aurélie. My Aurélie." He kissed me, and we lay quietly cuddling for a while. "I'm never going to get up again," murmured André, and stroked my back. "We'll just stay in bed, shall we?"

I smiled. "Don't you have to go to work?" I asked.

"What work?" he murmured, and his hand slid between my legs. I giggled. "You should at least let them know that you're going to stay here in bed for the rest of your life." I glanced at the little clock on my bedside table. "It's already nearly eleven."

He sighed and regretfully removed his hand. "You're a little spoilsport, Mademoiselle Bredin, I've always suspected it," he said, and tweaked the tip of my nose. "Okay, then I'll ring Madame Petit and say that I'll be late. Or . . . no, better still— I'll say that I'm sorry, but I can't come in at all today. And then we'll have a super wonderful day—what do you think of that?"

"I think it's a marvelous idea," I said. "You sort things out while I make us coffee."

"Then that's what we'll do. But I don't like leaving you . . ."

"It's not for long," I responded, and wrapped myself in my short, dark blue dressing gown to go into the kitchen.

"You'll be taking that straight off again," André called, and I laughed.

"You just can't get enough!"

"No," he replied, "I can't get enough of you!"

Nor I of you, I thought.

I felt so safe at that moment, oh dear, so safe!

I made two big cups of *café crème* while André was on the phone and then disappeared into the bathroom. I carried them carefully into the bedroom. I pushed Robert Miller's book, which was still on my bedside table, aside and put the cups down.

Was it possible that this was all the result of the *menu d'amour*? Instead of an English writer, I'd dined with a French editor, and all at once we had seen each other with different eyes—almost like Tristan and Isolde, who accidentally drank the love potion and could not live without each other ever again. I could still remember very well how impressed I'd been by the opera as a child when Papa had taken me to see it. And I'd found the business of the love potion particularly exciting.

With a smile, I picked up the clothes that were lying strewn all around the room, and laid them over a chair beside the bed. As I lifted André's jacket, something fell out. It was his wallet. It fell open and a couple of bits of paper slipped out. Coins rolled over the parquet floor.

I knelt down to collect the coins, and could hear André singing happily in the bathroom. Smiling, I put the coins back in the front of the wallet and was just about to slip the papers that were sticking out of the back of the wallet back in when I noticed the photograph. At first I thought it was a picture of André and, a bit nosily, took it out. And then my heart stood still for a terrible moment.

I knew the picture—it was of a woman in a green dress, smiling at the camera. It was a picture of me.

For a few seconds I stared blankly at the photo in my hand, and then the thoughts began flooding in and hundreds of little stills fitted together to make a whole storyboard.

I'd put that photo in with my letter to Robert Miller. It was in André's wallet. André, who had brushed me off in the hall of the publisher's office. André, who had put Robert Miller's reply in the mailbox at my home because the writer had ostensibly lost my address. André, who had sat laughing and joking in La Coupole and knew very well that Robert Miller was never going to turn up there. André, who hadn't said a word to me about the reading—the only time Miller had really been in Paris—and who could not drag the obviously bewildered author away from me quickly enough. André, who had appeared at Le Temps des Cerises with his bouquet just at the moment that Miller had got his agent to cry off.

Miller? Ha!

Who knows who the man that Monsieur Chabanais had got to call me had been. And Robert Miller's letter? How could the author have answered me when he'd never received my letter?

And suddenly I remembered something. Something I'd already noticed after the reading without really being able to make sense of it.

I dropped the photo and rushed to the bedside table. *The Smiles of Women* was there and Miller's letter was stuck in the book. With trembling hands I took out the handwritten pages.

"Yours faithfully, Robert Miller." I whispered the closing words of the letter softly to myself as I hastily opened the book and stared at the dedication. *To Aurélie Bredin with very best wishes from Robert Miller.* Robert Miller had signed his name twice. But the signature on the dedication was totally different from the one on the letter. I turned the envelope over—the little yellow Post-it note from André Chabanais was still sticking to it—and groaned. It was André who had written Miller's letter, and I'd had the wool pulled over my eyes the whole time!

In a daze, I sat down on the bed. I thought of how André with his brown eyes had looked at me so ingenuously the evening before in the restaurant. "I'm so sorry, Aurélie." I was suddenly filled with icy rage. This man had exploited my trusting nature, he'd had fun leading me around by the nose, he'd played his games with me to get me into bed, and I'd fallen for it.

I looked out of the window where the sun was still shining on the courtyard, but the lovely picture of a happy morning was destroyed.

André Chabanais had deceived me just as Claude had deceived me, but I wasn't going to let myself be deceived ever again, no way! I clenched my hands into fists and took short breaths in and out.

"So, my love, the whole day is ours."

André had come into the room wrapped in a big dark gray bath towel and his brown hair was dripping water.

I stared at the floor.

"Aurélie?" He came nearer, stood in front of me, and put his hands on my shoulders. "My goodness, your face is terribly pale. Do you feel all right?"

I took his hands off my shoulders and stood up slowly.

"No," I said, my voice trembling. "I don't feel all right. I don't feel all right at all."

He looked at me in confusion. "What's wrong? Aurélie . . . my love . . . can I do anything for you?" He stroked a wisp of hair away from my face.

I brushed his hand away. "Yes," I said threateningly. "Never touch me again, do you hear, never ever again!" He stepped back in shock.

"But Aurélie, what's wrong?" he cried.

I felt a wave of anger rising within me. "What's wrong?" I asked dangerously softly. "You want to know what's wrong?"

I went over to where I'd dropped the photo, picked it up in a single movement, and held it out to him.

"That's wrong!" I screamed, and rushed over to the bedside table. "And that's wrong too!" I grabbed the forged letter and threw it at André's feet.

I saw his face turning red.

"Aurélie . . . please . . . Aurélie," he stammered.

"What?" I shrieked. "Are you going to trot out yet more lies? Don't you think you've done enough?" I picked up Robert Miller's book and would gladly have beaten him around the head with it. "The only thing that makes sense in this whole tissue of lies is this book. And you, André, chief editor at Éditions Opale, you're the last man for me. You're even worse than Claude. At least he had a reason for deceiving me, but you . . . you . . . you had fun doing it . . ."

"No, Aurélie, it wasn't like *that* at all . . . please . . ." he said despairingly.

"Yes," I said. "It was indeed. You opened my letter instead of forwarding it. You delivered a forged letter to me, and then you were probably laughing yourself silly in La Coupole when I refused to tell you anything about the letter. All very cleverly contrived. My compliments!" I took a step toward him and looked at him with utter contempt. "In my whole life I've never met another person who so hypocritically feeds off the misfortune of others." I saw him flinch. "There's just one thing you need to explain—it really does interest me to know how you managed it. Who was it that rang the restaurant yesterday evening? Who?"

"It really was Adam Goldberg. He's a friend of mine," he said.

"Oh, he's a friend, is he? Well, that's just great. How many other friends like that have you got, eh? How many of them are laughing now at this silly naive little girl, *hein,* would you mind telling me?" I was getting more and more enraged.

André raised his hands in a defensive gesture, then lowered them again quickly as his towel slipped. "No one's laughing at you, Aurélie. Please don't think badly of me . . . Yes, I know

I've *lied* to you, I've lied to you *a lot,* but . . . there was no other way, you *must* believe that! I . . . I was in a terrible predicament. Please! I can explain it all to you . . ."

I cut him short. "Do you know what, André Chabanais? I can do without your explanations. From the very beginning you didn't want me to meet Robert Miller, you always got in the way and made a nuisance of yourself, but then . . . then you had a far better idea, didn't you?" I shook my head. "How could anyone think up such a deceitful plan?"

"Aurélie, I fell in love with you—and that's the truth," he said.

"No!" I yelled. "That's not the way to treat any woman you love." I took his clothes from the chair and threw them in his face. "Here," I said. "Just get dressed and go!"

He picked up his clothes and looked at me unhappily. "Please give me a chance, Aurélie." He took a tentative step toward me and tried to put his arm around me. I turned away and folded my arms.

"Yesterday . . . that . . . was the loveliest thing that's ever happened to me . . ." he said in a cajoling tone.

I felt the tears welling up in my eyes. *"C'est fini!"* I blurted angrily. "It's over! It's over before it really began. And that's good. Because I don't want to live with a liar!"

"I didn't really lie," he said.

"How can you not *really* lie? That's ludicrous!" I replied. He'd obviously thought up a new strategy.

André moved to stand in front of me in his gray terry-cloth bath towel.

"I'm Robert Miller," he said.

I burst out laughing, and even in my own ears my voice

sounded shrill. Then I looked him up and down from head to foot before saying, "How dumb do you think I actually am? *You're* Robert Miller? I've heard a lot of things in my time, but this takes the cake. It's getting more absurd by the minute." I put my hands on my hips. "Tough luck for you, but I've seen Robert Miller, the *real* Robert Miller, at the reading! I've read his interview in *Le Figaro*. But *you're* Robert Miller, of course you are!" My voice cracked. "Do you know what you are, André Chabanais? You're just *laughable*! You can't hold a candle to Miller—and that's the truth. And now just go! I don't want to hear any more, you're just making everything worse!"

"But you must understand—Robert Miller *isn't* Robert Miller!" he cried. "That was . . . that was . . . a dentist!"

"Get out!" I screamed, and put my hands over my ears. "Get out of my life, André Chabanais, I hate you!"

When André had left the apartment without another word and with a very red face, I collapsed sobbing on the bed. An hour before I had been the happiest person in Paris, an hour before I had thought that I was standing at the beginning of something absolutely wonderful—and now there had been a totally catastrophic turn of events.

I saw the two full coffee cups on my bedside table and broke out in tears once more. Was it my fate always to be lied to? Did my happiness always have to end with a lie?

I stared out into the courtyard. I had a full supply of men who lied to me. I sighed deeply. A long, dreary life opened before me. If things went on that way, I'd end up a bitter old woman taking walks around cemeteries and planting flowers on graves. Only I wouldn't be as cheerful as Mrs. Dinsmore.

Suddenly I saw us all again, sitting in La Coupole on Mrs.

Dinsmore's birthday, and heard her saying, "My child, he is definitely the right one for you."

I threw myself headlong onto the pillow and sobbed on. One unhappy thought gave rise to another, and I was forced to remember that it would soon be Christmas. It would be the most miserable Christmas of my life. The finger on the little clock on my bedside table clicked forward, and I suddenly felt very old.

Sometime or other I got up and took the cups into the kitchen. I brushed against the notes on my wall of thoughts and a thought fluttered to the ground.

Sorrow is a land where it rains and rains and yet nothing grows, was what it said. That was incontrovertibly correct. No tears of mine would undo what had happened. I took the little note and stuck it carefully back on the wall.

And then I called Jacquie and told him that an attempt had been made on my heart and that I'd go to the seaside with him for the Christmas holidays.

Sixteen

....

When a tentative knock came at the door and Mademoiselle Mirabeau came in, I was sitting as I had done for almost all of the last few days, bent over my desk with my head in my hands.

Since my inglorious retreat from Aurélie Bredin's apartment I was dumbfounded. I had staggered back home, I'd stood in front of the bathroom mirror and berated myself as the total idiot who had messed everything up. I'd drunk too much in the evenings and hardly slept at night. I'd repeatedly tried to call Aurélie, but her home telephone was permanently switched to the answering machine and at the restaurant the phone was picked up by another woman who informed me robotically that Mademoiselle Bredin had no desire to speak to me.

On one occasion a man picked up (I think it was that boorish chef) and bellowed down the phone that if I didn't stop harassing Mademoiselle Aurélie he would personally come round to the publishing house and would take great pleasure in punching me in the face.

I'd sent an e-mail to Aurélie three times, and then I got a

brief answer saying that I could save myself the trouble of sending any further e-mails, as she'd delete them unread.

In those last days before Christmas I was as desperate as a man could be. It looked as if I'd irrevocably lost Aurélie: I didn't even have her photo, and the last glance she had given me had been so full of contempt that I felt shivers down my spine every time I thought about it.

"Monsieur Chabanais?"

I raised my head wearily and looked toward Mademoiselle Mirabeau.

"I'm going to get a sandwich—shall I bring something for you?" she asked.

"No, I'm not hungry," I said.

Florence Mirabeau approached carefully. "Monsieur Chabanais?"

"Yes, what is it?"

She looked at me with her little mimosa face.

"You look terrible, Monsieur Chabanais," she said, hastily adding: "Please forgive me for saying that. Go on, eat a sandwich . . . just to please me."

I sighed heavily. "All right, all right," I said.

"Chicken, ham, or tuna?"

"Whatever. Just bring me anything you like."

Half an hour later she came in with a tuna baguette and a freshly pressed *jus d'orange* and silently put them both down on my desk.

"Are you coming to the Christmas party this evening?" she asked.

It was Friday, next Tuesday would be Christmas Eve, and Éditions Opale was going to be shut from next week until the

New Year. In recent years it had become the custom for all of us in the publishing house to go to the Brasserie Lipp on the evening of our last day at work to celebrate the ending of the year in an appropriate fashion. It was always a very jolly occasion with lots of food, laughter, and chatter. I didn't feel up to so much merriment.

I shook my head. "I'm sorry, I'm not coming."

"Oh," she said. "Is it because of your mother? She broke her leg, didn't she?"

"No, no," I answered. Why should I lie? I'd lied so much in the past few weeks that I'd lost all desire to do so anymore.

Maman had already been at home in Neuilly for five days, was able to hobble through the house quite nimbly on her crutches planning *le réveillon,* our Christmas feast.

"Her broken leg is getting better," I said.

"But . . . what is it then?" Mademoiselle Mirabeau wanted to know.

I looked at her. "I've made an enormous mistake," I said, and laid my hand on my chest. "And now . . . what can I say . . . I believe my heart is broken." I attempted to smile, but I don't think it really sounded like my best joke ever.

"Oh," said Mademoiselle Mirabeau. I felt the warm wave of her sympathy spreading through the room. And then she said something that kept on going round in my head long after she'd shut the door quietly behind her.

"When you realize you've made a mistake, you should put it right as quickly as possible."

It wasn't very often that the publisher himself appeared in the offices of his workers, but if he did, you could be sure that it was something really important. An hour after Florence Mirabeau had been with me, Jean-Paul Monsignac pulled open my office door and fell into the chair in front of my desk with a crash.

He looked at me piercingly with his blue eyes. Then he said: "What does this mean, André . . . I've just heard that you're not coming to the Christmas party this evening?"

I squirmed uncomfortably in my chair. "Er . . . no," I said.

"May one know why?" Monsignac regarded the Christmas party at Lipp's as sacrosanct, and he expected to see all the members of his little flock there.

"Well, I . . . I simply don't feel up to it, to be honest," I said.

"My dear André, I'm not stupid. I mean, anyone with eyes in his head can see that you can't be feeling too good. You don't come to the editorial meeting, cry off without giving any reason at eleven o'clock, then turn up here the next day looking like death and hardly ever emerge from your lair anymore. What's wrong? This is not the André I know." Monsignac eyed me thoughtfully.

I shrugged my shoulders and said nothing. What could I have said anyway? If I were to come clean with Monsignac, that would be my next problem.

"You can talk to me about anything, André, I hope you know that."

I smiled tensely. "That's very nice of you, Monsieur Monsignac, but I'm afraid that you are precisely the one person I can't talk to about it."

He leaned back in astonishment, crossed one leg over the other, and gripped his ankle in its dark blue sock with both hands.

"Now you've made me curious. Why can't you talk to me about it? What nonsense!"

I looked out of the window, where the spire of the Church of Saint-Germain thrust into a rose-colored sky.

"Because then I'd probably be out of a job," I said gloomily.

Monsignac burst out laughing. "But my dear André, what have you done that's so bad? Have you been stealing the silverware? Groped one of the female staff? Embezzled money?" he rocked back and forth in his chair.

And then I thought of what Mademoiselle Mirabeau had said and decided to make a clean breast of it.

"It's about Robert Miller. I haven't been totally honest with you about the matter, Monsieur Monsignac."

He leaned forward with interest. "Really?" he asked. "What about Miller? Are there problems with that Englishman? Out with it!"

I swallowed. It wasn't easy to tell the truth.

"The reading was magnificent. *Mon Dieu,* I laughed till I cried," Monsignac continued. "What's up with the fellow? He said he was going to give us his new novel very soon."

I groaned softly and put my hands in front of my face.

"What's wrong?" asked Monsignac with alarm. "Now, André, don't get melodramatic, just tell me what's happened. Surely Miller will go on writing for us, or were there problems between you two? Have you by any chance fallen out?"

I shook my head almost imperceptibly.

"Has someone poached him?"

I took a deep breath and looked Monsignac in the eye.

"Promise me that you won't fly off the handle and that you won't shout?"

"Yes, yes . . . now *tell* me!"

"There will be no next novel by Robert Miller," I said, and

paused briefly, "for the simple reason that in reality there is no Robert Miller."

Monsignac looked at me, astounded. "Now you're really losing the plot, André. What's up, have you got a fever? Have you lost your memory? Robert Miller was in Paris, don't you remember?"

I nodded. "That's just the point. The man at the reading was not Robert Miller. He was a dentist who pretended to be Miller to do us a favor."

"Us?"

"Well, yes, Adam Goldberg and me. The dentist is his brother. His name is Sam Goldberg and he doesn't live alone in a cottage with his dog, but with his wife and children in Devonshire. He has as much to do with books as I do with gold inlays. The whole thing was a setup, do you see? So that the whole story wouldn't come out."

"But . . ." Monsignac's blue eyes fluttered in alarm. "Who did write the book then?"

"I did," I said.

And then Jean-Paul Monsignac did start shouting anyway.

The bad thing about Monsieur Monsignac is that he becomes a force of nature when he gets worked up. "That's monstrous! You've deceived me, André. I trusted you and would have put my hand in the fire to guarantee your honesty. You've hoodwinked me—that will have consequences. You're fired!" he yelled, and jumped from his chair angrily.

The good thing about Monsieur Monsignac is that he calms down as quickly as he gets angry and that he has a great sense of humor.

"Unbelievable," he said after ten minutes in which I imagined myself as an unemployed editor with the whole industry pointing the finger at me. "Unbelievable, what a coup you two brought off there. Leading all the press around by the nose. Takes a lot of nerve to get away with something like that." He shook his head and suddenly began to laugh. "I must admit that I was a bit surprised when Miller said at the reading that the hero of his new novel was a *dentist*. Why didn't you tell me from the very beginning that you were behind it, André? My goodness, I had no idea that you could write so well. You really *do* write well," he repeated, and ran his hands through his graying hair.

"It was simply a sort of spontaneous idea. You wanted a Stephen Clarke, do you remember? And at that time there wasn't an Englishman writing amusingly about Paris. And we weren't intending to fleece you or do the company any harm. You know that the advance for that novel was an extremely modest one—and we made that back long ago."

Monsignac nodded.

"None of us could have suspected that the book would take off so well that anyone would be interested in the author," I continued.

"Bon," said Monsignac, who had been walking up and down in my office the whole time, and sat down. "That's sorted that out. And now we will talk as man to man." He folded his arms over his chest and looked sternly at me. "I withdraw your dismissal, André. And your punishment is to come with us to the Brasserie Lipp this evening, understood?"

I nodded with relief.

"And now I want you to explain to me what this whole intrigue has to do with your broken heart. Because Mademoiselle Mirabeau is really worried. And for my part I have the feeling that we're getting toward the heart of the matter."

He leaned back comfortably in his chair, lit a cigarillo, and waited.

The story turned out to be a long one. Outside, the first streetlights were coming on when I finally finished speaking. "I've no idea what to do, Monsieur Monsignac," I concluded unhappily. "I've finally found the woman I've always been searching for, and now she *hates* me! And even if I could prove to her that there really is no author called Miller, I don't think it would be of any use. She's so incredibly angry with me . . . her feelings have been so hurt . . . she won't forgive me for it . . . never . . ."

"Pah-pah-pah!" Monsieur Monsignac interrupted me. "What do you think you're saying, André? The way the story's gone so far, nothing is yet lost. Believe a man who has a little more experience of life than you do." He tipped the ash off his cigarillo and jiggled his foot. "You know, André, three phrases have always helped me get through difficult times: *Je ne vois pas la raison, Je ne regrette rien,* and not least, *Je m'en fous!*" He smiled. "But I'm afraid that in your case neither Voltaire nor Edith Piaf will be of any use, let alone slang words. In your case, my dear friend, only one thing will help: the truth. And nothing but the whole truth." He stood up and came over to my desk. "Follow my advice and write this whole story up just as it happened— from the first moment that you looked through the window of that restaurant to our conversation here. And then send the manuscript to your Aurélie, pointing out that her favorite author has written a new book and that it is very important to him that she should be the first person to read it."

He patted me on the shoulder. "It's an incredible story, André. It's just great! Get writing—start tomorrow morning, or better still tonight! Write for your life, my friend. Write yourself into the heart of the woman you already seduced with your first novel."

He went over to the door and turned round once more. "And no matter how things end up"—he winked at me—"we'll make a Robert Miller of it!"

Seventeen

....

There are writers who spend days on the first sentence of their novels. The first sentence must feel right, and then everything else will follow automatically, they say. I believe that there has now actually been research into novel openings because the first sentence, the beginning of a book, is like the first glance between two people who do not know each other. And then there are writers who say that they cannot begin a novel without knowing what the last sentence is. John Irving, for example, is said to work conceptually from the last chapter back to the beginning of his books, and only then to begin writing. I, on the other hand, am writing this story out without knowing the end, in fact without being able to exert the slightest influence on that ending.

The truth is that there is as yet no ending to this story, because the final sentence must be written by a woman whom I saw one spring evening about a year and a half ago through the window of a little restaurant with red-and-white-checked table-cloths in the Rue Princesse in Paris. It's the woman I love.

She was smiling behind the window—and her smile en-

*chanted me so exceedingly that I stole it. I borrowed it. I carried
it around with me. I don't know if such a thing is possible—that
you can fall in love with a smile, I mean. Nevertheless, that
smile inspired me to write a story—a story in which everything
was invented, even its author. And then something unbelievable
happened. One year later on a really horrible November day, the
woman with the beautiful smile was standing in front of me, as if
she had fallen from the sky. And the wonderful—and at the
same time tragic—thing about that meeting was that she wanted
something from me that I could not give her. She had only one
wish—she was obsessed with it, just like princesses in fairy tales
are obsessed with the forbidden door—and it was precisely that
wish that it was impossible to satisfy. Or was it? A lot has happened since then—lovely things and horrible things—and I
want to write them all down. The whole truth after all the lies.*

*This is the story as it really happened, and I'm writing it
like a soldier about to go into battle, like an invalid who doesn't
know if he'll see the sun rise tomorrow morning, like a lover who
has put his whole heart into the tender hands of a woman in the
rash hope that she will listen to him.*

Since my conversation with Monsignac three days had passed.
It had taken three days for me to get these first sentences down
on paper, but then all at once everything went with a rush.

In the following weeks I wrote as if I was being guided by a
higher power; I was writing for my life, as my employer had so
aptly put it. I wrote about the bar where a brilliant idea had
been concocted, about an apparition in the lobby of a publishing house, about a letter to an English writer in my mailbox, a
letter I tore open impatiently—and about everything else that
had happened in those exciting, remarkable weeks.

Christmas came and went. I took my laptop and my notes to Maman's in Neuilly, where I spent the holidays, and as we sat around the big table in the salon with the whole family on Christmas Eve praising the *foie gras* with onion confit that was on our plates, Maman was right for the first time when she said I'd lost weight and was not eating enough.

Did I eat anything at all in those weeks? I must have, but I don't remember it. Good old Monsignac had given me leave until the end of January—on a special assignment, as he told the others—and I got up in the morning, put on any old thing, and stumbled over to my writing desk with a cup of coffee and my cigarettes.

I didn't answer the telephone, I didn't answer the door when the bell rang, I didn't watch any TV, the newspapers piled up unread on my coffee table, and some days I walked through the *quartier* to get a bit of fresh air and to buy anything that was absolutely necessary.

I was no longer in this world, and if any disasters occurred they passed me by. I knew nothing at all in those weeks. I only knew that I had to write.

If I stood in front of the bathroom mirror I caught a fleeting glimpse of a pale man with disheveled hair and shadows under his eyes.

I wasn't interested.

Sometimes I walked up and down in the room to stretch my stiff limbs, and when I couldn't go on and the flow of the narrative faltered, I stuck the *French Café* CD into the player. It began with "*Fibre de Verre*" and ended with "*La Fée Clochette*"; all those weeks I listened to nothing but that CD.

I'd become fixated on it like someone autistic who has to

count everything that they come across. It was my ritual—when the first bars rang out I felt secure and after the second or third song I was back in the story and the music became a kind of background accompaniment that let my thoughts soar high over the wide seas like a white seagull.

From time to time it flew closer to the water, and then I was listening to Coralie Clément's *"La Mer Opale"* and could see Aurélie Bredin's green eyes in front of me. Or I heard Brigitte Bardot's *"Un Jour Comme un Autre,"* which made me think of how Aurélie had been deserted by Claude.

Every time *"La Fée Clochette"* played, I knew that another hour had passed, and my heart grew heavy—and tender at the same time—at the memory of that enchanted evening in Le Temps des Cerises.

At night I would turn out the lamp on my desk at some time or other and go to bed—often enough I would get back up because I thought I'd been struck by a fantastic idea—which next morning often turned out not to have been quite so fantastic.

The days became hours, and the days began to blur without any transitions into a transatlantic, dark blue sea where every wave is the same as the others and your gaze is directed at the thin line on the horizon where the traveler thinks he can see *terra firma.*

I don't think any book has ever been written as quickly as this one. I was driven by the desire to win Aurélie back, and I was longing for the day when I could lay my manuscript at her feet.

By the final days of January I had finished.

On the evening when I laid the manuscript at Aurélie Bredin's apartment door it began to snow. Snow is such a rare occurrence in Paris that most people are delighted.

I wandered through the streets like a prisoner on parole, I admired the displays in the brightly lit store windows, I inhaled the tempting smell of the freshly made crêpes from the little stall behind the Church of Saint-Germain, but then decided on a waffle, which I smeared thickly with cream of chestnut.

The snowflakes fell softly, little white points in the dark, and I thought about the manuscript, wrapped in brown paper, which Aurélie would find at her door that evening.

By the time it was finished there were 280 pages, and I'd thought long and hard about what title I was going to give the story, the novel that I hoped would win me back the girl with the green eyes forever.

I wrote down many sentimental, romantic, even kitschy titles, but I deleted them all from my list. And then I named the book, simply and poignantly, *The End of the Story.*

No matter how a story begins, no matter what convoluted turns and paths it takes, in the end only the ending is important.

My profession entails reading a lot of books and manuscripts, and I must admit that I have been most fascinated by novels that have an open or even a tragic ending. Well, you think about books like that for quite a while, whereas you forget those with a happy ending quite quickly.

But there has to be some difference between literature and reality, and I confess that as I laid the little brown package on the cold stone floor outside Aurélie's door I abandoned all intellectual pretensions. I addressed a quick prayer to the heavens, asking for a *happy* ending.

An open letter was included with the manuscript, in which I wrote:

Dear Aurélie,

I know that you have banished me from your life and do not wish to have anything further to do with me, and I respect that wish.

Today I lay your favorite author's new book at your door.

It is a completely brand-new, unedited manuscript, and it has as yet no proper ending, but I know that it will interest you, because it contains the answers to all your questions about Robert Miller's first novel. I hope that this will make at least some amends for the things I have done.

I miss you,

André

That night I slept deeply and well for the first time in weeks. I woke up with the feeling that I'd done everything I possibly could. Now all that was left was to wait.

I wrapped up a copy of the novel for Monsieur Monsignac and then made my way after more than five weeks to the publishing house. It was still snowing, snow lay on the roofs of the houses and the sounds of the city were muffled. The cars on the boulevards were not driving as fast as usual and even the people on the streets slowed their pace somewhat. The world, it seemed to me, was in a way holding its breath, and I myself was strangely filled with great calm. My heart was as white as if it were the first day of creation.

In the office I was welcomed extravagantly. Madame Petit did not just bring my mail (there were heaps of it) but a coffee as well; a red-cheeked Mademoiselle Mirabeau popped her head round the door and wished me a Happy New Year (I noticed a ring glinting on her finger); Michelle Auteuil greeted me regally when we met in the lobby and even condescended to offer a *"Ça va, André?"*; Gabrielle Mercier sighed with relief, saying it was good that I was back because the boss was driving her crazy; and Jean-Paul Monsignac pulled the door shut behind us as we went into my office and said I looked like an author who had just finished a book.

"What do they look like, then?" I asked.

"Completely wasted, but with that very special glint in their eyes," said Monsignac. Then he looked at me searchingly. "And?" he asked.

I handed him the copy of the manuscript. "No idea if it's any good," I said. "But it contains a lot of my heart's blood."

Monsignac smiled. "Heart's blood is always good. I've got my fingers crossed for you, my friend."

"Oh well," I said. "I only finished it last night, so nothing's going to happen that quickly . . . if at all."

"You might just be wrong there, André," said Monsignac. "I'm looking forward to reading this anyway."

The afternoon crept by. I looked through my mail, and answered my e-mail. I looked out of the window, where thick flakes of snow were still falling from the sky. And then I closed my eyes and thought of Aurélie and hoped that my thoughts would reach their goal even with closed eyes.

It was half past four and already dark outside when the telephone rang and Jean-Paul Monsignac asked me to come into his office.

As I went in he was standing by the window staring out at the street. My manuscript was lying on his desk.

Monsignac turned round. "Ah, André, come in, come in," he said, and swayed back and forth as his custom was. He pointed to the manuscript. "What you've written there"—he looked at me severely and I pressed my lips nervously together—"is unfortunately very good. Don't let your agent get the idea of going to other publishers and starting an auction, or you'll be out on your ear, do you understand?"

"C'est bien compris," I answered with a smile. "I'm really very pleased, Monsieur Monsignac."

He turned back to the window. "I bet that what's out here will please you even more," he said, and pointed to the street.

I looked at him inquiringly. For just one second I thought that he meant the snowflakes that were still floating around outside the window, then my heart began to beat faster, and I could have hugged old Monsignac.

Outside on the street, on the side opposite Éditions Opale's office building, a woman was walking up and down. She was wearing a red coat, and kept looking at the publishers' door as if she was waiting for someone.

I didn't even take the time to put on a coat, but just rushed down the stairs, pulled open the heavy front door, and ran across the street.

And then I was standing in front of her and for a moment I was almost unable to breathe.

"You came!" I said softly, and then I said it again and my voice was quite hoarse, I was so glad to see her.

"Aurélie . . ." I said, and gave her a questioning look.

The snowflakes were falling on her and catching in her hair like little white almond blossoms.

She smiled, and I reached for her hand, which was wrapped in a brightly colored woolen glove, and felt myself suddenly becoming quite lighthearted.

"You know what? I actually like Robert Miller's second

254 · NICOLAS BARREAU

book a bit better than the first one," she said, and her green eyes gleamed.

I laughed softly and took her in my arms.

"Is that going to be the last sentence?" I asked.

Aurélie shook her head slowly. "No, I don't think so," she said.

For a moment she looked at me so solemnly that I nervously looked for an answer in her eyes.

"I love you, you dope," she said.

Then she put her arms around me and everything melted into a soft, carmine-colored red woolen coat and a single kiss that never wanted to end.

Of course I would have found this sentence a little conventional in a novel. But here, in real life, on this little snowy street in a great city that is also called the city of love, it made me the happiest man in Paris.

Author's Note

·····················

When you've finished writing a novel, you're very relieved that it's over. (Thanks for listening to me, Jean!) And for that very reason, you're also very sad. Because writing the final lines of a novel also means saying good-bye to the heroes who have been your companions for such a long time. And even if they are (more or less) invented, they are still very close to the author's heart.

And so I watch Aurélie and André; who finally found each other in spite of a thousand trials and tribulations, going on their way, and I sigh emotionally, get a little sentimental, and wish them both every happiness.

A lot that is in my book is invented; some of it is true. The cafés, bars, restaurants, and stores really exist, the *menu d'amour* is always worth a try—which is why I've included the recipes, as well as the recipe for La Coupole's *Curry d'agneau* (both the original recipe, and the way Aurélie Bredin would cook it).

But the reader will search in vain for a restaurant called Le Temps des Cerises in the Rue Princesse.

Even if I did, as I wrote, have a very particular restaurant with red-and-white-checked tablecloths in my mind, let it remain a place of the imagination. A place where wishes come true and anything is possible.

The smiles of women are a gift from heaven, they are the beginning of every love story, and if I had just one wish, this is what it would be: that my dear friend U. should wear her new winter coat for many years to come and that this book should end for any indulgent readers—men or women—as it began: with a smile.

Aurélie's Menu d'Amour

FIELD SALAD WITH AVOCADOS, MUSHROOMS, AND MACADAMIA NUTS IN POTATO VINAIGRETTE

4 ounces field salad
4 ounces small mushrooms
1 avocado
10 macadamia nuts
1 tablespoon butter
1 red onion
1 large floury potato
2 ounces bacon lardons
4 ounces vegetable stock
2 to 3 dessert spoons of apple cider vinegar
salt
pepper
1 tablespoon clear honey
3 teaspoons olive oil

Clean and wash the field salad and then spin it dry. Wash, peel, and slice the mushrooms. Peel the avocado and cut into slices. Heat the macadamia nuts in a pan with the butter until golden brown. Cut the onion in half and slice thinly. Boil the potato in its skin until soft. Fry the bacon lardons in a pan until nicely crisp. Then boil up the vegetable stock and stir in the vinegar, salt and pepper to taste, honey, and oil. Peel the potato, add it to the stock and mash with a fork, then whisk everything with an eggbeater until smooth.

Arrange the field salad with the mushrooms, avocado slices, onion, and nuts on a plate. Sprinkle with the lardons and dress with the lukewarm sauce.

Serve immediately.

LAMB RAGOUT WITH POMEGRANATE SEEDS AND GRATINÉ POTATOES

1 pound boned leg of lamb
2 carrots
2 stalks celery
1 large eggplant
1 red onion
2 cloves garlic
seeds of 2 pomegranates
3 tomatoes
3 tablespoons butter
salt
pepper
1 bunch fresh thyme
2 tablespoons olive oil
1 tablespoon flour
1 cup dry white wine

For the Gratiné Potatoes
1 pound small potatoes (waxy)
1 cup cream
2 eggs
4 tablespoons butter

Remove any fat from the lamb and then cut into cubes. Peel the carrots and wash and clean the celery. Wash the eggplant and cut vegetables into small cubes. Peel the onion and garlic and chop finely. Halve the pomegranates, remove the seeds, and put them to one side. Briefly put the tomatoes into boiling water, then into cold water, and peel them. Remove the seeds and cut the flesh into cubes.

Soften the vegetables (except for the tomatoes and the pomegranate seeds) in a pan with butter. Season with salt, pepper, and the thyme.

Brown the lamb quickly in olive oil in a casserole, and season with salt and pepper. Then dust with flour, stir, and pour in the white wine. Add the vegetables, cover and braise in a low oven (300°F/150°C) for about two hours, adding more wine if necessary. Add the pomegranate seeds at the very end.

While the lamb is cooking, wash and peel the potatoes and cut into very fine slices. Grease a gratin dish with butter and arrange the potato slices in a circle in the dish, then season with salt and pepper. Whip the cream and eggs together, season, and pour over the potatoes. Dot with lumps of butter. Cook for about 40 minutes in the oven at 350°F/180°C.

GÂTEAU AU CHOCOLAT WITH BLOOD ORANGE PARFAIT

For the Gâteaux au Chocolate
4 ounces fine dark chocolate, at least 70% cocoa content
1½ ounces salted butter
2 eggs

2½ tablespoons brown sugar
1 packet vanilla sugar
⅛ cup flour
4 extra pieces of chocolate
Powdered sugar

For the Blood Orange Parfait
2 egg yolks
4 ounces powdered sugar
1 pinch of salt
3 dessert spoons of hot water
3 blood oranges
2 packets of vanilla sugar
1 cup whipping cream

Melt the chocolate and the butter in a double boiler. Whip the eggs until stiff and then add the brown sugar. Stir in the vanilla sugar. Fold in the flour and the melted chocolate.

Grease two ramekins with butter and powder with flour. Fill the ramekins two-thirds full, place two pieces of chocolate in each, then add the rest of the mixture.

Bake in a preheated oven at 420°F/220°C for 8 to 10 minutes.

The *gâteaux au chocolat* should be baked only on the outside and should be liquid in the middle. Dust them with powdered sugar and serve lukewarm, accompanied by the blood orange parfait.

Beat the egg yolk with powdered sugar, a pinch of salt, and hot water in the mixer until stiff. Then add the juice of two blood oranges. Whip the cream with the vanilla sugar until stiff and fold into the mixture.

Put into a mold and chill overnight. Decorate with slices of the third orange and serve with the *gâteaux au chocolat*.

Bon appetit!

La Coupole's Curry d'Agneau

(1927 RECIPE)

(SERVES SIX)

7 pounds leg or shoulder of lamb
3½ ounces sunflower oil
3 Golden Delicious apples, sliced (Aurélie uses 5 apples)
1 banana, sliced (Aurélie uses 4 bananas)
1 cup chopped onions (Aurélie recommends that you use twice the quantity of onions, so that it's juicier)
3 cloves of garlic, chopped
3 teaspoons curry powder (Aurélie recommends Indian curry powder and also suggests you taste to see if 3 teaspoons are enough)
1 teaspoon sweet paprika
¼ cup grated coconut (and another dishful served at the table)
¼ cup flour
2 cups lamb stock (or water)
1 bouquet garni
½ tablespoon coarse sea salt
1 pound basmati rice, cooked
1 large tomato, sliced

¼ cup parsley (flat-leaf, preferably in a bunch)
mango chutney, allspice, fruit and vegetable relishes

Gently brown the lamb in sunflower oil for about 5 minutes and add the sliced apple and sliced banana. Then add the chopped onion and the garlic. Cook for a further 5 minutes, then stir in the curry powder, the paprika, and the grated coconut.

Stir well and then sprinkle with the flour. Cover with lamb stock or water. Add the bouquet garni and the salt, then cook on a low flame for an hour to 90 minutes until the meat is almost completely cooked. (It can also be broiled in a casserole in the oven for two to three hours at low temperature [350°F/180°C], in which case the flesh gets really tender and there is no need to puree.)

Remove the meat from the liquid and puree the sauce. (It is not necessary to puree the sauce if you like to be able to taste small pieces of the ingredients.)

Serve with the rice, sliced tomato, and parsley. Accompany with little dishes of mango chutney, allspice, and relishes.

1. Aurélie is convinced that Robert Miller's book, *The Smiles of Women*, saved her life. Is there a book you have read at a certain point in your life that you felt similarly about? What was it, and how did it help you in that moment?

2. For Aurélie, there is no such thing as coincidence. What happens in the book that could be considered a coincidence, and where are the protagonists helping things along? Generally, do you believe everything happens for a reason?

3. Are there points in the book at which André could or should have come clean about his deception to Aurélie and his colleagues? Would this have changed the overall outcome?

4. Talk about the author's use of color in the book (the coat, the dress, eyes, etc.).

5. What are your favorite dishes to cook (or eat) for a special, romantic occasion, and do you believe certain ingredients or recipes have power beyond nutrition? Will you be making any of the recipes in the book with that in mind?

6. Have you ever developed a crush on someone before or without actually meeting them? What was it about them that attracted you? Their looks? Their talents? Their achievements?

7. Discuss Aurélie's grip on reality (or lack thereof) and what it is about her that makes people respond to her the way they do.

8. If you were to cast the movie of *The Ingredients of Love*, who would be your choices for the protagonists and minor characters?

St. Martin's
Griffin

9. Would you agree to play a role the way Sam does for a few nights? How would you have prepared for the potentially awkward situation in his place?

10. How do you pick books in a bookstore? Do you rely on recommendations from the bookseller, the way Aurélie does, or are you drawn to a beautiful cover?

11. Paris plays a very large part in *The Ingredients of Love*. Discuss how the setting is used to enhance the story, and talk about other cities you might have visited that have a similar or equally memorable atmosphere.

12. What do you think the ingredients of love are? Are they pretty basic and always the same, or do they vary from couple to couple?

For more reading group suggestions, visit www.readinggroupgold.com.